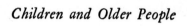

Children and Older People

By RUTH SUCKOW

Novels

THE ODYSSEY OF A NICE GIRL

THE BONNEY FAMILY

CORA

THE KRAMER GIRLS

Short Stories

COUNTRY PEOPLE

IOWA INTERIORS

CHILDREN AND OLDER PEOPLE

These are Borzoi Books published by Alfred A. Knopf

Children and Older People

Ruth Suckow

New York
ALFRED·A·KNOPF
1931

Thanks are due to the editors of *The American Mercury, Harper's Magazine, Good Housekeeping* and *The Country Home* for their permission to re-print these stories. "A Great Mollie" appeared in slightly different form in *Harper's Magazine* under the title "As Strong As a Man." All of the stories have received revisions.

Contents

Children and Older People

Eminence

M R. AND MRS. WATKINS were going to church on Christmas
Eve. Mr. Watkins was proudly carrying Florentine. Her
little white legs, dangling, bumped against his coat. Her curls
were carefully covered. Mrs. Watkins was carrying, wrapped
from the snow, the star and crown of silver paper.

"Be careful of her slippers, daddy!"

"I'm being careful."

Florentine took one bare hand from her muff and stretched
it out to the snow flakes. They were like dim soft little stars.
They melted with a cool delicious tingle upon her warm skin.
The flimmer of misty snow hushed for a moment the high excitement of being on the program.

"Oh, keep your hands covered, darling!"

The church was brilliant with lighted windows in the snowfall. With preoccupied faces, taking only an instant to smile
and half nod to this one and that, Mr. and Mrs. Watkins made
their way through the people flocking up the church steps.
They were thrillingly aware of the whispers all around them.
A man called out jovially, "What's that you've got there, Watkins?" Mr. Watkins said proudly, "That's part of the program!" Above all the heads was Florentine's small pale face
with starry eyes.

They went straight to the Infant Room, where the children
who were going to take part on the program were crowded.
Instantly they were surrounded. "Oh, here she is! They've

3

brought her!" Faces of Sunday-school teachers, of older girls, delighted, eager, were all around them. Boys watched, while they pretended not to, with aloof and silent admiration. At the edge of the group, withdrawn, solemn and watchful, were the other little girls in Florentine's class.

Mr. Watkins set Florentine on her feet. Mrs. Watkins sent him to find seats for them in the audience room. Her face was tensely absorbed as she laid aside Florentine's white wavy furs, drew off her white coat, and undid the scarf. She brushed out the pale-gold curls that were flattened, the little fine surface hairs roughened and glinting, from the pressure. She knelt to place the crown of silver paper, tipped at the center with a star, upon Florentine's head. Florentine was all in white. She wore white slippers and stockings and a little white silk dress with puffed sleeves.

"How darling! How dear! Mrs. Watkins, what is she?"

"The Christmas Fairy," Mrs. Watkins said.

She led Florentine over to the register, murmuring, "Come, darling, you must get warm!" The girls from the older classes circled around her in delight, with coos and cries of ecstasy, reaching out adoring fingers to brush Florentine's floating curls, to fondle her little soft wrists, and touch her silken skirts. "Oh, Mrs. Watkins, can't we look after her?" Florentine Watkins was the prettiest child in the Sunday-school. She stood on the register, a little princess, small, calm and sure of herself, but her face pale and her eyes like dark blue stars. She let one hold her hand and another lay all her curls straight, with one curl over each shoulder. Beneath her little smile, the glory of the occasion, of the moment, of the worship, was shining and singing through her—almost ready to break into fiery sparkles, as when she dragged her feet across the rug and touched the cat's

fur. She was well aware of being the star of the evening. The
scarf her mother had anxiously put about her floated and clung
to her puffed sleeves and her small chilly arms. The heat from
the register billowed out her full skirt, that clung like milk-
weed floss to the fingers of the girls when they pushed it down.
All the boys were aware of her, but awed, looking sidelong at
her and standing apart.

"Mrs. Watkins, let us take care of her!"

"Will you stay with the girls, darling?"

Florentine consented royally.

"You remember your piece, darling. You remember what
to do."

"I remember."

Still on the edge of the group stood the other girls in the
class, Lola, Kitty, Amy, Mary Louise. They were in their
winter dresses, black stockings and high shoes. They had
walked to the church. Their hair was crimped or braided, and
they wore big red ribbons. They eyed Florentine.

The noise in the audience room was growing louder. It was
almost time for the program to begin. The teachers were beginning to marshal the classes. "Now, Miss Morrison's class!" That
was the one to which Florentine belonged. She stepped into
line with a thrill of shining fear and expectation.

Lola, Kitty, Amy and Mary Louise huddled together behind
her with giggles and excited whispers. They clung to each
other. "What if I should forget!" "I know your part. I'll prompt
you." Florentine stood at the head. Now her fear had become a
great cold blankness that left her, in the midst of the envy and
the worship, all alone. The girls looked at her, but did not cling
to her. Her face was white and her eyes dark under her silver
star. If she forgot, none of them could help her. She had the

principal part. The exercise depended upon her.

The organ was almost hidden behind the Christmas tree, that was dark glistening green, laden with white packages, shredded over with sparkles of tinsel. The opening march sounded out through the branches. It spread through the air heated from the big registers and chilled by the wintry drafts from the door, spiced with evergreen, thick with the odors of the crowd in their winter clothing damp from the snow. All the heads turned to watch the Sunday-school march in.

Mr. and Mrs. Watkins sat near the front. Their eyes were set in a glaze of expectation. Mrs. Watkins clasped her hands until the knuckles were strained to white. In all the marching ranks—little boys and little girls, bigger, smaller, fair-haired, black-haired, awkward, pretty—they could see only one child. "There comes Florentine!" She had a little space to herself, as if made by the shining of her silver star and the dainty floating of her silken skirts. Just for one transported instant the little face passed them, pale, unconscious of them, under the silver star. Then they sat back. With shovings, rustlings, scuffings, and orders from teachers, the Sunday-school was seated. She was lost to them among the other children.

The exercises began.

"Joy to the world, the Lord has come . . ."

The music roared through the branches of the Christmas tree and filled the room. When the audience sat down again, the front seats reserved for the Sunday-school quivered with hair ribbons.

All bowed their heads, but they were not listening to the minister's prayer. It was just something that came at this time on the program. Parents were craning and straining their eyes

to see their own children. The children had their eyes on the
packages heaped about the tree. They nudged one another to
see that big package propped at its foot. "Wonder whose that
is?" The prayer ended, the audience moved and shuffled, and
the superintendent stepped forward and announced the first
real number of the program. Now those who were to take part
became self-conscious, looked down and twisted their shaking
fingers, with their lips silently repeating the opening lines of
their pieces.

"A song by the Infant Department."

Pulling back, stopping and wandering, whimpering or looking about with widely innocent eyes, the infants were herded
upon the platform. The little ones were pulled to their places
in front. Some were too large and awkward among the others.
A shock-headed boy, with holes in his stockings that showed
white patches of winter underwear, stood grinning at the end
of the line. The little threads of voices followed the voice of
the primary teacher, on and off the key. When the song was
over none of the infants knew enough to go down. They stood
smiling with engaging foolishness at the audience until the
teacher began to marshal them off the platform. Some wandered
down, others came with quick little steps, while the audience
laughed and clapped, the men grinning, but ashamed, at the
exhibition of ingenuousness.

Mr. and Mrs. Watkins smiled slightly and clapped perfunc-
torily. They could not give ready applause until Florentine had
had hers.

Exercises, songs and recitations—pieces by children whose
mothers would be offended if they were left off the program:
good or bad, the audience clapped. Here a clear little voice got
a momentary sharpness of applause; or a lisp or a stutter drew

a ripple of laughter. Mrs. Watkins listened, clasping her hands. Once she was angry. It was when Howard Hopkins "forgot." He stood staring at the audience with a bright, bold, unabashed gaze, and when he could not go on, suddenly grinned and said, "Guess that's all!" and marched nonchalantly down. The roar of laughter and appreciation beat upon Mrs. Watkins' jealous ears. It was not fair. It did not really belong to the program. This boy had no right to come in, not even able to speak his piece, and take away some of the applause from Florentine.

In the third row from the front, Miss Morrison's class waited, all crowded together. Their exercise came near the end of the program. It was the principal one. They were old enough now to know how to do things, but still small enough to be "cute." And then, they had Florentine Watkins. They wiggled and squirmed through the earlier numbers. The other girls whispered together. But Florentine sat still, her eyes brightly fixed, whispering over and over to herself with rapt intentness the first line of her piece. At times she forgot about it, and it fled away from her, and then, after a cold moment when the world shook, it sounded clear and true in her mind. She felt all the eyes upon her silver star. Through the earlier part of the program, that elated her and made her hold her small golden head high. But now it quivered through her with terror. Her turn was almost here. She was Florentine Watkins. The whole church expected her to do well. The teacher depended upon her. The girls would wait for her. Her mother and father were listening. Her lines started to vanish and her mind made a leap and caught them. The lights and the sparkles on the Christmas tree dazzled together. She could not breathe or live until this was over. She moistened her lips and moved one cold little hand. She was the most miserable one on the program. If she could

be Kitty with only four lines to speak, that girl in front of her
who had already given her recitation—be a child of whom no
one expected anything—Beany Watters, that boy with the holes
in his stockings! The shining of the silver star on her forehead
was a bright terror. The next . . . her heart began to
thump . . .

"'The Christmas Fairy'—an exercise by Miss Morrison's
class."

Florentine rose at the head of her line, made her way daintily
down the aisle and up the steps, padded with white and bor-
dered with evergreen, and crossed the enormous space of the
platform. Her knees were trembling, but a strange spacious
coolness was upon her. She would get through her part, and
then die.

In shaking silence the little girls took their places about
Florentine. Mr. and Mrs. Watkins were staring straight ahead.
Mr. Watkins cleared his throat. Mrs. Watkins saw her child
through a wavering shimmer of dizziness: little delicate white
figure in the flimsy shine of the silken dress, silver star tipping
the golden head—was the dress all right? Long enough? the
crown straight on her head? Mrs. Watkins dug her nails in
ecstatic agony into her palms. Then silence. Florentine stepped
forward. Her voice came out clear and small, tremulous—like
the shaking of a tiny bell—in the rustling hush of the room.

> "Dear children all, I heard your wishes,
>   And o'er the world I flew
>   To bring my happy Christmas message
>   To all the world and you. . . ."

Her mother's eyes were fixed in an agony of watchfulness on
that small face. Every word seemed to turn and twist in her

own heart.

Florentine was getting through it. Her little bell-like voice rang out the words small and clear and pure. Her knees had stopped trembling. Her coolness was fired with happiness. Why, it was going to be over too soon! In a blaze of elation she wanted to go all through it again. Now the eyes upon her were a bright intoxication. Just for this little moment, she was the Fairy—silver star and white slippers, silken dress and silver crown—herself and beyond herself. . . . It was over. She had spoken the last word. She was standing—she was going down the steps—sliding into her pew. The applause was a roaring sea in her ears. It was not until she was seated, breathing quickly and clasping her warm trembling hands in her silken lap, that she realized in a burning glory that the applause was for her!

Mr. Watkins was smiling broadly, unable to hold in his pride. Mrs. Watkins' heart steadied into a happy, elated beat as she drank in the applause. Their child, their child—the best on the whole program! Moisture stung in the mother's eyes, and warmth flowed over her. Now she could be happy. Now she could be easy. She could smile at the rest of the program.

The children were growing restless. They did not want to hear the superintendent's announcements. They were watching, turning—but the little ones shrieked when they heard a jingle of bells from the entry and a stamping of feet. Santa Claus came running down the aisle. He shouted in an enormous jovial voice, "Well, children, Merry Christmas! Did you think old Santy wouldn't come?"

Clapping, laughter and cat-calls answered him.

"Well, Santy pretty near thought so himself. I'll tell you how it was. One of Santy's reindeer got a stone in its hoof and we

had to stop and see the blacksmith down there at Grover. Well
sir, and all the presents I was bringing to the good little girls
and boys in Mahaska—Santy don't give any presents to bad
children, no sir, but you're all good, ain't you? (A little trust-
ing voice piped up, 'Yes, Santy!') Sure you are! I knew it! Well,
all the presents rolled out, and those children in Grover—I guess,
they hadn't seen any things like those!—they came pretty near
getting the whole lot of them."

The little children sat with starry eyes of wonder and expectation. It was Mr. Heggy. The big boys were whispering
that it was only Mr. Heggy. And yet, could they be sure? There
were the buffalo coat and the fur cap, the white woolly beard
and rosy cheeks, the jingle of sleighbells from up his sleeve.
. . . They watched breathlessly while the first presents were
taken from the Christmas tree. "Aw, it ain't either Santy. It's
just Hr. Heggy. Because there's another Santy at the Meth-
odists! They ain't two Santys, is they?" Still the little ones were
not convinced. They murmured, "I bet it *could* be Santy,
though!"

The big boys in Mr. Pendleton's class were distributing the
candy—hard Christmas candy, little colored curley-cues and
squares and round white logs with flowers in the center glistening red and sticky white. Every child—visitors and all—got one
of the little cardboard packages. Florentine accepted hers. She
was glad·to sit back for a little while in the obscurity that Santa's
speech made for her, but still with the radiance of her great
moment warmly upon her.

Santa had come to the packages. He was reading the names
in a loud voice as he took them from the tree.

" 'Helen Vincent!' Anybody know Helen? Oh, that's Helen,
is it? Hold up your hand, Helen, this looks like a pretty nice

present. . . . 'Mamie Runkle!' Now I wonder who could have given Mamie a present like that? Must have been some one who likes her pretty well! . . . 'Mrs. Peabody. From her Sunday-school class!' Well, well, I guess those boys know a good teacher when they get one."

The boys rushed about, waving the packages, sending them down the aisles from hand to hand. Children were gnawing at the hard candy, with loud snaps, as if teeth were breaking. Papers were strewed untidily over the church. The Christmas tree was shining but disheveled. Santa was just calling the names now. The big box at the foot of the tree had not yet been given out. It had been saved for the last. The children were still pointing to it, and hoping and whispering about it.

Santa lifted it. A hush in the buzzing and talking and rustling followed. The package was big enough to catch the last jaded attention of the audience. He looked it all over for a name. The room became still. Respectful, wondering, eager glances were turned toward the box. Santa took his time.

"Well, this is quite a little bundle! Glad Santy didn't have to carry this very far. Guess this must go to Santy himself—must be a token of appreciation. . . . No, sir! I'm mistaken there. This seems to belong to a little girl. I'd oughta brought my specs along from the North Pole to read this. Let's see if I can make it out. . . . 'Florentine Watkins!' Well, well! A big box for a little girl! Here, boys! The little girl with the silver star on her head."

The sound of wonder, envy, disappointment, and excited laughter swelled. Mr. and Mrs. Watkins sat suffused with happy pride. Florentine's face was pale as she held out her arms to take the package. "Open it, open it!" She heard the whispers all around her. The girls pressed close. Some one had to help her untie the string. . . . The string was loose, the white paper off—tissue paper, crackling and soft, and wadded into it, an enormous doll! . . . There was a long sigh from the children crowding to see. The doll lay revealed—closed, waxy-lidded eyes and golden-brown lashes upon pink bisque cheeks, golden curls matted upon its cold bisque forehead, dress of pink satin, pink stockings, gold buckles on its tiny shoes. . . . "Oh, look!" A moan came from the girls. They crowded about to touch the hair and the satin gown. "Florentine, will you let me see? Is she jointed all over? Can I just *touch* her?" Heads through the audience craned to see, people half rose, the room was a buzz.

Florentine sat holding the big box. She was mute with a surfeit of bliss. Nothing else could happen after this.

In the loud hubbub of leaving, people were all crowded and talking at the door. Children came running on padding little feet up the sloping aisles, and bumped joyously into parents. "Oh, here you are, are you?" A father put his arm around a little shoulder, squeezed a flaxen head against him and held it there while he went on talking, and the other persons smiled. "See all the things I got, papa!"

"Well, well!" He didn't really see them. "Santy Claus was pretty good to you!"

Mothers had gone down to the front rows to find their own infants. They sat down in convenient pews and tried to drag small, stiff, black overshoes over little feet limp in their laps. The white sheeting on the platform was marked all over with footprints, the evergreen trimmings were pulled out from their tacks. The Christmas tree stood sparkling but denuded. From it spread the odors of pine needles, hot wax, popcorn and paper.

Mrs. Watkins had taken Florentine at once into the Infant Room to find her wraps. Mr. Watkins waited in the audience room near the register. He talked in a manly way with Mr. Hollister—also waiting—about the effect this snow would have upon the ground; but his ears were straining with shamed eagerness for the words that were occasionally spoken to him: "I should think you'd be pretty proud of that little girl tonight, Mr. Watkins!"

In the Infant Room, where tired mothers were finding wraps in the piled mountain shaking and toppling on an old discarded pew— "How can we *ever* find our own things in this jam!" Mrs. Watkins took down Florentine's white wraps from their special hook. "Are you tired, darling?" she mourned. Even when she was drawing on the little coat, and her back was turned to the room, she was tinglingly aware of the notice of the others and the glory shed upon her by her child. She pretended to think only of the hurry of getting home. As soon as she turned toward the room, she expected the congratulations to break out. With careful, proud, reluctant hands she lifted off the silver crown and star.

A woman came searching through the Infant Room with a big-eyed little child clinging to her hand. "Oh, here she is!" She encouraged the child, "Ask her! I think she will!"; and then she said to Mrs. Watkins, "Here's a little girl, Mrs. Watkins, who thinks she can't go home until she's seen Florentine Watkins' big doll!"

"Why, of course!" Mrs. Watkins said with radiant graciousness. "It's in the other room. Mr. Watkins has it. You come in with us, Lucy. Florentine will show it to you."

"I want to see that, too! Mamma, I want to see it, too! I want to see the big doll."

Now all the crowd who had been pawing over the wraps and staying away from Mrs. Watkins and Florentine out of respect, diffidence and envy, came flocking around them.

"These children want to see the doll, daddy!"

"Want to see the doll?"

Mr. Watkins opened the box. The little children gave great sighs. Mothers had to clutch little reaching hands and warn, "Oh, mustn't touch!" while Mrs. Watkins smiled graciously, but alertly. Mr. Watkins set the box upright, and the bright blue eyes of the doll flew open between its golden-brown lashes. Lola Hollister cried with an anguish of longing, "Oh, mamma, look! The doll's got *real* little gold buckles on its shoes!" Mrs. Hollister said in a slight, withdrawn voice, "Yes, I see!", and gave a painful little smirk. She compared this doll with the doll Lola was going to get in the morning. Her heart was rent with a painful anguish of jealousy for her child. Mr. Hollister tried to be admiring, but it shamed him, shamed his adequacy as a father, when he too compared this doll with Lola's doll, which he had bought. Some of the crowding faces were artlessly adoring. Others had a look of reserve which Mrs. Watkins' alert eyes caught. At last all the wondering childish eyes were satiated with the vision. Hands of mothers drew little figures gently back and voices murmured: "Well, are you satisfied? Have you seen the big doll?"

Long-drawn sighs answered them.

But there was something that made Florentine wonder. Mary Louise did not come to look at the doll. "I saw it before!" she said snippily to Lola, and ran off. The doll was too much. The Watkinses, on the very peak of glory in showing it off, did not know. Even some of the admiring ones went away from the church saying: they shouldn't have bought the doll; they shouldn't have put it on the Christmas tree; it was too expensive for a little girl; the Watkinses made them tired trotting out that child; next year they hoped some other child would get a chance.

The chief families of the church, with the minister and his wife, stood talking at the door. Mr. Watkins had set Florentine in a pew, and she stood leaning against him while he kept his arm around her. As people passed him, going to the door, they stopped. "My, but you must be proud of her tonight!" Florentine touched his cheek with a little princess air. The great doll was asleep in its closed box. The room glittered in tinsel and evergreen, and her presents were heaped on the pew beside her.

Freddy Perkins, being dragged out by a father who wanted to get home, called back eagerly, "G'night Flor'ntine!"

"Goodnight!" she answered with starry graciousness.

Old ladies moving slowly to the door, stopping to pat her little woolly sleeve with thin fingers, murmured, "Wasn't she dear? Just *like* a little fairy!" Florentine accepted the homage with sweet, childish royalty. But in her mind, under all the glory, was a tremulous, shining wonder that craved to be reassured.

Mrs. Watkins was flushed. She drank down the praise that burned her like a fiery wine. "She was simply perfect, Mrs. Watkins!" "I know you're proud tonight!" But the first perfect bliss of the applause that followed Florentine's exercise was marred. Florentine had won, and yet there were people who went away unconvinced, who seemed to have other, strange values. Already the atmosphere of universal praise had slackened. She was jealous of the laughter that still followed any mention of Howard Hopkins. "Wasn't that kid funny? Say, he was great!" Could there be people who had enjoyed him more than Florentine? She hated the minister's wife, who kept repeating, with effervescing tactfulness:

"They were *all* good!"

It was time to close up the church. The people who were talking over the program, the expenses, the success of the evening, began to look about for their children; and the Watkinses were beginning to realize that they had heard all the praise they were likely to hear for this evening. Lola and Mary Louise and Kitty were playing a game, chasing each other through the pews and down the aisles. "Come! It's time to go home! Remember, tomorrow is Christmas!" They came scampering up to the register, flushed, with disordered hair, panting and giggling together. "What are you little girls up to?" some one asked tolerantly. Kitty pinched Lola, and they laughed; but when they looked at Florentine, their eyes grew sober and aloof, considering.

"You go get your wraps on, young lady!"

Kitty ran off. She turned to call back to Mary Louise, "Don't you forget about tomorrow!" Mary Louise answered, "I won't! Don't *you* forget, Lola!" "I won't." They were going to see each other's presents. Lola gave a timid look at Florentine, but did not ask her to come. Florentine's big doll was so wonderful —finer than anything they would get. Florentine, in her white dress and slippers, noticed by every one, was no longer one of them.

Florentine stood silent and cool. She could not make a move toward the other girls, but she looked after them with a strange loneliness; and all at once it seemed to her that they had been having the most fun in the world playing together. She was suddenly very tired. Her eyes blinked under the dazzle of the lights. She no longer cared what people said to her. The program was over. She had her doll. What more was there? Christmas would be nothing after this evening.

Mrs. Watkins said commiseratingly, "Hurry up, daddy. She's tired."

Mr. Watkins picked Florentine up in his arms again. As they went outside the warm church into the snow, her disheveled little head drooped upon his shoulder. Mrs. Watkins was carrying the doll, and she was saying with anxious caution, "I was so afraid some of those children would do something to this doll! Daddy and mother had to send away off for it. It isn't to play with every day—just on special occasions. And Florentine, you must never let any of the girls handle it, no matter if they do ask you. You can't trust other children with it. Remember how Kitty ruined your little piano! This doll is much too expensive for that."

Florentine did not answer. All down the silent street—it had stopped snowing now, the ground where the corner light shone was covered with a soft, white, diamondy fluff—she snuggled down against her father's shoulder. To be carried by her father, and give way to the strong shelter of his arms, was all she wanted now. When they came up onto their own porch, stamping the snow from their rubbers, he set her down. They were going into the house, proud, happy and satisfied; but by the hall light they saw her sleepy face under the bright dishevelment of hair, drunk with the glories of the evening, forlorn now and bewildered, able to bear no more. Her eyes almost closed. It was as if they had never realized until now how small she was.

Her father said heartily, "Well, the big night's over!"

But her mother cried, in an anguish of adoring pity: "She must go to bed this minute! She'll be all tired out if she doesn't. We mustn't forget that tomorrow will be here."

Susan and the Doctor

SUSAN started going with the boys early. Too early. Her mother had died, and there was no one to look after her. Her father had affairs of his own on his hands.

Susan's escapades, from the time she was thirteen, had been a source of talk in the town where she lived. But they seemed all to have happened in a past that was now incredible. People had almost forgotten that she had once gone with Buddie Merton and Carl Flannigan and Chuck Myers and Pat Dougherty —her affair had been going on for so many years with the Doctor.

And it had obscured not only her relations to other men, but almost everything else about Susan. People did not think about the long and steady efficiency of her position in the Farmers Bank, where she had risen from clerk to assistant cashier, and where she was actually a stand-by. When they went into the bank, and up to Susan's little barred window, they did not see her—slim, shining-haired, immaculate—as the cashier who dealt out nickels and dimes and bills with swift, experienced, white fingers. They did not recall how her present security was due to herself alone. She had never depended upon her father for a living. She had never depended upon any one. She had borrowed money and taken a business course and then asked old Henry Houghton for a place in the bank; and it was upon that first meager and grudging admission that she had lived and put money aside and paid for the always fashionable

perfection of her tailored clothes and the smartness of her hats.
They looked through the little window at her white hands and
smooth hair, and thought:

"I wonder how her affair is coming on with the Doctor!"

Oh, yes! Susan was handy, and she was bright. She made
some of those pretty clothes herself—knitted scarves when
scarves were in fashion, and embroidered collar and cuff sets
when they were the thing. She kept her two rooms and kitchenette at Mrs. Calverton's in exquisite order. Women did admit
that. And there were men in town who said that no one in that
bank knew as much about its business as Susan. But all that
seemed irrelevant to the consistent interest of her love affair.

It obscured the rest of her life to Susan herself. There was
never a moment when she was not aware of it. At the bank,
when she was making up accounts with swift and practiced
accuracy, it was there in her breast, something unsatisfied, an
ache and a craving; it was there behind the businesslike rhythm
of the adding machine; and when she sat at the big table in the
back room where the sunshine lay slantwise in the morning its
sweetness enveloped her in dreamy pain. She could never give
herself up to the warmth of the sunshine. Her white fingers
had to keep at work to ease the craving and subdue the thoughts
that drew to their tight, inevitable center in her mind.

"Always at it!" old Tommy Munson, wealthy farmer and
nominal vice president, said to her jovially when he came into
the bank.

He was the only person in town who thought of Susan as
cashier and seemed never to have heard of her affair with the
Doctor.

It was with her when she went out on the street at noon.
She frowned at the outdoor brightness. Suppose the Doctor

should come past! The possibility of it blinded her for a moment, with tense persistence of desire; and she would have liked—if she could have liked!—to stay in the shelter of the bank, where it was shaded and apart. She might be with Nita Allen, the stenographer; but her eyes could not be restrained from their restless, watching alertness. She must notice every car on the street. She must look down the narrowing vista to the building where the Doctor had his office on the fifth floor, and must strain for a brief and unsatisfying glimpse of the small and distant figure of a man who might be the Doctor himself coming out of the building. In Wessel's drugstore, where she had her tuna-fish sandwich and glass of malted milk at the shining new counter, she had to talk gay and brightly, in the usual ironic repartee, with the crowded line of stenographers and young business men, above her restless preoccupation and the constant small wear of pain.

"Hello, Susan! How are you?"

"Fine."

"Where do you keep yourself these days?"

In the busy street of the growing town she felt almost a stranger—she, Susan, who had lived here all her life and knew every window display in every store! But her affair with the Doctor had set her apart from the rest of the town—from the old crowd, her own crowd: Elsie Adams, who was married and had two babies; Letha Grove, who lived with her parents and hadn't changed since high school days; Mary Wilson, who came back now and then from her work in Chicago. Susan seemed never to have known another man than the Doctor; and at times, when she heard in the drugstore the animated chatter about dances, she would wonder if she could actually be Susan—the one whom the boys used to fall over one another to ask to dances, who chose this one or that with imperious freedom, who was the most popular girl of her day.

She was tense and defiant in her loyalty—and the thing had been going on, how many years?—but all the same, her eyes could not meet the curious or carefully incurious eyes of older women, her mother's friends, whom she might pass on this street and who would ask her, "Well, Susan, how are you getting along?" The consciousness of her affair with the Doctor hung between them, clouding the old neighborly relationship. Mrs. Andrews had tried to "speak to her" once about it. She had talked about Susan's mother while Susan stood with head up and lips haughtily closed. But it made Susan dread the street.

When she went into the bank again she would sometimes stand for a moment, humiliated and hurt through every nerve, because this one thing must claim her whole being. The spirit of independence, upright and narrow, that lived in her slim body rebelled. She thought of the time when she used to say airily to Carl Flannigan, "No, I can't go anywhere—I've got to do some work for the bank"; and of the later days when, after one of those excitingly perilous meetings with Pat Dougherty, who was just getting his divorce, she used to go back to the bank, and think with cool exultancy, "Well, here I'm by myself!" She, Susan, who had always been so sure, imperious, efficient, cool . . .

"I won't stand this. It's got to end."

But then the far more torturing fear that it might end shot through her in pain.

But when she went home after work—home? well, back to Mrs. Calverton's—at half-past-five, through smoky twilights of fall or the veiled tenderness of spring, resentful wonder would come over her again. Had there actually been a time when she was her own self, Susan, free and wild and belonging to herself; when she could walk swiftly through such a twilight, breathing the acrid smoke, or linger and lift her face to the damp spring air, with love left over for the little leaves and the tulips, with nothing to come between her and the night?

She went up the same gray-painted steps of the large, neat porch. She put her hand on the same bronze knob of the door. Inside, the house odor, orderly and slightly aging and remote, never quite that of home, enveloped her in dreariness. She could not stand the board that creaked on the stairs and the hot-water faucet that ran a meager and maddening trickle.

How could she endure this place a day longer? She had certainly never meant to spend all her life in a rooming house. Independence was all right. She wasn't going to have to ask anybody for things. But Susan had always planned, being methodical and worldly shrewd, that when the time came, when she was ready, she would marry and have a home of her own, the kind she wanted. And here she was, well along in the twenties, with nearly all the other girls in the crowd settled, and she still living in two rented rooms at Mrs. Calverton's! Sometimes it seemed as if her whole scheme of life were going astray.

But when she entered her room, with its waiting orderliness of cushions and reading lamp and cigarette trays placed here and there, the dreariness vanished. Her impatience sternly curbed itself. Mrs. Calverton was used to the whole thing. The Doctor could come, and she let them alone. A move—one little thing like that—and the whole perilous, precious status of the thing might be lost.

Besides, the Doctor would be here in a little while.

Susan went into the kitchenette. The shelves were filled with things of his own special choice—Mocha coffee, fig preserves, salted almonds. Susan saw these things, and they brought back the beloved and secret intimacy of a hundred little dinners. She used to love to put on her best clothes and go out to dinner with men, to the dining room of the Melrose, the most expensive place in town, where she would see people and be seen by them. But there was a painful kind of delight in giving up these old pleasures of hers—her own special pleasures. She wanted them again at times; but there was the same delight in sacrificing them to his demands for secrecy and seclusion.

Anyway, he would be here in a little while. She would be with him.

He came up the stairs, into the living room, into the doorway of the kitchenette. Susan felt the vital largeness of his presence, warming the whole place into life; although—with her old manner of cool concentration—she did not turn from her work at the small gas stove. His arms were around her, and she was drawn backward.

"Susan! Aren't you going to tell me you're glad to see me?"

Through his arms she felt the straining domination of his need.

The dinner was exciting and happy and cozy—one of their own little dinners, at the card table with the linen cloth that Susan had embroidered in her leisure time, with the favorite dishes she had kept from her own home, and with the orange candles and the green-glass candlesticks that he had brought her. The shades were down. Their voices were low, so that even Mrs. Calverton could not hear. He told her his professional troubles and leaned upon the cool practicality of her advice, even while he was demanding from her the sympathy that her pride would not seem to yield him. The old atmosphere of troubled splendor was about him, blinding her clear-sightedness, and forcing devotion, that was half maternal, out of the independence she could not admit that she had lost.

And then, when dinner was over, he wouldn't permit her to wash the dishes, upset the precision of her routine to her anger and delight, and drew her to him.

But after he had left, Susan lay in her narrow bed aching and alone. Her tingling body was tense with resentment. No matter how they parted, her body was left tense and aching—for he went away, he left her alone, she could not stay warm and at ease in his arms and wake up beside him in the morning. She hated him.

Then she turned and tossed. Her sleep seemed always to be shallow and tense. She craved wildly to break away from him. Why must her own need be sacrificed to his? Her life was passing. But it was as if he had sown within her the seed of his trouble. She could not wrench it out of her. In the night, in the darkness, she could let her coolness be diffused with aching tenderness. This was the only way that it could be for him —so he thought; and she, Susan, was the only woman in town with courage to take him as he must be taken. She thrilled with pride of his largeness, handsomeness, and splendor; and she would rather have him secretly, equivocally hers than to have all the common, tame little men whom the other girls had married. The straight and narrow loyalty that made her a stand-by in the bank held her to him in tense, undeviating devotion.

The affair had begun in quite a different way.

Susan, for the time being, was free of all her men. In

disgust she had broken the last frayed end of her brief but hotly melodramatic "case" with Pat Dougherty. And she didn't want to go with any one for a while. It seemed to her that she had tried nearly all the eligible men in this town, and that there was no interest in any of them. There wasn't a one whose silly devotion could make up for the loss of her position in the bank or who could give her anything that could surpass it.

"I'm hard-hearted," Susan said coolly and with a slightly malicious enjoyment of power, to the wistfully sentimental Letha Grove. "If I ever get married, I'll marry for money. I'll marry a man who can get more for me than I can get for myself. At present—I'll stay as I am."

In idleness and in revulsion from the extremely hot persistence of Pat Dougherty, Susan had looked up some of the old high-school crowd again. She took pleasure in going with Letha Grove and "the girls" to concerts and basket-ball games. There was in it a defiance of the men who admired her, and a challenge to them. Never had she enjoyed her work at the bank so much. She exulted in the rapid, ceaseless click of her adding machine. Whenever she thought of Pat Dougherty, it was with a wild, glad sense of escape. At this time Susan used to wake up and look out at the dew-wet grass of Mrs. Calverton's lawn, with a feeling as cool and free and fresh as the morning.

However, such a state of affairs could not last for any one used to as much excitement as Susan. She began to get restless and to make excuses when the girls wanted her to go somewhere with them. She wanted—what did she want?—she didn't know. But something.

"I'll tell you what's the matter with you," Mrs. Calverton said. Susan used to go downstairs sometimes and talk to Mrs. Calverton in the evening. "You've never been in love. That's what's the trouble."

"I!" Susan exclaimed. "This is about the first time I've been out of it."

"You think so," Mrs. Calverton said.

She rocked. She was mending curtains, while Susan embroidered a stamped pink nightgown that she had bought in the "art goods department" of Stephenson's store. She ducked her mouth and bit off a thread.

Susan laughed. It was funny to hear Mrs. Calverton talking to her!—Mrs. Calverton, shapeless and faded, whose husband (every one knew) had been good-for-nothing, never kept a job, went out with other women, and had left Mrs. Calverton to take in roomers and keep this old family home of hers going.

"That's so," Mrs. Calverton insisted. "I know what I'm talking about." She added, with that portentous mysteriousness in talking about men and marriage that older women affected, and that Susan had always laughed at, "You'll see some day!"

Susan laughed gleefully again. But when she went back upstairs to her room, that she had taken such delight in arranging and keeping just as she wanted it, she felt restless and lonely. She resented Mrs. Calverton. Old married women always pretended to know so much. Besides kindness, and a sad dwelling upon past mysterious events, it seemed to her that there had been resentment in Mrs. Calverton's tone, and a gloomy looking forward to seeing Susan leveled down at last with other women. But, superior as she felt, what Mrs. Calverton had said—her tone and her look of quiet, mysterious knowledge recurred sometimes to Susan; and again she felt that restlessness.

She began to look at men with a different eye, although she was scarcely aware of it. Town seemed all dull and too familiar to her, and she thought of going away somewhere. She was jealous of her present freedom, and tired of it. At any rate, she couldn't stand "the girls" any longer!—their twitterings, their secrets, their eager veiled interest in every man who appeared. They all seemed silly to her; and there was even more interest in the saddened, subdued, mysteriously completed presence of Mrs. Calverton.

Not that Susan thought much of Mrs. Calverton's great wisdom!

One day she happened to pass the Doctor on the street. She had never really thought, before, of how handsome he was— and interesting, too, and mysterious! Living in that big old brick house, in the great lawn that was dark with trees, and with the dimly romantic legend of the "not quite right" aunt and invalid mother. She hadn't really thought of his good looks or noticed them because she hadn't considered the Doctor within the realms of possibility. He had never gone with a woman in this town. He never appeared at dances. Susan began to amuse herself by wondering about him and speculating half idly about him. When she hurt her arm, in a fall from the rocks at a picnic, she wouldn't let Ross Crabtree take her to Doctor Bradley's office when they got to town; but the next day, in a spirit of mischief and daring, and she didn't know what else, Susan went to the Doctor's office.

She hadn't exactly meant anything at first—or nothing that could be put into words. She hadn't thought when she began it that it would be essentially different from her other wild and yet carefully controlled affairs that never went too far. . . . Or had she meant something more? Had she been restless, wearied, impatient, tired of her cold and narrow hardness, wishing to be forced somehow into change? . . . At any rate, she had meant nothing like this. She hadn't dreamed, seeing that handsome face upon the street one day and wondering what the Doctor would be like if she knew him, how the sullen humors, the regal gloom, and lordly gayety, the insistent warmth of his intimate presence could break into her shining hardness; and how at last her cool strength, at the appeal of his sudden childishness, could diffuse into a passion of tenderness. She had no idea when she started deftly, and with a subtly cool speculation, to draw him to her, that the thing could ever be real—that he would want more of her, and that she would give it, with the future—always so clear to Susan—lost in haze.

Dissatisfaction, certainly, hadn't come in at the start! There had been first—looking back, when she happened to be alone, over the long, half buried, only half comprehended course of the whole affair—first that subtle and slightly malicious pleasure, then amazement, fear, defiance, shame, and glory. She had grown closer and closer to him; and her first imperious overriding of difficulties had changed imperceptibly into defense, support, and compensation for his bonds.

It was a long while before dissatisfaction had actually begun —a tiny, gnawing restlessness at first, and then a never-ended craving, and now a mingled long resentment and sick tenderness. In the beginning she had found a dramatic pleasure in taking him and yielding to him in spite of difficulties. The impossibility had added to the intensity in a way that shook her with a wild, rapturous surprise, while at the same time that small, subtle, calculating part of her mind had kept thinking that the same impossibility left her ultimately free. Free! Well, she had learned something since then. Mrs. Calverton, had Susan admitted it to her, might well have been satisfied. Slowly, quite beyond reason, seemingly beyond her own desire, it began to enrage Susan that he did not simply burst the bonds, cast off those two old women, and be hers entirely. Always now, until his arms went round her, drowning her in rapture and tenderness, she was angry that he held her so, in this long suspension of living, that he would not finally take her or finally let her go.

But to her amazement, her shaken and furious incredulity, whenever she finally determined to bring the affair to some conclusion, she was stopped, in breathless terror, by the still more unbearable thought that she might lose him entirely. Beyond that she could not go.

Other girls in town, girls living at home and managing only a "date" now and then with an unattached man, envied Susan and the Doctor. They saw the two driving off in the Doctor's car, not to a dance—they never went to dances—but all by themselves for a long, mysterious ride. People had seen them sitting, or wandering slowly, under the trees in Dawsons Grove. The intimate apartness of the ambiguous couple, with the wonder and speculation that surrounded them, seemed to these girls so much more romantic than the open and inevitable companionship of the married couples in town. Letha Grove, if Susan had known it, looked at her with that furtive dubious- ness not because she disapproved of her, but because she admired her, and because Letha felt herself humble and colorless beside Susan. The audacity and mystery of the unexplained relation- ship gave Susan a kind of glitter in the eyes of the town.

But Susan herself could scarcely realize how the situation and the relationship between them had slowly changed through the years.

She remembered, with brooding nostalgia now—a wonder if she could have made things end differently—what he used to tell her at first.

"You're the only thing I've got in this town. The only thing I've got in this damned, futile existence." And then his voice broke, and his big handsome body was twisted and crumpled in pain and longing before her awed, incredulous eyes. "Oh, God, Susan—give me some happiness! You're free. You can do as you please with yourself. And I'm held in this damned— oh no, God, I can't call it that!—but I can't live in it any longer, they never let me out of it."

Yes, that was true. It was she who had been the free one, the incalculable one, at first. He used to tell her that she lived in the open daylight and he always in shadow. She was the only ray of daylight that he had. Was it through a long, underground persistence of craving, then, to right the balance and assert his final necessity of domination, that he had slowly bound her to him and taken her freedom with her love? By the giving of a free gift she had bound herself. But that she, Susan, should be conquered and held at last by tenderness!—what an amazing overturning of nature and fate.

Gradually, what he said to her came to be:

"But how can I? You knew how things were in the beginning. Well, it's just the same. They're still alive. And you wouldn't live with them."

Even that was true. The old imperious Susan could not even have contemplated being shut up for a night with those terrible women in that gloomy house.

But it was his contentment, she thought now, that made her resentment burn. (But wasn't it she who had made him so?) Nevertheless, it was his contentment, under the long habit of sacrifice to those women, with the unfailing, romantic comfort of Susan's love—no matter how he might burst out into terrible despair at times, and at times cry brokenly in her arms.

She wondered if he had grown to enjoy the gloom of misanthropy, his dark and dramatic aspect of it, fostered by the shuttered gloom of the big brick house. Sometimes it seemed to Susan, bitterly, that that was all her love had done for him. He was content to live in the aging splendor of the old home and then to come for happiness to the bright, small orderliness of Susan's rooms, to eat their perfect little dinners, to force out of her slim hardness a poignant comfort for all his wrongs, to remain with her—it might be—an hour in fierce and secret rapture, and then to break away and take the wholeness of himself back into the familiar gloom, leaving her broken. . . .

"My god, Susan, I can't change things! I wish you'd keep still."

She was not too loyal to wonder sometimes, now, if the hold of the two old women was still so inevitable. She had made him a different person from the solitary man she had passed upon the street. The compensation and sustainment had done their work. That terrible hold did not sap all his strength or turn his energy into hopeless brooding. He had a secret pride. And although he still shunned dances and social meetings—and made Susan shun them—in his old misanthropic way, he was no longer afraid to meet other men. His training and study, after all these years, were at last beginning to show; and people in physical extremity did not care about the equivocal reputation of their surgeon. He was making money now. Susan knew how much that meant; and fear had slowly grown into her that he could make a place for her if he would. But she dared not quiet the fear by an assurance that would force the last of her pride to break away from him.

And was there joy in her love for him any more? Yes, she had actually come to question that. Joy, which had made her look out at the familiar world through Mrs. Calverton's window one March morning upon thawing patches of snow which shone with a blinding brilliance, and feel that the song of the first spring robin had bubbled in sheer happiness out of her own body and heart? Tenderness which had melted the clear hard edges of her well-known little world and watered the dry exactness of her vision with a living freshness and wondering depth of comprehension? . . . Or had she yielded so much to him that she simply had nothing left for herself?

Then, perhaps, she would get a new dress or discover in a magazine a new kind of cushion she could make for her room. She would shampoo her hair and put in with her skillful fingers just the perfect suggestion of a finger wave. She would be feeling well. The whole affair would change its aspect for her. She would pity those two old women, who clung to the presence of their son, while Susan herself had all the best of him. She could look forward to the time when he would be hers altogether—when she could go to sleep beside him in a warm sweet luxury of ease, and wake up still beside him in the morning.

And she thought that she was glad—yes, ultimately glad. His need, his domination, and his terrible dependence upon her, had forced out of her the sweetness of a compassion she had never known that she possessed. It held her to him with a tightness nothing more equal could have done. Mrs. Calverton was right—Mrs. Calverton knew after all. His dominance, more imperious because more needful than her own, had crushed out of pain a strangled fragrance that without him she would never have known.

His mother died. Susan heard it at noon in the drugstore. Fred Jefferson told her.

"I hear the Doctor's mother died last night."

Things irrelevant to that statement were the first that came into Susan's mind: Fred Jefferson's eyes, curious and cold, betraying the tone he had taken, and the calculated shock of his statement (Fred was an old beau of hers, he had always taken a sneering tone about her affair with the Doctor); and then a painful thrust of anger because she must hear from other people this news affecting the man who was hers. The news seemed to have no other significance, although a kind of sickness made her food tasteless to her.

It was not until she went out of the drugstore, into the open light of the street, that she stopped still—for the barest second—while the meaning of the event opened up dizziness before her.

"The Doctor's mother died last night."

A wildness of impatience thrilled through her. It was agony to go on with her work at the bank. She walked home through a changed, incredible world—it was June, lawns were fresh, roses were out. Susan hadn't noticed that until now. The low sunlight of half-past-five lay across Mrs. Calverton's lawn. The green thick stalks of the peony bush bent over and laid flushed thick blossoms against the cool earth. For the first time in years, Susan thought of the woods . . . in the deep green filter of sunlight, the flush of wild geraniums. . . . Cars sped down the wide bright street. She heard voices of children playing. All the town, all the world, was coming out of the tightness and uncertainty of spring into the open and sunlit freedom of summer.

There was a summery light in Susan's room. A pleasant light lay over the mirror. She stood and looked. Eagerness made the brown eyes sparkle out from the fine lines that were beginning to surround them. It flushed the cheeks and ripened the lips.

Her whole white body in its pink summer dress was flushed and open and warm, like the roses, and the peonies, and the wild geraniums. She had not yet lost the youth of her girlhood, but womanhood curved the slight lines of her form. She was at her best this warm sweet hour of late afternoon . . . let him come, let him take her now, claim her, keep her. . . .

He telephoned the bare news to her—a guarded voice, withdrawn and strange. He could not see her just now. He would manage it tomorrow. But after all these years, on this perfect night, it was terrible to be thrown back again into the old tense suspension of living. She ate a solitary dinner, stood at the window awhile, and went to bed.

The news made its small uproar in the town. Not because of the Doctor's mother herself—she had been, in her own person, almost forgotten—but because of the way her death would affect the Doctor and Susan.

"What's been the matter with her?"

There were very few who could actually say. "She used to be quite a beautiful woman. The old Doctor did everything for her." It was rumored, but never quite substantiated, that the old Doctor had taken his own life. But they only knew that for years she had absorbed the care and money of her son; and all reminiscence of her ended:

"I suppose now the Doctor will marry Susan."

And Susan, accepted for some time in a role seemingly static, became a heroine of a sort in the eyes of the town again. Her old challenging interest came back to her. She seemed no longer set apart from the town's life. Again she was appreciated in her shining and immaculate slimness; although now the memory of the affair, the never-ending curiosity and speculation as to exactly how far it had gone—its culmination indignantly denied by the innocent and insisted upon with secret delight and outward cynical derision by the knowing ones—shed a deeper and more significant aura of romance about her.

But the summer went on and the thing still hung fire. The Doctor stayed on in the brick house. Susan went daily to her work at the bank and back to her rooms at Mrs. Calverton's. The roses were gone, the peonies shed their petals on the grass; there were only bitter-smelling yarrow and boneset in the woods. People wondered, laughed cynically, or were indifferent; women who had loved Susan's mother talked angrily about the selfishness of men; and the rest of the force in the bank, getting their heads together, declared:

"Susan ought to give him a jacking up!"

There were so many things to think of, the Doctor said. There was the old home. There was Aunt Agnes. She trusted him. After all these years, he could not put her in an institution. And when Susan, hard and resentful in her balked desire, would not agree, he called her cruel and cold. Susan, with the heat and confidence of her fresh bloom upon her, fought with him, almost in the old arrogant way.

"It can't stay as it is. Don't you see? That's all I'm saying."

Almost—but without the old straight and clear direction of her free imperiousness—because beyond that statement she dared not go. She was sobbing and angry; her hands still clutching with weakened passion at the edges of the couch, but a feeling of brokenness lay within her. The Doctor sat in the big chair that he claimed as his. His voice was husky. He was almost too tired to speak.

"Susan, I'm tired. I've got to have some time to myself. I've had this strain for years. I can't think of anything. I can't do anything now."

Then go, then go, Susan wanted to say. But it was only telling herself to go. She was bound up in him. The old habit of passionate consolation remained; and she could not keep her strength or her anger at the tired appeal of his hands loosely clasping the arms of the chair, and the bright remoteness of pain in his eyes. She went over and put nerveless arms about him and laid her wet cheek against his hair.

After he had left she lay on the couch; and then tired, more tired than he could be, more tired than anything in the world, she struggled up through a daze of weakness to take off her clothes, fold them neatly, wash her face, brush her hair—as her stern sense of orderliness still commanded—and lie down, on her single cot—lie down to the old dissatisfaction turned now into apathy.

The next morning the lawn outside the windows was not so bright. The green, still thick and deep along the edges, beside the sunken coolness of the old cement walk, was fading into dry brown at the center. The leaves had a look of dustiness.

The Doctor came to see Susan as always. But a sense of estrangement, an actual thing, not the old resentment that had made her turn more passionately to him, had crept between them. Or was he a little more cautious and infrequent, now that the eyes of the town were curiously upon him, and that something else might be expected of him?

Susan was no longer a glittering figure to the town. How had it happened? . . . She was good-looking still. The clear features, the slim, straight figure, the smart perfection still were left. Her red-gold hair was smooth. But the fresh attraction of her bloom had faded out of her. How and when had it gone? A little while ago, and Susan was "looking better than ever." But now when she stared into her mirror it was with a sense of dry and hopeless helplessness. The brown eyes stared back, with the sparkle worn out of them, from a face not altered from its familiar contour but from which the living texture had faded. Her swift white hands had settled into a mechanical rhythm at their work in the bank. The warmth of sympathetic interest that people had felt for a few weeks was gone. They were thinking, while they looked at her curiously, "I wonder if he will marry her!"

For imperceptibly the light which shone upon that image of two had shifted and brought out the figure of the Doctor into relief. The lifting of the strain was beginning to tell. He looked fresher, freer, more vigorous. The gloom had lifted so that his handsomeness was no longer mysteriously perceptible through his aloofness. Any one could see it now. He met people with an awakened interest. Nothing held him back from them —nothing but the still secret, unacknowledged pull of his affair with Susan. And they felt a new respect for him, for it was plain that he was his own man at last.

"Well, the poor fellow," men often said, when women accused him of dealing selfishly with Susan, "he's been tied down ever since he was a kid. Let him stretch himself awhile before he gets tied down again."

Women, on the other hand, to men who still admired and stood up for Susan, often said with a hard, small clarity of perception:

"I think he could do better than Susan now."

So that no one was really surprised when he started going with another girl.

Susan knew it long before she consciously knew it as a definite actuality, long before her tortured imagination began to settle and dig its talons into the actual image of now this girl and now that. She could only turn at night in a restless fever of conjecture and rejection of the fact itself. She wanted to know, and at the same time skirted all possibility of discovery, until finally her torture of uncertainty grew more unbearable than knowledge itself, and forced her to say to him—a laughing hint that couldn't possibly be true, "I believe you must be going with some other girl!"

He answered her impatiently and without sympathy, "Well, good heavens, Susan, you played around long enough! We can't shut out the whole world forever."

He to say that! But when he had been bound and moody, it was just what she must do!—until now, forced into the way he had made for her, she wanted no one but him. Another of her accusations against him. They were piling up into a weight of pain that lay upon her and ruined her happiness with him. Still, they did not suffice to permit her to be the one who broke the tie. Susan had been as calculable as quicksilver with the other men whom she had known. But her rectitude and loyalty, once demanded, once actually forced and given, held her with a grip beyond resentment.

That answer, little as it told and incredible as it seemed, was an admission. And now the torture of her imagination was worse than anything she had gone through before. She did not know who it was. People were thoughtful enough to avoid all mention of the name, and even of the Doctor's name; but she could see their knowledge in the curious, conjecturing glances of their eyes. Her natural swift directness made her crave to go straight to the point and learn the fact. But that long suspension of action seemed to have bound her into itself so that she was unable to move hand or foot out of the new agony of suspense.

Susan was too clear-sighted to deceive herself with false reasons for the longer and ever more irregular intervals between his visits. In these intervals she wondered bitterly why she wanted him to come at all. She had allowed—they had allowed—that brief brightness of recovered June to die out of the summer, and since then it had never been the same. She felt as if their love were going as irresistibly and irrevocably as the summer itself. She tried fiercely to wrench what sweetness she could out of every meeting, giving up in the end to her failure with the same dry hopelessness that came upon her when she looked at her fading image in the glass. She was out of step— could not catch the new rhythm—had responded for so long to his need that she had no response for his new desire for light-heartedness.

But she could have responded! Why, she used to be known as the gayest girl in town! All the boys had said of her, "You can have the most fun with Susan." And after all the years of passionate submission to his unhappiness, that old brightness had been alive in her only a little while ago. It was perhaps her worst accusation against him that he had, at that time—her time —forced out of her tenderness and consolation again instead of fulfilment.

Now, what had she left? But she could not let him go.

Fear had crept into the place of dissatisfaction in the tense center of her mind. It gnawed at her all the time, no matter what she was doing. Sometimes she would stop work for a moment in the bank, caught in an inexplicable breathlessness of fear. She dreaded having him come and dreaded just as much that he might not come. Every meeting might be their last. Then why not make it the last? . . . She understood Mrs. Calverton now.

Still, outwardly, the affair seemed to go on pretty much as it always did. They had their little dinners together. The warm weather lasted on into the fall; and on Sunday they were to drive as usual to the Four Corners.

Susan dragged herself out of her tired inertia and got up in good time on Sunday morning so that she could bathe, wash and wave her hair, and press her white-silk sleeveless dress. Now, in the bright daylight, she wondered why she should dread this meeting. She thought of their long time together. One meeting like this could not really end it—not with the leaves still on the trees, dahlias still scarlet out in the garden, only one red branch on the big soft-maple tree. She tried to wrest confidence out of the immaculate slimness of the figure in the glass—when she turned just that certain way, the long lines of the form seemed perfect, and the brown eyes were dark and bright in the white skin under the faint shadow of the white hat. But she knew that she dared not risk turning and letting the light fall this way and that. The same inexplicable fear kept gnawing under her expectation.

She looked out of the window and saw the Doctor coming up the walk. His roadster stood out in front. He looked handsome, large, well-dressed. Susan felt even more than the old thrilling leap of pride. She wanted to tell every one that this man was hers. The time had long passed when it was enough to know this sweetly in secret. The familiarity of going down the walk together and getting into the car made her fear look small and foolish, like a night terror dragged into daylight.

"Have a good time!" Mrs. Calverton called. She stood and looked after the couple.

All the same, Susan had the feeling that the large, well-kept surgeon's hands upon the wheel were not hers to touch. The profile was strange. She chattered recklessly to keep him from speaking.

The Doctor seemed, after a little while—and that might have been only because the motor wasn't acting well—to be responding to her. It was just like all of their drives, so that, when they came to the top of the One-Mile Hill, turned aside from the main road, and stopped in the midst of the tangle of fall flowers, the silence brought back fear to her with a shock of surprise which blinded her. She sat in incredulous stillness; but her heart was pounding. She tried to say that she would get out and pick some goldenrod.

"Susan, look here."

Even her breathing was suspended. The world was stopping.

"We've had the best out of this. Don't you think so, too?"

Silence.

He turned toward her, and something like the old pleading broke through the strained huskiness of his voice. It was almost like an accusation.

"You must have known this was coming as well as I did." Silence. . . . "My God, I wish you'd say something!"

Through her dry throat, Susan forced a muttered, "What?"

"Well, just a response. You make me do it all."

"What is there to say?"

That was all there was to it. Susan felt it, in a terrible tiredness, as she sat with her slim hands loose in her silken lap. The great autumn landscape of brown fields and tufted trees spread out beyond the hill. She saw it. But she could not even feel pain for the difference between this chance final view and all the other happy ones.

The Doctor felt it. He did not even try to explain. There was so much to be said that there was nothing to be said. And yet there was little after all. The thing had come to an end. He sat hunched loosely over the steering wheel and stared at the autumn landscape, too.

There was a sort of ease between them as they drove back to town, the ease of mutual understanding again, and of apathy. But for the Doctor, the apathy was only for the moment. It was the temporary conclusion of one thing. There lay beyond it the fresh and eager beginning of another. Brightness lay just beneath the tired glaze of his eyes.

Susan could not go beyond her sense of final completeness—to her, it was relief, if it was anything at all. When they reached town, she saw the Sunday streets, empty and stony, of the familiar business section, and thought that now she was entering them for the first time in years with love and pain gone from her. There was no emotion in the thought.

It was the Doctor whose face, Susan noticed with wonder, when they stopped in front of Mrs. Calverton's again, was broken up with pain; and he begged her before he could let her out of the car to tell him that she felt as he did about it and understood. They had both had the best out of this, hadn't they? What was the use in dragging it on? And he had never, in his whole life, felt a moment of freedom to be himself. . . .

"I want you to tell me that, Susan."

"Tell you what?"

"Well . . . that you feel this as much as I do."

"Yes . . . I guess I do."

She smiled at him quickly. But she got out of the car bitter with her final resentment. He could not even leave her without her reassurance; and she could not help giving it.

She took off her white hat at the mirror and stared at herself in bleak bitterness. He was right. Why should he care for her now? She hated him because he had forced out of her a tenderness that was beyond her nature. And then, still staring with dry, dark eyes at her faded face, she hated herself as much. It was what she had wanted—what she had asked for—the change, the something beyond herself—the something that would break into her and make her over again. It seemed to her that she had not really understood what Mrs. Calverton had meant until now.

The affair was broken. The small anticlimax of the ending had proved final.

Susan kept on with her work at the bank. She still dressed smartly and immaculately, kept scent of the new styles in hats and scarves and beads and, after a little while, had an occasional date with a traveling man or even with one of her old beaux. But they asked her without much ardent interest—because she was a good dancer and because Susan had always been a man's woman and because she was at hand.

The hard truth was that Susan was passée. Young girls no longer adored the sheer perfection of her clothes. Men coming into the bank no longer had the pleasantly disturbing sense of an exceedingly attractive girl. They did not try to linger at the window when they took the money from her white fingers. Letha Grove spoke to Susan now as an equal, perhaps even an inferior—because Letha herself was full of new interests, planning for a trip abroad that was going to change her whole life. . . . Why? Susan was not old, still good-looking, not much changed. It was only, perhaps, that a suggestion of spareness had hardened the slimness of her form, a set dryness the clear features of her face, and about her clothes and her hair

there was some finality of precision from which the interest was
gone.

"Yes," Mrs. Calverton thought, "that's the way it goes."

She looked for a moment at her own face in the darkened
mirror of the oldfashioned parlor. She saw it faded, sad, old,
wise with a wisdom she could not be without, and yet that she
might wish she had never had to learn.

The whole town, of course, knew that the affair—whatever
it had been—was over. They blamed the Doctor and felt sorry
for Susan, but without much conviction, at that. Not nearly as
much as one might have expected. "She ought to have brought
him to time sooner," the men at the bank agreed. They had
always, for the sake of Susan's usefulness and the bank's re-
spectability, taken the line that it was merely a case of "going
together," and "not yet able to get married." The Doctor was
beginning to show an interest in Marjorie Pratt. She was only
three or four years younger than Susan, but gay, wealthy, fresh.
The Doctor was having a good time for the first moment in
his life. Who could blame him? His affair with Susan was
bound up with the old days. She wouldn't make the best wife
for him now. She had worked too long at that one job in the
bank. There were plenty of men who were indignant; but
there were others who said, "Well, we don't know the inside of
these things."

The older women who had known Susan's mother, and
always taken a particular interest in her because of that, were
unhappy to see that the long affair, which they had regarded
so fearfully and about which they had tried to give their warnings, had come to nothing. They wondered about Susan. They
should think it would break her heart, they said. For reluctant
as the innocent and kindhearted among these ladies were to

credit "anything bad" about Susan—a girl whose family they had known intimately—they all agreed that "men were selfish" and that there was little hope of happiness in these long engagements.

Nevertheless, Susan did not die when the affair was over. In fact, she was aware of other powers in her that had never been brought to fullness. In spite of the bleak dreariness in which she moved, she resented the finality of her aspect in the eyes of the town.

She was alive. She had to think of what to do with her life. At times she considered marrying. There was even a touch of grateful warmth in the thought of a home. Pride—the obviousness of the reason for the change—was all that kept her from moving away from Mrs. Calverton's. She had domestic and managing instincts that had never been given free play. And if the freshness and ease of her attraction were gone, there was enough of her old sure confidence left to tell her that she could marry if she would. A home . . . she would put everything into that, not into the man; forget the Doctor.

For a while, she looked at the men who came into the bank with a faintly reawakened interest. She would have to work now to get one of them; but that would be all the more reason for doing it. There was old Tommy Rumsey. His wife was dead. He had always liked Susan, if he was not quite so apt, now, to pat her cheek and squeeze her hand. To him, however, she was young. He was a rich old codger. The town would have to yield her, involuntarily, a place among the matrons if she married him; and sometimes it amused one side of her mind—an earlier side, belonging to the old Susan, having nothing to do with the Doctor—to conjecture what she could make him do. Could she force him out of that big old house in the

country and into a new one in town? Susan thought she might.
Now, when she was walking home at night, she made long,
interminable plans about what she would do if she married
Tommy Rumsey—only to lose them abstractedly, if her eye
caught sight of a new car or a strange person or just anything.

And her intention of attracting him—sometimes seriously
decided upon—always failed when he came into the bank in
his bluff, sentimental, aged person. What was the matter with
her? Had she found that love left her with much? But she
could not make marrying Tommy Rumsey for a home seem
worth while.

And the other men—the bank examiner, whom she knew to
be a bachelor; a certain pleasant traveling man; Sid Bartley
who had started out as a mechanic, but now, with a garage of
his own, was a new possibility—they were not worth while,
either.

In fact, Susan felt with an amazement about which she
could do nothing that she didn't want to marry any one. She
resented the patronage in the tone of her old beaux—she wasn't
done yet!—and the pitying tone of the older women, the way
in which the town took it for granted that she was still thinking of the Doctor. In the bleak clarity of her vision, she had admitted the truth when he had said that it was ended. Sometimes she wondered . . . if she had told him this or that at
such and such a time . . . but she had waited too long until
expectation had frayed out into nothing. His need and demand
had crushed out of her more tenderness and passion than perhaps she had possessed. Why should just she, Susan, the most
unlikely one, have been sacrificed to that need? But she understood Mrs. Calverton in that, too. She could not really wish it
had never been. She might be happier, but she would not be

what she was now, not this Susan.

Her love for him had gone too long balked, half fed, unsatisfied. It had sucked her dry. All that it had really left was her practical capability. She took refuge in the shelter of that, away from feeling. It grew restlessly. She was no longer contented in her work in the bank. She began to talk about going West and finding something else to do. Nothing seemed interesting now, but she could foresee—at the end of a long dim vista of change—how an interest might open up. She was not finished.

But it was finished—her affair with the Doctor . . . her heart; yes, her life after all. . . . The Doctor was marrying Marjorie Pratt. He was building a new house and sending off the old aunt to an institution. His practice was enlarging. People took him as he was. But as long as she lived in this town, they would never look at Susan without thinking of the Doctor.

Good Pals

A LL the way through the meadows of wildflowers, ever since
they had come out from the canyon, Ray and the boys had
been on the look-out for a camping place. At last Ray cried:

"Ha, boys—look there!"

He drove the car into a rough, tiny off-road and parked it
among the pine trees. The boys kept up a fire of "Where, dad?
Are we going to stay here, dad? Dad, is this the place?" Ray
let them know by his silence that the place was here. He hated
regular tourist camps. He liked to get off alone with his family.
They sat looking about them at the great trunks and branches
of the pines, the sunny quivering shimmer of aspens, and the
wildflowers along the road. The mountain stream made a clear
watery singing in the stillness. Ray kept his hands on the wheel.

"Hazel, how's this?"

The boys were already out of the car. "Well, here goes
again!" Ray slid out from under the wheel. Hazel got down
feeling stiff and suddenly exhausted. They all started in to set
up camp again as they had been trained, and under Ray's directions. The dusty khaki bundles were untied from the running
board.

"You fellows gather wood—rustle around, now. Mother, get
out the grub."

Hazel heard this with resentment. Her legs ached and her
hands were trembly as she set up the little folding table again.
She was silent except when she had to ask Ray for his knife or

to bring her some water. The drive through the narrow, rocky canyon along the very edge of the dark roaring water had been a torment. All the way she had been planning how, if they met a car and something happened, she could get her hands on both boys at once. She had braced her feet and kept her mouth shut, because it would have killed her to have Ray and the boys think that she wasn't a good sport. She was weak from that experience yet. And here was the everlasting old necessity of cooking again, the minute they stopped! Building camp fires was fun for Ray, but cooking was no novelty for her. Ray didn't have to keep the boys in mind minute by minute—just step in with a voice of authority when they got beyond control.

"Oh, that fire's so slow tonight."

"No, it isn't—anything of the kind!" Ray protested indignantly.

He put on the wood that the boys had brought. The good smoke went up and curled among the pine branches. At the smell of bacon and coffee they all knew that they were famished. Stedman danced on one foot with impatience. "Oh gee, mom, when are we going to eat?"

They were so ravenous that they devoured their food in silence at first. A steam went up from the dark bright coffee that turned a smooth thick yellow when they poured in the condensed milk. They fished out tiny insects with their spoons and threw them to the air. "*Get* out o' here—you little fool!" They began to feel warm and relaxed and contented, although the mountain air was getting chill. Their little table looked cozy set with the camping dishes. "More toast, anybody? Hazel?" "Oh Ray, I believe I do." Hazel began to see with wonder and amused shame that it was hunger and weariness that had ailed her. Why couldn't people ever learn that? She sat with her back against a tree and let Ray fill her coffee cup.

Faint friendly jeers came to them from a car going past on the road. Ray answered, and then the boys shouted joyously: "Hi, there! Hi!" until he had to tell them: "That's enough now. Don't need to keep it up forever." Having other people pass by made them feel more than ever that they were one family, one camp—off by themselves in their fine little place, but with other little camps scattered through the great wood. They were content with each other. Replete with good hot food, they sat around their fire. The whole family wore khaki.

"Golly, this is a fire!"

"It's going down, dad."

"Well, you kids rustle a few sticks. Let your old dad rest."

With happy jeers, the boys scurried off into the dusk. Ray said, "Come on, mommy, I'll help you stick things away." The two adults rose stiffly and, hobbling, folded up the table. Ray spread their old college army blanket in front of the fire.

"That's the boys! Now watch her burn!"

They all sat down on the blanket, Ray stretched out, the boys sitting up and hugging their knees. The red-gold of the fire shifted and changed, and the boys lifted their heads to watch the smoke going up through the pine trees into the fathomless dark of the night.

"Dad, how far do you s'pose you could see our fire?"

"Oh, I don't know. Quite a ways."

Ray was humming. He rolled over on the blanket. Stedman told him: "You must feel good, dad."

"I feel musical. Songs are swelling in my throat."

"Dad," David pleaded, "sing that funny song you used to, when I was little. You know. About that goat."

"A man named Wurts—" Ray sang,

"A friend of mine—"

He laughed. "What made you think of that? It's so far in the past I can't remember it. Mom'll have to help me out."

"Oh gee, mom! Go on. Help dad sing it."

Hazel remembered only half the words, and the duet got tangled. Besides, David was asleep. Sleep came down upon the boys as suddenly as the cold night upon the mountains. Persuaded and herded and commanded, they were stuffed at last into the warm new sleeping bags. They lay on the ground just outside the circle of the fire. Hazel could dimly see the little sleeping faces. The coffee kept her awake and she stayed on at the fire. Ray came back and sat down beside her.

"Well, Hazel, how's this? Think you can climb a mountain tomorrow?"

"Certainly. If you can," she answered with spirit.

"You're a pretty good old sport, aren't you?"

Hazel leaned her head against Ray's arm and they looked into the fire together. This was like their college days. No wonder that Ray had taken to singing of that ancient friend, the man named Wurts. They used to drive out, then, with the famous old gray horse and the red-wheeled buggy from the livery barn to picnics at Maple Sugar Grove. Hazel made the sandwiches, Ray supplied the beef steak, and after dinner they sat on this same army blanket near the fire and Ray read Kipling aloud.

"Well, sir, pal, we're here!" Ray said in exultant wonder.

Hazel's eyes shone up at him in the firelight.

This was their first real summer vacation since Stedman was born. They had just gone on little trips here and there with the car. The Bensons would only do things that they could all do together. Ever since Ray and Hazel were married, they had planned to drive to the mountains. Ever since they were first engaged, their ideal had been to watch the sunrise together from a mountain peak. They had gone to college on the prairies. Now, they were camped at the foot of Black's Peak.

Ray said, "We might be back in school. This is great. This is living."

Hazel answered jealously, "But we wouldn't have the boys, then!"

She snuggled up to Ray, glad that he wanted to be with her. But it hurt her that he could seem to want, or even to imagine, life without the children. It was like leaving them out. It was too dark now to see the little sleeping faces, but they were there, just within the firelight.

The boys had found out, of course, that their parents meant to climb Black's Peak, and that they were to be left behind. Then there was a turmoil.

"You said I could climb mountains, daddy! You said if I let my heel be lanced, it was so I could climb mountains."

"Well, you are going to climb mountains. Didn't I say I'd take you up Lone Pine?"

"Lone Pine!" they both wailed in concert. Stedman scoffed: "That little bitty mountain!"

"Well, you're little boys. You can't go up Black's Peak. It's too high for you."

"It isn't, daddy! Why can't we go up?" Stedman sobbed: "That's why I got my big high boots!"

"Oh," Ray cried in exasperation at last, "we'll give it up! We won't any of us go! You can't climb it if we do let you go, but you just won't let mom and dad have a little fun on their own. We'll give up the whole thing!"

"No! *No,* dad!" they wailed now in despair.

Hazel pleaded and argued with the boys, pleaded and argued with Ray. She was torn between them. She knew that Ray had set his heart on this one thing, that she had promised him, and that she simply couldn't fail him. But half her heart was with the boys. She couldn't stand their disappointment. She wasn't sure that, even to keep her promise to Ray and her conscience and her own old desire, she could be hard enough to go off and leave them and take her own pleasure. But it would have been too great a tragedy to have the plan given up. At last the whole thing was compromised and rearranged as usual. The boys were to go. They were all to go. But the boys were to stop—"willingly now, without any fussing"—when they got to timber-line. They were to spend the night at the Halfway Cabin with Jack the ranger, and let their parents go on up the Peak without them—willingly, and without any fussing, on Hazel's side, Ray stipulated.

"You'll do that, now, will you?"

"Yes, dad. We will."

The parents knew of old those wide-eyed, starry-eyed, ready promises. But it seemed too hard and cruel to doubt them.

And after all, the thing worked out well. It was better than the other way. They had always done things together. For two weeks, the family went into training. "Boys can't eat themselves sick and then expect to go up Black's Peak!" David dropped the cooky he had been stealing from the camp larder. It was the whole family again, a common cause. "Eight o'clock every night if you expect to reach timber-line." Ray and the boys planned together. "What kind of staffs are you going to make us, dad, to go up Black's Peak?" Hazel was secretly relieved of that torturing, reasonless fear she knew she would have had to

feel if she had gone up to the Peak with Ray and left the boys
behind at the inn—ever since, by ill luck, she had read of that
little boy being lost in the North Carolina mountains. At least,
she would be on the same mountain with her boys. Both parents now felt that it would have been treachery to leave the boys
behind.

"This is the day for the great stunt!"

The boy who counted automobiles had promised to look
after their camp. When they dressed that morning, it was like
starting on their trip all over again. It was even more wonderful. Going to the top of a mountain! It would be something
they had never done in their lives. It might change everything.
They joked and laughed and talked excitedly as they all got
into their khaki. The boys danced around, crying: "Dad, when
we going to start?" They tried out their new aspen sticks. Ray
cried at last:

"Now the procession moves!"

All in their khaki, with their sticks and knapsacks, they
crossed the hot sunny open space in front of the inn. "Going to
try the Peak today?" goodnatured people asked them. The
boys strutted with their dazzling importance. Other boys were
looking on—little sissy boys who stayed at inns and didn't
know how fine it was to be camping. They were proud of each
other. Dad was the tallest man around. The boys in their high
laced boots, dressed just alike, looked so dear. Hazel had got
brown camping. She was still girlish and rather thin, but getting too broad through the beam, so she often feared, to look
"cute" any more in knickerbockers. But the bob had changed
her. On this bright morning, she looked not so much girlish as
childish—with her short curling hair, her eager sunburned face,
her ankles trim in her laced elk-skin boots.

"Oh gee, dad, aren't you glad we're going?"

They passed the inn with its conscious rusticity, its cars, and its leisurely wealthy people strolling about and sitting on the verandas. They entered the trail. But still they were on known ground. The path was wide and well-trodden. They kept meeting hikers and strollers, who gave them casual glances—although one very elegant young couple in beautiful outing clothes had to laugh and break the well-bred surface of their indifference when David cried out irrepressibly to them:

"We're all going up the Peak!"

Ray cautioned: "Now, boys!"

They obeyed him like little soldiers, still remembering their promises. When he gave the order, they flung themselves flat. David rested with such determination, and breathed so hard, that Hazel and Ray had to turn toward each other a little and smile. His eyes were squeezed shut.

"Now up, everybody—and onwards!"

Up and up. The path was so beautiful now that it kept them hushed and intent. They were all climbing into wonder. The pure high air charged them with its primal freshness. The sunlight shifted down through great pine branches, lighted up columns of bronze trunks, struck out clear bright red from an Indian pink. All the way, the water sang beside them, until at last they reached the waterfall.

The boys went fairly crazy. They plunged and plunged their hands into the cold white swirl of foam. They caught handsful of the tumbling water to throw over their burning faces. All of them were light-headed with beauty. The roar of plunging water in the mountain stillness thrilled them with delicious fear. The boys ran forward to let the chill spray from the falls beat against their faces, and then ran back again. The greenness and the silence—even that small steady thunder of water within the silence—hushed them. They rested. The ground was hard, clean and dry, slippery with pine needles. Lying flat upon it, mystically content, they looked up through great brown tree-trunks, great green branches, to lacy bits of far blue sky. The sun burned on the warm needles.

The boys were up before Hazel and Ray. They were playing with the foam again, getting wild as they threw water into each other's faces. "Come, boys!" It was harder to get the whole flock herded together and started again, after the long, delicious rest.

It was harder to keep them together, too. They were demoralized by their brief freedom. The boys kept making side excursions, and Ray called them sternly back. "Boys! We can't stop for those things now." Their attention was scattered. They wanted to run after every wildflower and chipmunk and bird; to stop every other moment to drink from the cold rushing stream, flat on their bellies, their little warm beaks open to gulp it in. "Well, I'm thirsty, dad! You've got to let me." "No, you're not. You can't be. You'll blow up and burst before you reach timber-line if you drink any more water."

But threats, reminders, enticements were getting worn out under the unexpected length of the strain. In spite of promises, it was too much for the boys. The path was no longer fresh to them. Pine trees, Indian pinks, chipmunks, waterfalls had lost their shining newness of the morning. The path was steeper and steeper and all the same. Their feet hurt, they had nails in their shoes. They whined and couldn't go on.

"Daddy, wait!" Hazel pleaded. "They can't go so fast."

Ray cried in exasperation: "We'll never get there at this rate!"

At last they gave out altogether. The party was halted. They were all tired, all with aching backs, smarting feet, burning faces, weary ankles. Ray sat down and hugged his knees, feeling that that helped him somehow to hold in his helpless anger. He had known it would be this way! Hazel's face wore a look of distress. She wanted to go on, hated to keep Ray waiting, and yet she brooded over the aches and pains of the boys and was secretly indignant with Ray. It looked as if the whole splendid excursion would come to nothing, and almost in sight of the first goal. Finally Ray said:

"Well, we'll go down if you boys want to. We'll give the thing up. But we'll hear no more about mountains on this trip."

Stedman sobbed and sniffed; but then he began to get his second wind. It was David now who was the stubborn one. He simply lay flat and refused to budge. He wouldn't look at them, wouldn't answer, wouldn't say whether he meant to go up or go down. They coaxed, prodded, cajoled and threatened. There he lay. Even Stedman began to urge him now:

"Brother, come on, brother. You want to see timber-line. What makes you *act* so, brother?"

Ray cried in uncontrollable anger: "I knew how it would be! What's the use of going on their promises? They'll promise anything."

Hazel glared at him, defending the little tired bodies. She bent over and pleaded again, and it made Ray still more angry to hear the coaxing, brooding, maternal tone of her low voice. He wanted her to be as angry as he was, to uphold him.

"All right. If David won't go up or down, we'll leave him here."

Then, all at once, it was over. David was sitting up. He was permitting his teary, smudgy face to be wiped by his mother;

his damp hair to be smoothed back, his cap to be straightened, his boots to be re-tied. He was sniffing and coming to life. Ray's anger melted.

"That's the boy. Of course he wants to go on. He wouldn't give up. Now, come on, we'll give him a boost."

They all felt rested and ashamed of their tempers. They were ready to go on and finish the thing.

And after all, they were closer to the goal than they had thought. The long monotony of the path was broken. The dark ranks of marching trees were scattered. They were getting smaller and gnarled. There was a different, wilder coldness in the air. Here was a tree split by lightning—a gaunt, silver skeleton.

"We're getting there, boys!" Ray exulted.

"To timber-line, dad?"

"Almost to timber-line!"

Now the plodding, toiling, endless climb had changed to thrilling expectation. They felt a hugeness in the air. Their aching limbs had a mysterious lightness. They could keep on going forever now. They were coming into another world. The green trees were getting fewer. Those that had survived were stunted, twisted and bitterly warped. At last there were no living trees at all. The climbers were moving now through a silver forest of death. The stark branches were blinding white against a sapphire sky, drawn with a singing, fierce exultance. And then all at once the climbers were beyond even the forest and saw only rocks before them.

"Dad, is it timber-line?"

"It's timber-line!"

The little troop broke ranks. With wild whoops the boys scrambled over the tumbled rocks. The log-built fastness of the Halfway Cabin was humanly snug and small in the savage hugeness of the landscape. Jack stood outside it with the sun glinting in his eyes. The air had the tingle of snow, and snow itself was streaked in the hollows. The boys ran madly here and there. This wild shining bleakness was beyond the beauty of the green place and the waterfall. This was on the edge of sublimity. . . . Tiny flowerets, chill and fresh as the snow, just tinged with blue, grew among the rocks, blooming in the midst of immensity.

"Oh, Dave! Gol! Look at the snow!"

Whooping and yelling, the two little figures, so human, so absurd, slid down the long white shining streaks. Hazel laughed wildly to see them. She was not afraid any longer. Here, no one could be afraid. Ray shouted:

"Come on, mom!"

He spread his arms, and Hazel, laughing, panting, shrieking, balanced with madly waving arms, slid down into them. He caught her at the base of the slide. She was squeezed up against his chest, her chin lifted, her open eyes dazzled with sunshine—he kissed her. The boys shouted.

"Oh, look at mom and dad!"

Jack stood outside his cabin and grinned at their madness. He was used to either the madness or the deadness of the people who reached timber-line. Ray began to pelt Hazel with snowballs. Snowballs in August! "Go after her, dad—get her!" "No sir, don't you hit mom!" Hazel ducked and defended herself. The wet cold snow spattered against her hair. Cold shining bits clung in the curly meshes. Her cheeks stung. She spat little grains from her lips. She bent and scraped her cold fingers into the tingling snow. With a wild throw at Ray, she turned and fled panting into safety among the rocks.

She sat there, getting her breath. Her eyes glanced brightly about. The wild air tingled in her lungs. Getting up, she began to wander about the huge gray sunlit rocks. Such immensity made her exultant. The first beautiful hour when they drove through the meadows flooded with purple flowers was nothing to this. Here she was free, wild, beyond herself. She stooped to touch small flowers, to touch the warm side of great rocks. She paid no attention to the others. She was delirious with joy, but her head had never been so magically clear. Clear as crystal, as the flashing water, as this mountain air. She could take in the universe in her vision. She could take in the whole of life, drawn like a map before her inward eyes in lines of light. . . . And up, up to the very peak they were going! She had come through the strange white glory of that skeleton forest into this wild freedom. There was nothing, nothing to fear. She had passed through death and death was beauty. She didn't care now if the others saw her wandering. In such beauty and glory as this, she was herself, exultant, solitary.

But she loved her own family madly because they had been feeling it too. Separate but sharing. She heard Ray's voice ring out. She laughed with love that hurt her at the cold pink cheeks and shining eyes, the mad puppy excitement of her boys, as they came scrambling over the rocks to find her. She could stand it that they were so small when the world was as huge as this. She was proud that her own family—the Benson family, from Iowa, from home—could feel the wonder and be transfigured by it.

"See the little bits of flowers, mom!"

The sudden mountain twilight came down piercingly cold. The shadowed tumbled rocks were grayish-green. The snow patches were without light. The world had grown pre-historic, and the Bensons turned away from it and went into the cabin.

Jack had a fire in the big stone fireplace. They huddled gladly about it, but with the joyousness still upon them. Hazel crossed her knees and took an easy pose in Jack's rustic chair. They felt liberated by the glory of the climb and the last wild hour, from all old disabilities—felt young and strong and even rich. Ray got out the wildflower guide, and Stedman, his face bent eagerly and flushed with firelight, searched for the flowers he had caught sight of along the way. David drowsed against his mother's arm. Another party broke into the cabin—laughing, talking shrilly, dazzled still with their climb through the silver forest. The Bensons, older comers, settled and rested now, looked at them with sympathy but superiority: quite at home now in Jack's cabin. Held down under the surface of Hazel's mind was the memory of her transfigured hour. Ahead of her was the climb to the Peak, dangerous, arduous, splendid. More splendid than this hour alone, because she and Ray would take it together. It was for both of them. Together they would watch the sunrise. Hazel caught her breath with the wonder that opened up in her mind. Tears came to her eyes and she bent her head and blinked her lashes. She smiled. It was like—when she was a child—Christmas Eve with Christmas morning to follow.

Jack's larder had nothing much but baked beans. Baked beans were the grandest food in the world. David was just able to rouse himself enough to eat. The other people, too, were going on to the Peak—all but a plump woman with a red face and gray hair wildly short who made them all laugh by her husky, pop-eyed declaration that this was high enough for her! She would stay, she said with puffing vivacity, and look after the little boys.

Hazel and Ray lay on their bunks, dressed, and in spite of the cold alert and taut with readiness for the climb. The moon would come up at midnight. The boys slumbered innocently and appealingly. Hazel did not relax her determination. Jack called them cautiously. They heard the other people laughing and scrambling up and lacing their boots in the next room of the cabin. The time had actually come. Ray whispered loudly:

"Getting ready, Hazel?"

"Yes!"

Breathlessly she was pulling on her boots with cold hands unsteady with excitement.

"Haven't lost your nerve?"

"Don't you think it!"

They giggled together, happy conspirators, as they did on Christmas Eve. Hazel gave one quick look at the little sleeping faces, afraid of letting herself look too long—had one grinding pang of fear and tenderness as she left them there in the dark.

Then they were outside in the strange cold moonlight. The other party, like a flock of spirits, was shadowily visible climbing ahead of them in the dimness. The gray expanses of tumbled rocks were lighted with a cold, titanic glow. Ray's flashlight shot a tiny, intimate path of light ahead of them.

Their sleepy reluctance to start the climb had all worn off. A queer exultance held both Ray and Hazel. The presence of the other party drew them together. They were like college chums again—pals. Hazel looked slim and mischievous in the moonlight. Ray was excited by the glint of her eyes, dark and bright, as she looked up at him. The fluffy-haired girl in the party ahead gave little plaintive cries when she came to bowlders. She stopped and halted the whole party by virtue of her soft appealing hands and fluffy hair. Ray called back to Hazel:

"Coming?"

"Coming!" Hazel answered sturdily.

He was proud of her and tender toward her. She scrambled over the rocks like a little Trojan and scorned making him stop for her. Ray waited.

"You're a pretty good kid, aren't you?" he said in a low, intimate, teasing tone. He held out his hand to help her up and it was good to Hazel to feel it tighten into iron under the tug.

Hazel felt the way she used to feel when they all went out in sheets, with pumpkin faces, on Hallowe'en. Only that this was exalted, splendid. She and Ray were boy and girl, together again. She scrambled up breathlessly over the cold, savage bowlders, saying nothing when she scraped her hand, determined to come up to Ray's expectations and not to hold him back. She liked to loiter and to look at things, but Ray, when he had a point in mind, wanted to go straight to that point. They seemed to be climbing in a savage waste. There were no directions, no here or there, only giant stoniness.

The party ahead was resting, and they rested, too. Ray said: "How you like it?"

"It's gorgeous!" she panted. She wouldn't say he had gone too fast for her. If she could have stopped every now and then, cuddled down on a rock and closed her eyes, she could have gone farther and better and faster in the end. But it wasn't Ray's way of climbing. It made him impatient to have little wayside stops.

"Gosh!" he murmured, in a sort of wonder. "Think how many years we've waited for this!"

The romance of their youth was back with the words. They could see their whole career now as romantic. Hazel sat close to Ray. They looked out over the titanic barrenness of the rocks which they would cross together. They were content, for a moment, to rest. But the mountain cold poured like water through their bones. The other party had gone on. Ray stretched and rose.

"Well, we'd better travel!"

He gave her her aspen staff, pulled her up, and again they started. It was going to be difficult now. They did not talk. Hazel, intently silent, climbed over the bowlders after Ray, not seeing the rocks, not seeing the moon, conscious only of her hot labored breathing and the little niches where she could set her staff. They lost track of time and place.

There was a faint shrieking below them. Hazel stopped, and suddenly knew that it had been going on for sometime. Premonitary knowledge flashed into her, and she was sure. She called sharply:

"Ray!"

"What!"

"Listen!"

He stopped, poised and listening. Then he said:

"Somebody else coming up."

He started to go on. Hazel followed, and then called to him.

"Ray! Wait! It's for us!"

He halted at the sharpness of her tone. Hazel was frozen with the intentness of her listening.

"It isn't—" he began scoffing.

"It is!"

At that moment the cry came faint but piercingly audible. "Ben-son!"

She turned, and with a harsh sobbing panting began to scramble back over the rocks. She had not a thought of going on. Ray tried angrily to hold her back. "We're coming!" She

screamed. "Hazel!" he said to her. His anger and stiff reluctance were wrenched to belief, to shame, and then to fear.
"Gosh!" he muttered under his breath. He followed Hazel,
still angry that she had been so swift to go, but relieved his
complicated feelings, his unadmitted disappointment by calling
to her so sharply— "Wait! We won't gain anything by breaking
our necks!"—that she stopped. She forced herself to stillness.
Wildly intent, they made their precarious way down over the
bowlders.

"BEN-N-N-son!"

"Coming!"

They could see the shadowy figure of Jack, and far below
him the cabin. Hazel heard:

"Mrs. Benson . . . the little boy . . ."

Hazel only existed now until she could get to the cabin. She
was wildly furious at herself for leaving her children here in
this cold strange place without her. In the cabin doorway, she
saw the scared face and protruding eyes of the plump woman
under a wild dishevelment of hair. "Oh, Mrs. Benson, I'm so
glad we found you—" Hazel pushed into the cabin. Ray, with
a frightened face, followed her. They could hear Stedman's
voice wild with sobbing.

"We're coming! Mother's coming!"

The instant she saw him—little unfledged figure, sitting up
in his bunk, his face streaming with tears, his red mouth piteously open, his little arms stretched out to her—Hazel's agony
of fear gave way to the first relief. He was here! A swarm of
hideous possibilities melted instantly.

"What is it? What is it, darling?"

At the sight of the two faces, the mother's tense with passionate comfort, the father's scared, Stedman's crazy sobbing

increased. All the others were in a hub-bub of explanations.
David's eyes were round and bright, the eyes of a bird wak-
ened in its nest. The plump woman, stood huddling her coat
around her. Jack looked scared and awkward in the doorway.
"He cried so terribly—we couldn't find out what was the matter—so terrified—!" Hazel, saying nothing, was holding Stedman tightly. Ray was demanding in a frightened tone: "What
is it, old fellow? Come on! What is it? Tell daddy."

Stedman lifted bright, drowned eyes. His sobs were louder
than ever, but the scream of agony had gone out of them. Hazel
knew it, with that swift premonitory knowledge, although the
scared onlookers did not. They were still pleading. The sobs
hushed enough for her to hear the plump woman's explanation,
interspersed with eager sentences from David.

"Just a little while after you were gone, Mrs. Benson! Woke
up screaming. Thought he *must* be in pain."

"Oh, he just *howled,* mom!"

Ray begged Stedman, "Were you sick? Did something hurt
you?" The woman kept gasping, "I was so afraid of appendi-
citis!"—saying at intervals, "I knew you'd never for-*give* me,
Mrs. Benson!" Hazel said nothing. She held Stedman to her,
comforting him, defending him against impatience to come,
letting him feel by pressure of her arms that she understood.
She knew Stedman so well—a knowledge subtle and enfolding,
fathoms deep, beyond all words, beyond all reason. Once, years
ago—Ray had forgotten it—this same thing had happened.
Stedman had waked in a strange place, screaming, at his grandmother's.

At last they had all begun to realize. They showed, in different ways, reaction from the torturing anxiety. Jack was
sheepish. "Well, I didn't know, I thought maybe the boy was

sick," he said. The plump woman was pop-eyed with assur-
ances. "Why, I really thought the child was in pain," she declared over and over again. They all tried to reassure Stedman,
until Ray—weak, at first with relief, then with a sense of let-
down—had to smother his impatience, still half ashamed because it was too soon to admit or even feel it. Hazel, defensive
already, held Stedman to her, guilty because she had left him,
because she could realize through all her being what he had
felt when he woke up in this strange wild place alone—and
only she.

He began at last to be comforted. The plump woman went
back to her bunk. Hazel sat holding Stedman yet, and brooding over him. Ray, as he looked at them, uncertain how to take
this or what to do, felt a thrust of mingled jealous anger and
distaste at their look of being one. He said:

"Well, I suppose the trip's up!"

Hazel did not answer.

"Was that all?" Ray demanded, rather piteously. "Were you
only frightened?"

Stedman raised his wet eyelids, looked, drooped them again
—nestled deeper into the warm comfort of his mother's arms.

Ray said bitterly, after a moment, "It's no use trying to do
anything when you have kids!"

Hazel did not reply. Her lips quivered. She felt with Ray—
she felt with Stedman. Neither of them understood the other.
She understood both. She was guilty, through all her knowledge, for she felt that Ray always blamed her when he
blamed the children, as if she and they, at such a time, were
one. It was true. She took the justice of the blame.

Jack looked in at the door, saw that all was quiet. He said,
"Excuse me, Mr. Benson, but I didn't know whether you

wanted to get up to the Peak?"

Ray looked startled. "Why, they've all gone on!"

"They stop quite a lot." Jack grinned. "That young lady'll take some help before she gets there. If you wanted to catch up with them before sunrise, I guess you still could."

"Oh, no! No!" Ray said hastily. "Thanks, Jack. I guess I'd better not."

There was silence when Jack had left the room.

Ray said: "Well?"

"Why don't you go?" Hazel asked him. She scarcely moved her lips, and her arms pressed Stedman to her.

"Will you come?" he demanded, unbelieving.

She did not reply. If she left Stedman now, the pressure of her arms would be treachery. But Ray's voice shamed her.

"Can't we wait now?" she pleaded.

He answered, with vehement bitterness: "I don't want to go at all unless we can get there for sunrise! You know that."

Silence again. He broke out: "There's nothing the matter with that boy! We've come back, he knows it's all right now. If you'd insist, he'd let you go." But all the same, he knew that she would not go, could not go. "To make us give this up—like everything else—"

Hazel said in a low passionate voice: "You can go! I'm not keeping you."

He paused. "I think I *will* go!"

"Well, *go*. I'm not keeping you."

He went to the door. She heard his voice.

"Jack! Think you can get me up to where those people are?"

Hazel stayed on with the boys. She had told Ray to go, had wanted him to go—yet she couldn't help resenting that he had obeyed her. It was his willingness to go that she resented. How could he want to do it if he really cared about the boys? He thought that she had failed him; that she was weak and let the boys have their way with her; that she couldn't hold out; that because he could leave them, he was the stronger. She wanted to run after him, seize him by the shoulders and tell him: it isn't because you're stronger that you can go; it's because you're blind; you don't see; you don't feel. He was a child to care so much about his own little way.

Still, she had wanted to go with him. It had been their ideal. She had never meant to give it up—couldn't understand, even as she looked about the little cabin room in the moonlight, how it had come about that he was going on and she was here. Their splendid climb together had come to this! Ray was going to the Peak and she was left, with the children, at the Halfway Cabin.

Bitterness engulfed her in a great wave. It was not that she could not, did not want to, reach the Peak. She loved to climb. She had prided herself upon keeping up with Ray: his pal—with him in every endeavor. What it came to for her was the Halfway Cabin. Halfway mother, halfway wife, halfway person, every one's helper. It would have been better, she thought with bitterness, to have stayed at the bottom and never started to climb at all. She turned passionately to Stedman, but he turned away his face with a little impatient movement and did not respond. He had had what he craved from her. Now he wanted to sleep.

Hazel got up, went over to her own bunk, and lay down alone.

Now she could have gone. The boys did not need her any longer. It would only mean missing the sunrise. But then— the sunrise was the thing they had come to see. The sunrise was just the thing she would always miss.

Sounds roused her. She supposed it was Jack getting back to the cabin. Their door opened, and Ray came into the room. Hazel struggled up, wide-eyed in the moonlight. It was actually Ray. He came on into the room.

"What happened? Couldn't you find the others?"

He was trying to look unconcerned, but a disarming boyish sheepishness, that she knew of old, struggled through his manly composure and sounded in his voice.

"I let 'em go."

"Why, but—! Were they too far ahead?"

"Oh, I guess I could have caught 'em. . . . How's the boy?"

"He's gone to sleep."

Ray wandered restlessly about the room. He paused, looked at her and blurted: "Oh, I didn't want to go up there without you! It was with you I wanted to see it. I didn't care about it alone."

Hazel felt stricken with guilt. She wailed indignantly:

"Oh, but Ray, I *told* you to go on!"

"I didn't want to," he answered gruffly.

Hazel, raised on her elbow, stared at him with distress. She didn't know whether to love or to hate him for this. He was none of the things that she had called him. Her huge splendid grievance was upset. Yet he was all of those things. He was half impatient, she could see, and disgruntled and disappointed yet. He had a right to be disappointed. She stared at him with remorse and guilt; with anger; with pity. She was half ashamed, in spite of her deep resentment, that his ruthlessness was softened and spoiled. She and the children had done it. Now it would be too late for the sunrise.

"You could have gone," she asserted.

"Oh, well. We'll both go in the morning."

She was silent.

Ray blurted again, in the last flare of his anger: "Oh, we can't do anything with these kids and we might as well know it! I'll climb Lone Pine and get the sunrise. That won't be so much of a jaunt. We can all do that. You and I'll go on up to the Peak in the morning. How'll that be, old girl?"

With remorse and yielding, he pressed her to his shoulder as he sat down beside her on the bunk, and roughly fondled her chin. Hazel yielded to him; but her eyes kept their distress. It was a compromise, both of them knew. He thought he was making it for her; she thought she had made it for him. Ray was ashamed of himself—Hazel remorseful about herself. In any event, they had given up the sunrise. They felt old . . . and they felt like two lost children comforting each other. But there *was* comfort in it. She let him press her cheek to his and said, rather quaveringly:

"All right."

The Big Kids and the Little Kids

M R. AND MRS. THOMPSON had gone to call on Grandma Brewer this beautiful summer evening, too beautiful for any one to stay in the house. They had left the girls washing dishes in the kitchen. Jessie washed, since she was the older one, and Doris wiped. Jessie was in a hurry to get through, but Doris wanted to make it take as long as it could. Dish-washing was the best time for playing their special games which they couldn't play with any one but each other. It was the time when the little sister could have the big sister's attention all to herself.

"Sister, listen, you've got to tell me! If you could have twenty-five children—"

"I never would have, you little idiot!"

"Well, some of them adopted. Twenty-five girls and twenty boys. What names would you choose to call them? What name would you choose for the first girl and the first boy, and then the next-oldest girl and boy, and then the other ones?"

Sister always knew such wonderful names, that actresses and countesses might have, so much finer and fancier than Doris could think of for herself.

"Oh, I'd start at the first of the alphabet and go along."

"Tell me some of them. Please, Sister. I want to hear what you say."

"Well, then—Angelica, Barbara, Cynthia—Diantha—"

"That isn't twenty-five!"

73

"Oh, Dorrie, it takes too long. When I get the names said, then you'll want me to tell you how they're going to be dressed and all the rest of it. We've done all that so often. I don't want to play that tonight."

"Why not, Sister?"

Jessie kept glancing toward the screen door. Outside it was clear and cool and dusky, with just an exciting thrill of autumn in the air. Vacation was almost over. School would begin next week. Doris was away down in the lower grades, but Jessie was going into high-school. Somebody whistled out there. Jessie tried to look careless, as if she hadn't noticed it. But Doris was suspicious at once. More whistling—sweetly shrill, enticing through the dusk—and then above it sounded the long-drawn-out, piercingly hideous call of the crowd, Sister's crowd, the big kids. . . .

"PHEE-EE-ee-bit!"

Jessie wrung out the dish mop and hastily washed her hands. She had finished, but there was a whole stack of plates still to be wiped.

Doris was wild. "You're going to play outside tonight. The big kids are."

Jessie would not answer.

"Wait for me, Sister. Wait! You know I'm not through. I can't do it as fast as you can. Don't go off without me!"

"That wasn't for you."

"I don't care, I'm coming along!"

In wild haste she put away the plates still wet, although she knew her mother would scold when she found them all sticking together in the morning. She flew out of the house, let the screen door bang, jumped down the steps onto the cement walk that sent a jar all through her teeth and joggled the loose ones. Mabel and Bee had come past for Jessie. They were all three almost to the corner now. Doris went running down the walk after them, stopping once to hold her side, sobbing and frantically calling:

"Sister! You've got to wait. You can't go off and leave me at home all alone. Wai-ait!"

The three big girls turned. Doris had nearly caught up with them now, and they saw her straining eyes and woe-begone, tear-stained face.

"You go back!"

"I won't do it."

"I'm not going to look after you."

"I don't have to be looked after."

"Oh, well, I suppose we'll have to let her tag along."

They were going to play in the vacant lot. The little kids had that all to themselves in the daytime, but when the big kids wanted it in the evening, the little ones had to skedaddle. Some of the little kids were there now, playing pom-pom-pullaway. It was still light outside, and until it began to get dark, the real big kids, like Red Bishop, scorned playing. But they were beginning to gather. The little kids didn't have much time left. Even if the big kids had been willing to let them stay, the mothers would be out calling them.

"Why don't you play with those kids?" Jessie asked.

"I don't want to."

"Well, you needn't think you can be in our game. You'll just have to sit here and watch. You won't like that."

Doris didn't answer.

The three big girls were walking about now, Jessie in the middle with her arms around the waists of the other two. The boys were watching them, and they knew it. A subtle, new delight had crept into their old wild enjoyment of the games this summer, making it more thrilling than ever before to play out on the vacant lot in the evening. But the games were not quite the same.

Doris kept by herself at the edge of the walk. She liked pom-pom-pullaway She had been caught only twice this summer, and both times by Robert Nichols, who was such a fast runner it didn't count to be caught by him. But pom-pom-pullaway was so tame compared to the big kids' games, the kind you could play only at night, in the darkness or by moonlight. She didn't want those little kids to get hold of her.

The three big girls came back on their promenade.

"They're calling you, Dorrie," Mabel said. "They won't like you if you don't play with them."

"You could have so much more fun," Bee coaxed her. "You could keep up with them. You can't run fast enough to play with us. You'll be left 'way, 'way behind, and just think how lonesome you'll be!"

"Oh, let her alone," Jessie said severely. "She'll have to find out."

It was dark now in the street under the shady trees, but the vacant lot still lay in a clear twilight. The dresses of the little girls flashed white as they ran. "Pom-pom-PULLaway!" But there was a minor tone now to the cry—the players were dropping out—the game was ending.

They were trying to keep on, but a long call sounded from across the street through the evening air—"El-see-EEE!"—and one of the big kids said, "Your mother's calling you." A woman came picking her way through the dewy grass to get her two, and one of them went scampering ahead of her, while the other pulled back and was wailing.

Jessie said to Doris, "If mamma knew you were here, that's what would happen to you!"

Word had been sent from one of the big kids to the other, "Going to play outdoors tonight!" They were gathering now from all sides, running and flocking.

"Why don't we begin?" some one asked impatiently. "Make those little kids stop playing."

"We can't begin until Red gets here."

He was coming down the street now. His carroty hair flamed even in the dusk, and they could see his white shirt and recognize the masterful ease of his swinging stride. He was the fastest runner and the biggest boy. The crowd never did anything without him.

"Hey, Red!"

"Hey!" He leaped the ditch and came over to the crowd. "Looks like the gang's all here, huh? Hey, kids, you beat it. We want this place."

The little kids tried to act as if they didn't hear him—except Bennie Salter, who was always obedient and scary, and who scampered at once. Billy Godolphin smartly stuck out his tongue. But there was a scared bravado in his smartness. He ran around a circle all by himself on the playground, after the others had scattered, but in a few minutes he had faded out like the rest of them.

"What are we going to play?"

The big kids were crowding around Red. Pete had come, too, another big boy, and some of the bunch were ready to listen to him. Some of them wanted Beckon. But the word had already gone around that Red said it was to be Run-Sheep-Run tonight. Such a night couldn't be wasted on any other game.

Besides, it might be the last good chance they'd have. School began next week. Somebody might have put up a house on the vacant lot by next summer.

"Who says Beckon?"

Two hands went up—found themselves the only ones—wavered . . .

"How many vote for Run-Sheep-Run?"

"AYE!" came in a great roar.

"Run-Sheep-Run has it."

Red and Pete were to be the leaders. That might make a few others jealous, but the leadership belonged to them. Pete was a great big fellow. He weighed a little more than Red. But all of them—the girls especially—wanted to be chosen on Red's side. They were pretending to be airily unconscious, but the watchful, hopeful glint of their eyes gave them away. Only Jessie Thompson, to the secret envy of the others, could be really unconcerned. She was sure of being chosen. She was the fastest runner of the girls, the prettiest and most popular. Already there was a young-lady look about the little swish of her skirts as she went down the street. Mabel and Bee were chattering with great animation. They didn't seem to notice that sides were about to be chosen now. But there was a breathlessness in Mabel's shrill laughter.

"Who's going to play? Everybody here? Now get out, you little kids."

The few little ones who remained—those Whaley kids, whose mother didn't care how long they stayed out—had withdrawn into a watching, respectful row at the edge of the lot. The big kids were too much absorbed to notice Doris. She stood on the rim of the crowd, her eyes dark and bright, praying that somehow she would be chosen.

"Let me be chosen—oh, please, please, please, dear God and Jesus!" she prayed.

She kept her eyes shut tight, feeling that if she couldn't see she might not be seen. She was in the bunch, anyway. They were wrangling over the sides.

"Who has first turn?"

"Pete. Red chose last time."

"Aw, get out!"

"That's the truth!"

"But Pete has to hide first. Don't you remember?"

"Well, don't you know—?"

"Aw, go ahead. Somebody choose! Let's get going."

Every one knew it was because Red and Pete both wanted Jessie Thompson. That made some of the boys tired. Jessie could run fast enough for a girl, but not as fast as lots of the fellows. When that kind of business got into it, games were spoiled. Jessie thrust out one foot, pointed as if for dancing, and fastened back a curl with a tiny hairpin. She was afraid the hairpins would all fall out when she ran tonight. Pete was the one who got her this time. Jessie gave Red a long, sidelong look as she stepped daintily over to Pete's side. Red chose Bee then, just to show her. When Doris finished her prayer and opened her eyes, most of the crowd were on one side or the other. They were getting down to the undesirables. Robert Nichols was such a fast runner that they had let him stay; and now with proud nonchalence, superior to his short trousers, he swaggered over to stand beside Pete. Mabel had not been taken. She was too fat to run. She was pretending not to be aware of her unhappy isolation, but when Red glanced toward her, she made little conscious movements.

"Well, I guess I choose Mabel," Red drawled.

She proudly joined his flock, with a triumphant glance at Jessie. At least she was on Red's side. She knew that was where Jessie would rather be.

"Are we through now? Everybody chosen?"

Only Doris was left, desolate and small.

"Who's that kid?"

"Oh, it's just Dorrie!" Jessie said that with disdain. "She tagged along. She doesn't need to play. Don't bother about her."

But somebody else was coming—Chink Watson, and a good runner, too! "Hey, folks, hold on!"

They had to wait for Chink.

Then that left one too few on Red's side. It wouldn't be fair. "Why not take Jessie's kid sister?"

"She's too little. She couldn't run fast enough."

Her heart, so aching and forlorn a moment ago, now was beating fast. And Robert Nichols, her old enemy, was standing up for her.

"She's a fast runner. Honest. I can hardly catch her sometimes."

"Aw," said Pete, disgusted, "we don't want any of those little kids."

Oh, how she hated Pete! She wished he'd fall down in the long, wet weeds and never get out until morning. And she hoped Sister would fall down too—or anyway, that some one would catch her—saying so impatiently, as if it didn't matter:

"Oh, Dorrie doesn't know how to play this!"

"I do! I do know how to play! I've played it lots of times. Haven't I, Robert?"

And she had, but a little kids' Run-Sheep-Run, in the afternoon or just after supper—not the perilous, mysterious, exciting glory of the real Run-Sheep-Run at night. This one, one night—oh, she couldn't bear not having them decide; her breath seemed to choke her with eagerness, and she was praying frantically inside again, to God or Jesus, either one or both —one of them ought to help her.

Red looked over at her standing alone.

"Aw, let her play," he said easily. "What does it matter? Come on, kid. You can be on our side."

Pete's side went out first. Pete was getting all the luck tonight. Red's bunch stayed at the goal. They were watching, guessing, surmizing.

"They're going east!"

"Yes, but that doesn't mean anything!"

"Bet they're headed for the ravine."

"Too hard to get out of there."

Doris was dumb with happiness. It was enough just to be admitted. The Whaley kids were still staring from the edge of the lot, a stubborn, forlorn, unwanted little tribe. And she was one of the big kids! Well, anyway, they were letting her play with them.

Once Red looked at her and tweaked a lock of her hair. "Think you can run, kid?" he asked her.

She knew she could run! She would show them. Oh, how she worshiped Red! She would do anything for Red. She would catch Sister for him. How wonderful if she could be the one to find where the other side was hidden! They would all be glad, then, that she had been chosen. She was a little bit afraid of that fast Robert Nichols. But maybe she could keep away from him in the dark.

How different the vacant lot was at night! She had crossed

it this morning going to town—crossed it, watchful for snakes, by that little diagonal path all the neighborhood had trodden. Then it had lain bright under the morning sun, still a little shine of dew on the thin-stemmed weeds that left mouths all wryly full of knobby seeds when the children made "mustaches" with them. She had stooped down to pick a dandelion and blow the feathery top to see if her mother needed her— but to blow very softly, so that she would have a good excuse for lingering. In the afternoon, she and Elsie and Vinnie and Blythe had played Going-to-New-Orleans. She wouldn't play that now! Or any of those games played in the daylight with just a bunch of little kids.

Dark and significant stood the lone elm tree that they had chosen for the goal. Doris glanced at it nervously. Could she ever reach it when it was her turn to run? A thrill of delicious fear shot through her, making her hair prickle all over her head.

Red's bunch was getting impatient. The other side had been out a long time now. They were choosing a hard hiding-place. Common fear and danger drew the watchers close, the girls shivering and giggling, the boys stepping out on little scouting excursions as far as the rules would let them go.

"See anything of them?"

"Not a sign."

But it couldn't be long now.

"Listen here, kids." Red gathered them all about him. "We're going to run this thing right. We're going to catch just as many of that bunch as we can. Get me? We've got to beat that crowd tonight! It may be the last chance this summer. Now, I want every one of you to do exactly as I say."

They were in a cluster now in the dusk. Each could hear

the other's breathing, catch the gleam of eyes. They all belonged to the same side. Red's voice was low, fierce and vibrating. It sent a shock through them. His shoulders were tense, his arms freckled and strong below the short white sleeves, his red hair burning even in the twilight. He was their captain, their leader. All their dependence was upon him.

"I want every person on this side to go after one guy and get him. Now, all of you listen! Let the easy ones go. It's the fast ones we're after. I want two of you to run down that Chink Watson and catch him if you have to break your gol-darned necks."

"Who are you going after, Red?"

Red said with a deep, slow satisfaction, "I'm going to get that Jessie Thompson!"

Doris tried to crowd in with the others. Her eyes looked up at Red with shining, utter worship. She begged him:

"Who shall I catch? Red! Who shall I?"

She would run—she didn't care if all her blood vessels burst, if she did really and truly run her legs off; she could run faster than any of the big kids, she felt now.

Somebody laughed. Red looked down at her. His eyebrows lifted in a funny way.

"Gee, I forgot we had you on our side!"

Some one—that horrid fat Mabel—said impatiently, "Don't let her run. She can't catch anybody."

If they should leave her out now!—they were all looking at her.

"Aw, she can run," Red said grandly. "What does it hurt? You run, kid. Go after anybody you see."

Some one said, "Sh!" They saw Pete coming. He was trailing around the edge of the lot, but that didn't mean anything. He thought he could fool them. Red drew them about him again with an imperious gesture and gave his last, low, hurried instructions.

"All follow me and all keep close watch—remember . . . and the minute Pete calls 'Run-Sheep-Run'—!"

Pete sauntered up to them, carefully nonchalant.

"We know where you've left them. We can go straight to them."

"Think so, do you?" Pete answered the jeers.

"Well, let's get off, gang!" Red said impatiently.

Red struck across the vacant lot, and his flock trailed after him. The long, wet grass swished stealthily about their shoes. Pete, still nonchalant, sauntered as far as he dared in the rear.

No one paid any attention to Doris. She trotted along. She kept her eyes on Red's white shirt ahead of her in the dusk. To be playing, actually playing Run-Sheep-Run with Sister's crowd! In the passion of her devotion to Red, she hated Pete and the other side. She felt as if she could be a heroine and bring in the whole other side as captives. But as they kept on their stealthy search, going Indian file, her heart began to trip faster and faster and the sound of her own breathing frightened her.

Pete sang out, "Blue! Blue!" That was the first of the signals.

"Colors, is it?" Red said. "All right, old boy, we'll soon know what your blue means."

"Sh!"

Pete bent down to pick a long weed and to show that he wasn't worried. They had left the vacant lot now. Red was taking them across Hibbard's lawn. At every little sound—a branch moving, a footstep on the walk—there was a nervous twitter from one of the girls. The other side might be anywhere—in the shadow of the porch, behind those lilac bushes . . .

"PURPLE!" Pete shouted suddenly.

At every one of those warnings a shock of fear went through Doris. Her knees trembled, and she wanted to run back to the goal. But she must stand it—she was one of Red's bunch. Next it would be her own side that was hiding—in the dark, left behind by their leader, all crouched and breathing together. She shivered with a thrilling terror.

"Lie low!"

The long cry sounded hoarsely above them and trailed away into a moan of warning. Then the others must be close about! The barn, with its perilous shadows? In the long grass of the orchard? There were glints of watchful eyes in the dusk—the frightened breathing all subdued—the feet treading softly through wet weeds. Doris's blood beat in her throat. Her little heart choked her. She saw Red's gesture of warning—his lifted head . . .

"RUN-SHEEP-RUN!"

Screams from the girls, a mad stampede—the wild, glorious terror of that shout! From behind White's barn next door they say the dark figures running. "Get 'em! Go after 'em!" Bolting madly through the grass, leaping the walk, swishing through the lilac branches—they had all started before Doris knew which way to run. She went scudding wildly after them—after some one, she didn't know whom, one of her side or one of the other . . . Her breath ached in her straining throat, and her thin little legs began to hurt and get weak at the knees. Oh, she couldn't keep up! She must. Away off ahead of her she saw Red's white shirt and Sister's light dress. Red was going after Sister, and she had to help him. Her forehead pushed against the rush of cool night air, and her hair blew back as she plunged madly through darkness.

The cement walk, a long pale line glimmering in darkness . . . and bang into two people! She tried to go on—they caught her.

"What's this? Why, it's Dorrie!"

It was mama and papa!

"Let me go, papa, please! We're all playing Run-Sheep-Run. I'm catching somebody."

Like a little fish, plunging and straining, she struggled in their hands.

But they couldn't understand. "Why are you out here?" And in the dark? Didn't she know how late it was?

"We're playing, mama! Let me go!"

Mama said, "Oh, no, you must come with us now."

She tried to explain through sobs. It was Run-Sheep-Run. She was on Red's side. Red had chosen her. There wouldn't be enough without her. The game would be spoiled if they took her away. And her own side hadn't gone out yet—the game was just starting!

But bearing her along between them, each grasping a little hot hand, papa and mama just couldn't understand her. Even her crying couldn't stop them, they were so comfortably sure— like older people!—that they knew all about it and were right.

Stay and play? Oh no, it was too late. It was far too late for her. The game would go on without her, they assured her. She was too little, anyway. These big children didn't want her. How she hated their comforting but relentless hands! She could just see a play of dark figures about the elm tree—laughter, a girl's shrill scream that sound like Sister's—and she had to go home with papa and mama!

All the way home they had tried to console her.

Mr. Thompson said, "You little kids have the vacant lot all to yourselves the whole day long. I saw you playing there when I came home to dinner."

What did they suppose those little games mattered—Old Witch and Statuary—when she had felt the wild taste of the chase in the darkness? She never wanted to play those little kids' games again.

But when they reached home and got into the light, and saw the woebegone tear-stains on the little face, the parents' hearts smote them. They tried all their comforts. Did she want mama to make her a nice glass of lemonade? She was so hot!—Mrs. Thompson sighed, pushing back the damp hair from the flushed forehead. Trying to keep up with those big children! Perhaps there was still a piece of that candy? Papa, look in the top drawer of the buffet. The candy for which she had begged this morning, which mama had watchfully secreted— she wouldn't even say she wanted that. She let mama put a piece of it into her hand, but she held it slackly and refused to look at it. She sat in forlorn isolation and let the tears stay thick in her lashes.

Now the parents were at a loss. Each wanted to say to the other that she might have been allowed to stay a little longer, if it mattered this much; but it seemed that such words wouldn't do. They must preserve the cheerful falsity of their omniscience.

They pleaded with her. "Don't you see, we have to bring you home, so that you can grow up and be a big kid?"

"You let Sister stay."

"But, darling, Sister's a big girl now!"

"So am I."

"Oh, no, you aren't." Mama tried to stroke her hair. She begged, "Don't you want to be our little girl any longer?"

Papa cried with false, hearty cheer, "Of course she does! Why, we couldn't get along without her. We'd be two old folks, if we had to have two big girls right away. Like Grandma and Grandpa Brewer. Don't you want to keep your parents young?"

But he couldn't make her smile at his little jokes.

"Sister," mama mourned, "will soon be too big a girl to play." She thought for a moment of Jessie, wishing that by some magic they could keep her playing there forever, but knowing it wouldn't be so. "After she's through," mama promised, "it will be your turn."

"I want it to be my turn now!"

That was all they could get out of her. Couldn't she see, they asked her, that if they let her stay so late now and play so hard, she couldn't do it when she did get big? If she got everything too soon, how could there be anything left? There would be plenty of other nights—plenty of time to play Run-Sheep-Run. Yes, but they wouldn't be *this* night. That was the answer which none of the consolations could console.

At last there was nothing left to do but carry her up to bed so that she could wake up happier in the morning.

Her little legs dangled and bumped, and she wouldn't put her arms around her father's neck. She permitted herself to be undressed, but she turned her face away from kisses. Stricken, the two guiltily righteous parents looked down at the desolate little figure, finding it small comfort themselves that what must be must be; and, admitting the failure of their own wisdom as consolation, withdrew in favor of the kitten. Mr. Thompson had called and chased the little rascal all through the back yard, plucking him finally by guile from a tree; and now came upstairs holding him by the furry middle with four helpless paws dangling. At sight of that, Doris held out her slack arms and took the kitten to her. She squeezed his softness against her cheek, in love of him and reproach of mama and papa, and at least had the comfort of crying her last few tears into the fluffy warmth of his fur.

The parents stole downstairs. They could set up no claims to rival the kitten's. There was nothing for them to do now but wait until Jessie chose to come home. Next time they would have to let Doris stay. They could not tell her the sweetness of having things before her instead of behind her; and wistfulness for the big child mingled with humorous remorse for the little one. The game was still going on. The cries came distantly through the clear, cool darkness with its sharp touch of autumn, that seemed to say this was the last night any of them would be playing Run-Sheep-Run. Jessie's voice sounded shrill above the others. The parents, sighing and waiting in the lighted room, could hear it from across the vacant lot, like the last sweet call of her childhood through the deepening summer night.

Upstairs in her own little room, Doris heard closer than the cries of the players the familiar stirring and brushing of the maple tree outside her window. She pressed the kitten's warm side to her and felt a mournful comfort in the tickle of his little whiskers.

But he didn't want to stay. He had been snatched from freshly discovered cat pleasures of his own out among the dark trees in the garden. No longer was it bliss enough for him to lie in his little mistress's arms and purr. He was motionless, then he began a mute struggle.

She begged, "Stay, kitty!"

Then, with mournful acquiescence, she opened her hands and heard the soft thump of his little body on the floor and the pitter-patter of his feet down the stairs.

The Valentine Box

WHEN Betty had her mind set on a story, it was just as well to give up at once.

"Mother's told you all the stories she knows. Long ago."

"No, you haven't." Betty's trust in her poor little repertoire was inexhaustible.

"Mother can't think of any new ones."

"An old one, then. I don't want a new one. I want to hear about when you were a little girl. When you were a little girl and thought you wouldn't get any valentine."

"That old story again?"

"Yes!"

"Mother hates to tell that."

But light little fingers stroked her hand, soft as feathers, insistent, merciless. The mother sighed helplessly, staring into the dusky, pretty room. Betty echoed her sigh, but with satisfaction. She settled securely against her pillow. Her eyes, too, took on the fixed and darkened look of her mother's, anticipating the sorrowfulness of this many-times-heard story, as she, too, stared into the dusk.

"Well, once on Valentine's Day—"

"No! That isn't the way you begin it."

"How does mother begin it?"

Betty set her right inexorably. " 'Once when mother was a little girl' . . . That's the way you must tell it to me."

"Oh, dear, then I suppose that's the way it must be! Well,

once, when mother was a little girl grandpa sold his business, and we had to move away from the town where we were living and move to a different town. It was early in the winter, and grandma and grandpa said that mother must start into school again right away, so that she wouldn't get behind in her studies. And so she had to go all by herself to a new school where she didn't know any of the little girls or any of the little boys."

A sigh of gusty mournfulness from Betty.

"She had to leave her little chum—"

"Lois?"

"Yes, Lois. And she hadn't any little friend of her own."

"Tell about the first day at school."

"Well, and so, on the first day, mother had to go to the new school all alone."

"But why didn't grandma take you?"

"Because grandma was so busy getting the new house settled. And anyway, mother was supposed to be a big girl and not to mind going to school alone."

"But you did mind it."

"Yes, but grandma didn't know it. So mother started out."

"Tell about how you were dressed."

"She wore a little red plaid dress, and a little gray kitty hood that was tied with red ribbons."

Betty stroked her mother's hand, thinking mournfully of the kitty hood.

"Mother was very proud of that little hood. Well, grandma didn't know that in this town school started ten minutes earlier than it had in the other town, and so when mother got to the building, she found that she was tardy. All the other children had gone inside, and she had to open the big doors and go up the big stairway all by herself."

"And the stairway creaked!"

"Every single step of the way! And the worst of it was that mother didn't know where to find her own room, and she was such a silly little girl that she was afraid to ask anybody, and she thought that if she were to open the wrong door, and all the strange children were to look at her and know that she had made a mistake, she would die."

"But you did find the right room?"

"Oh, yes. Mother went on her tiptoes all through the long halls until at last she found Number Five."

She heard the small sigh of relief.

"But she had on her coat and hood, and she had to leave those in the cloakroom."

"Tell what it was like."

"It was a long room, and there was a row of hooks on each side, the girls' hooks on one side and the boys' hooks on the other."

"And all the hooks had numbers!"

"Yes, a number for every one. And the only vacant hook was Number Fifteen. I've always remembered that Number Fifteen. So mother had to take off her gray coat and her gray hood—"

"Your *kitty* hood!"

"—And hang them up on Number Fifteen. And then she made a dreadful discovery. In the town where mother came from, all the little girls her age were wearing kitty hoods just like hers; and grandma had crocheted this one for her at Christmas time, and it was fluffy and new, and mother thought it was beautiful. But that was a little town, and this was a big town! It had two railroads and a whole thousand more inhabitants. And here the little girls weren't wearing kitty hoods.

They were wearing caps."

"Round caps?"

"Yes, round caps. Every hook had a coat, and above every coat hung a round cap. So mother felt worse than ever. But there was nothing else for her to do. So finally she took off her gray coat and hung it on hook Number Fifteen. And then she did something that made her ashamed. She took off her little, fluffy kitty hood, that was just as soft and gray as the kitten she'd had to leave behind in the other town—"

"Because this was too big a town to keep so many cats."

"That was what grandma and grandpa had told her . . . And she hid it away under her coat, so that not even the shiny red ribbons showed. Then she stood a long while. She couldn't go back, for then grandma would have been ashamed of her. So she gave a little knock on the door."

"Loud enough for the teacher to hear it?"

"It must have been, because the teacher came."

"Was the teacher nice?"

"Nice enough, I think, but I've forgotten now just what this teacher was like. Mother's had so many other teachers . . . And so—oh, there was a great deal to it, too much to tell, but at any rate the teacher decided that mother could stay in that room. But I remember that she had to stand at the desk while the teacher asked her questions, and looked at her report cards, and tried to find a seat for her—and all this time the children in the room were staring until the teacher said, 'Go back to your lessons, class.'

"She gave mother the one vacant seat and all morning long mother sat there. She didn't know what these children were doing. They were using different books, and they were studying different lessons, and even her tablet paper was the wrong kind—so all she could do was sit.

"When recess came, mother marched out to the playground with the other children. She watched, and did just what they did, and followed the other little girls. But none of them knew her. So she had to pretend she didn't care about their games, and sit down in one of the basement windows where no one could notice her, and watch the other children play. The rest of the morning went just the same, and when mother went home to the new house at noon, she cried and told grandma she wasn't ever going back to that school."

The mother laughed easily and yet with a slight ruefulness.

Betty reminded her, "But you did go back!"

"Indeed I did! Grandpa said that mother needn't go, but grandma wouldn't hear of such a thing."

"Was grandpa nicer than grandma?"

"Well—perhaps mother thought so then. But I don't know just what grandma and grandpa could have done with her if they hadn't sent her back to school. So she had her face washed, and grandma held a wet towel to her eyes and her little red nose, and in the afternoon back she went."

In silence Betty contemplated the story. "Now tell me about the Valentine Box."

But the mother was not quite through with her introduction. She laughed again, softly.

"Go on," Betty urged.

But she sat looking into the dusk. She was remembering too many things to be told—how her father had promised to take her uptown that very night after school, to the big stores that filled her with awe, and see that she got a round cap exactly like those the other girls wore; how her mother had agreed, if she would be willing to wear the kitty hood when she played outdoors on Saturdays; and how she herself had apologized and explained to the little kitty hood, in a moment of shamed remorse, when she had come home triumphant in her new round cap and put the hood away in a drawer . . .

"The Valentine Box, mother!"

Yes, of course, she must get to the real story. That could be told, and these were things faintly stirring the darkness of her remembrance that no one would ever know but herself. There was too much bound up in them. . . . She turned away.

She said severely, "But you know you always cry, Betty."

"I won't cry this time," Betty promised hopefully.

"Why did I ever tell you this story in the first place? Well . . ."

And she began, she rather hoped for the last time, to tell the story of the Valentine Box.

"So mother got her round cap, and the right books, and the right kind of tablet paper, and she even began to understand what the class was doing in arithmetic. But none of the little girls had ever spoken to her. At recess she had to go and sit alone in the basement window, and after school she stayed and asked questions of the teacher so that she wouldn't have to march out with the others and see the girls go skipping off together. Of course, they might have spoken to her if she hadn't been such a silly, bashful little girl—"

"You aren't silly!"

"I hope not so silly as I was then. Anyway, it was about the first of February, and one morning, when mother went to school, she saw valentines in the drug-store window; and when she got to school, a whole group of little girls were standing together in the cloakroom and talking about valentines. After that, valentines were all she saw or thought or heard of. Last Valentine's Day, she had had the best time in the world. Lois had painted a little valentine for her, and she had painted one for Lois. And there had been a party, and a little boy named Dewey Boggs had given her a candy heart that said 'Love me.' Mother had kept it because it was too pretty to suck, and then finally it was too dirty!"

"Mother, Dewey Boggs wasn't *daddy?*"

The mother laughed. "Oh, no, he wasn't daddy! You know what daddy's name is, you foolish child!"

"I know it. Now tell me about the valentines."

"But this year everything was so different, and mother didn't want Valentine's Day to come."

She felt the soft clasp of Betty's arms, comforting her in advance.

"Now, Betty, you promised not to cry."

"I remember." The little voice was doleful.

"Then you mustn't. Or mother can't tell the story at all. She shouldn't anyway . . . but . . . Well, the worst of all was when the little girls began talking about the Valentine Box. At first, mother didn't know what they meant. She heard it in the cloakroom and on the playground and everywhere. 'Are we going to have a Valentine Box?' 'What do you think you'll get in the Valentine Box?' And finally one of the little girls—"

"That Gertie?"

"That Gertie it was! You remember, funny little midget, don't you?"

"Yes, because I don't *like* that Gertie."

"Oh, Gertie probably wasn't so bad as mother thought she was then."

"But she was *loud.*"

"She was. She had the loudest voice on the playground. And when the little girls chose sides, she always had to be the first to choose . . . Well, that Gertie began waving her hand in the air—"

"Show me how, mother. Do it."

"Oh, like this."

Betty giggled delightedly.

"And when the teacher said, 'Well, Gertie, what is it?' she hopped up from her seat and said, 'Teacher, are we going to have a Valentine Box this year?'

"That was the first mother had ever heard of a Valentine Box. She wondered what it could be. She was so silly that at first she thought it meant the teacher was going to give valentines to all the children—and she took her arithmetic home every night, so that the teacher would like her and give her a nice one."

"What had the teacher said to Gertie?"

"I think she'd said, 'We'll see.' "

"The way *you* do, mother."

"Do I? Yes, I suppose I do, funny one. And the teacher meant just the same thing that mother does—that she didn't much want to have the Valentine Box, but she supposed she'd have to agree! Because a few days later, after school had begun, she rapped with her rule on the desk and said, 'Class, attention!' "

Betty wiggled into a listening attitude.

"And then she said: 'On Valentine's Day, next Friday, there will be a Valentine Box in this room. All of you may bring your valentines here, and put them in the box, and we will take a half-hour in the afternoon and distribute the valentines.' And all the room clapped and clapped."

"Did you clap, mother?"

"At first mother clapped, because all the rest did and because she thought it sounded lovely, too. But afterward, when she thought about it, it didn't seem so nice to her. She began to wonder who would give her a valentine. At first, she thought about it just a little bit. Because she didn't really believe such a thing as being the one to get no valentine could happen. Not to her. And when she went past the drugstore, she would think: 'That's a pretty one! What if I should get that in the Valentine Box?'

"But the nearer the day came, the more she thought about it. There was a pretty little girl in her room named Fidelia. She wished Fidelia would give her a valentine. But she was such a silly little girl, as I told you, that instead of trying to know Fidelia better, she was all the more shy of her now, for fear Fidelia would think it was just a valentine she wanted.

"There was the little boy who sat behind her and who whispered to her and untied her hair ribbons. She even thought *he* might give her one. It would probably be one of those dreadful comics, but she didn't care, if only there was a valentine in the box for her. But one of the boys said to this boy, 'Hey, you going to give any valentines?' and he said, 'Naw, I ain't going to give any old valentines.' And then both the boys laughed and swaggered. And the next time he untied her ribbon, she looked fiercely at him and said, 'You stop that!'

"But there was Lois. Surely Lois would remember and send her a valentine. She would give it to the teacher and say, 'My little chum sent me this and said to put it in the Valentine Box.' It would be all the nicer because it had a stamp on it and had come through the mails.

"So mother went to grandpa's office and told him she wanted

a nickel to buy Lois a valentine.

" 'Lois!' he said to her. 'Well, what about the little girls here?'

"And he gave her a whole quarter! But what was she to do with it? Grandpa thought she was the nicest little girl in the world, and he would have been angry if he had supposed every one else didn't think so, too. Mother had to take the quarter, and kiss him, and go away wondering what she could do with it.

"But no letter from Lois came. Every day she ran home from school, and every day there was nothing. She wouldn't ask grandma about it, because she couldn't bear to have grandma know. She had sent Lois a pretty valentine with a picture of a gentleman with powdered hair handing roses to a lady in a puffed-out skirt. Friday came nearer and nearer, and she didn't know what she was going to do. She woke up in the night because she had dreamed the teacher had a great big Valentine Box and was calling out every name but her own. She couldn't stand it. She went and sat on grandpa's lap, and she thought she would ask *him* to put a valentine in the box for her. But she couldn't. Then grandpa and grandma would know all about it, how she didn't know anybody at school, and how even Lois had forgotten her, and she hadn't told them a single word. So when grandpa said, 'What does this little girl want?' she told him, 'An apple.'

"Then it was Valentine's Day itself. It was the loveliest bright winter day. The sun was shining, and the water was dripping from the icicles, so that they looked like what mother and Lois used to call 'diamond fingers.' 'What are you going to have to eat at your party?' Lois would ask mother when they were on the way to school. And mother would say, 'I'm going to have snowsparkle pudding and diamond fingers.'"

Betty said, "That's what *I'm* going to have some day!"

"So that at first mother didn't know why she felt so funny. There was a funny feeling in her stomach."

"Why was it in your *stomach,* mother?"

"I don't know, but that's where it was."

"What was it like?"

"Oh goodness, Betty, mother can't stop to remember. It was there—and then mother knew it was because this was Valentine's Day. At first she thought she wouldn't go to school. When she went down to breakfast, she told grandma she didn't feel well enough to go to school today. But grandma said, 'Let me see your tongue!' And then she said that she guessed this was 'Friday sickness,' and mother would be all right when it came time to play tomorrow morning. And there wasn't any letter from Lois—"

"Why not?"

"Well, mother had been away a long time—several weeks— and there were so many other little girls in the school . . . All the way to school she wondered what could happen so she wouldn't have to go. Maybe a fairy would come with her wand and tap on the Valentine Box—or maybe one of the gods and goddesses would send a cloud to hide her. Of course, she knew none of these things would really happen. She still had part of her quarter unspent. And so, when she came to the drug store, she went in and said to the man, 'I want to buy a valentine.'"

"The pretty one you saw in the window?"

"Oh, no, that was gone long ago. But a pretty one, too, with paper embroidery all around the edge, and little hearts and cupids, and a verse that said the person who got this valentine was very pretty and some one's love. The man said, 'How's this one?' and she said, 'It's all right.' And she went through the alley, instead of through the street, and she looked to see that no one was coming, and first she shut her eyes tight and prayed, 'Oh, dear God, please let the teacher call out my name!' and then she wrote a name on the valentine. She kept it in her arithmetic all morning.

"But that afternoon she went to school very early. She told grandma she had to work on her diagrams. Nobody was in the room but the teacher. The teacher had on a pretty dress, and there, on her desk, was a great, big Valentine Box all covered over with red crêpe paper and with a beautiful bow of white.

"'See our Valentine Box!' the teacher said. 'Do you have any valentines to put in it?' Mother said, 'Yes, ma'am.' And she dropped in her valentine. Then she went to her seat and worked on her diagrams."

"Tell me how you felt, mother."

"Well, it was a very funny feeling."

"In your *stomach?*"

"No, little funny one, I think all over. It was too much of a feeling to be any one place."

"Now tell me the rest of it."

"Well, pretty soon the other children began coming into the room, and all the little girls brought in valentines and dropped them into the box."

"Didn't the boys bring in valentines, too?"

"Some of them did. But you see, it didn't matter so much if the boys didn't get any valentines."

"Why not, mother?"

"Well, darling—just because it doesn't! Anyway it was the

little girls who cared.

"All afternoon none of the children wanted to get their lessons. They whispered and wiggled in their seats. Little girls wore their best dresses and best hair ribbons, and even that little boy who sat behind mother had slicked down his hair! And finally, at three o'clock, the teacher said, 'You may all put away your books.' "

Betty gave a deep sigh.

"And then when everything was quiet, the teacher opened the Valentine Box. It was all cram full of white envelopes and a great big sigh went over the room. The children craned their necks to see and they all wondered whose name would be the first one called."

"Whose was? Not yours, mother?"

"Oh, no, indeed it wasn't mother's name! Whose do you think it was? The teacher's! They had given her a beautiful, big valentine with lace paper and a red satin ribbon. The most beautiful valentine in the box. So every one was satisfied with that.

"But then came the other names. There were a few valentines for a few little boys—comic valentines, most of those, and you ought to have heard the children laugh! But most of them were for the little girls, and pretty soon it was the same names over and over again. 'Gertie' and 'Helen' and 'Fidelia,' and then 'Gertie' and 'Fidelia' and 'Helen' over again. Every time a name was called, up tripped the little girl to the desk, and back she came with her valentine. Pretty soon their desks were covered with white envelopes and bright pictures and paper lace. There was only one little desk that didn't have anything at all on it. All this time mother was listening—although she pretended not to—but the teacher never said 'Alice'!"

Betty's face was woebegone.

"At last the teacher came to the very bottom of the box. All the little heads were turning and waiting for the bell to ring. All the little girls were showing their valentines to each other. Every child in the room had one—even the little girl whose braids were tied with string and who lived on the other side of the railroad tracks. Every little girl but one—"

"Who?"

"You know who. Her heart was beating so queerly all this time. Her desk looked so empty that she took out her tablet and her books. She looked straight over all the heads and pretended not to see or hear anything. And then, just when it was time for the bell to ring, the teacher found the very last valentine and called 'Alice.'

"And then all the room stared while mother went up to the desk."

Betty gave a long, sobbing sigh. She settled back in her soft blankets. The mother hugged her tightly for a moment. Then her arms relaxed into a dreamy hold. Betty, struggling up a little shyly, saw the darkness in her eyes and a strange little smile on her lips. She burrowed her head against the warm shoulder, made little reminding sounds and movements. The mother looked at her again, laid her cheek against the smooth head, and the darkness in her eyes melted into tender brightness.

"I want to hear the rest of it, mother."

"But mother got her valentine. Isn't that the end?"

"No, I want to hear the rest of it."

"Well, then . . ."

She told it quickly, lightly, as if holding the story at a distance from her, something careless and forgotten.

"Well, then, all the children in the room marched out with their valentines. And as soon as they were out of the building they began to talk about them. 'Who gave you this one?' and 'Who gave you that one?'—and Gertie said she had twenty-nine. But they could all see that mother was carrying a valentine. She walked like a proud, cool little girl and paid no attention to them at all. They looked curious and respectful, as if they would like to know her now, because it seemed that some one must like her very much. You see, it was a very nice valentine. And when she was going down the walk, that Gertie came up to her and said:

" 'Won't you let us see your valentine?'

"Mother took it out of the envelope. They all said it was very nice. Fidelia said it was lovely. But mother, although she was pleased, kept wanting to cry. And then Gertie said:

" 'Who gave it to you?'

"And mother said, 'I'm not going to tell.' And she marched straight off home."

Betty was silent. Then she begged, "Is that *all* the story?"

"No, perhaps it isn't quite all. No, there was lots and lots more to it than that."

The mother pinched and patted the little cheek. But there was a tinge of bitterness in her voice. She smiled, too. She knew what the little voice was pleading for.

"No, because when mother got home, she went up to her room, and took the valentine out of the envelope again, and looked at it. She knew that she was saved from being disgraced. She knew that now Gertie and the other little girls were interested in her. They would ask her to play with them. But somehow she didn't care so much about knowing them, after this. It didn't seem so much to matter. She didn't care anything about her valentine, and she went down and put it in the kitchen stove, and when it was all burnt up, she got a book and read a story."

"Mother." The little voice was just a whisper. "Mother. Who gave you the valentine?"

"You know who gave it to me. Mother gave it to herself."

There was a sigh and a long silence. "And is *that* all?"

"Well—it's all of it as a story."

"But did the little girls play with you after that?"

"Oh, yes. They played with me."

"And *some*time other people gave you valentines?"

"Lots of times. Oh, yes, indeed!" She hugged the little figure repentantly. "You mustn't feel sorry for mother after that."

"But why didn't *daddy* give you a valentine?"

"Because daddy didn't know mother then. And one year he did!" She laughed. "An enormous big valentine, sent through the mail, in a box, not an envelope! A great, big valentine shaped like a banjo with golden strings. The biggest valentine he could buy!"

In silence Betty contemplated the splendor. She gave a sigh of satisfaction. Then her arms tightened again. Her voice breathed into her mother's ear.

"If *I'd* been there, *I'd* have given you a valentine. . . ."

The Little Girl from Town

I WONDER who that is, coming here," Mrs. Sieverson said looking out of the kitchen window.

"Somebody coming?" Mr. Sieverson asked from the sink. "Oh, I guess that's Dave Lindsay, ain't it? He said he'd be out."

"Yes, but he's got some one with him. Oh! I believe it's that little girl from back East somewhere that's visiting them. Leone! Children!"

Mr. Sieverson went outdoors, and then Mrs. Sieverson, and by the time the car stopped, rounding the drive, all four children were on hand from somewhere. Even Marvin and Clyde, the two boys.

"Anybody home?" Mr. Lindsay called out jovially.

"You bet!"

They were all looking at the little girl in the car beside him. They had heard about this little girl, and how "cute" she was. Her mother was some relative of Mrs. Lindsay's. Leone and Vila looked at her eagerly. The boys hung back, but they wanted to see her. Mr. Lindsay was proud. He said:

"Well sir, I've got somebody along with me!"

"I see you have!" Mr. Sieverson answered, with shy heavy jocularity; and Mrs. Sieverson asked, "Is this the little girl been visiting you?"

"This is the little girl! But I don't know whether she's visiting or not. I've just about made up my mind I'll keep her!"

They all laughed appreciatively. Leone pulled her mother's

107

dress. She wanted her mother to ask if the little girl couldn't get out and play with them. "Now, don't. We'll see," Mrs. Sieverson whispered. The little girl was so pretty sitting there with her soft golden-brown hair and her cream-white dress that Mr. and Mrs. Sieverson were both shy of saying anything directly to her. Mr. Sieverson cried, still trying conscientiously to joke:

"Well, ain't you going to get out?"

Mr. Lindsay asked, "Well!—shall we, Patricia?"

The little girl looked gravely at the other little girls, and then nodded.

"All right, sir! Patricia's the boss! I've got to do as she says."

She consented to smile at that, and the two boys giggled. Mr. Lindsay lifted her out of the car. She put her arms around his neck and her little legs and her feet in their shiny black slippers dangled as he swung her to the ground. The children felt shy when he set her down among them. Mr. and Mrs. Sieverson didn't quite know what to say.

"*There* she is! This is the first time this little girl has ever been out to a farm. What do you think of that, Marvin?"

Marvin grinned, and backed off a few steps.

"Yes, sir! But she and Uncle Dave have great times driving 'round together, don't they?"

The little girl looked up at him, and then smiled and nodded her head with a subtle hint of mischief.

"You bet we do! We have great times."

The Sieversons all stood back in a group shyly grinning and admiring. Leone's eyes were as eager as if she were looking at a big doll in a store window. They had never seen any child as pretty as this one—and Mr. Lindsay knew it, and was brimming with pride. Her short dress of creamy linen, tied with a red silk cord at the neck and embroidered with patches of bright Russian colors, melted its fairness into the pure lovely pallor of her skin. The sleeves were so short that almost the whole of her soft, round, tiny arms were bare. Her hair was of fine gold streaked and overlaid with brown—the color of a straw stack with the darker, richer brown on top—but every hair lay fine and perfect, the thick bangs waved slightly on her forehead, and the long soft bob curved out like a shining flower bell and shook a little when she moved her head. Her skin wasn't one bit sunburned, and so white and delicately grained that there seemed to Vila, in awe, to be a little frost upon it . . . like the silver bloom on wildflower petals, picked in cool places, that smudged when she rubbed it with her fingers.

Mr. Lindsay became businesslike now that he was out of the car. "Well, Henry," he said, "you got it all figured up and ready to show me? I think we've got Appleton where we can make a deal, all right."

"Yeah, I guess it's ready."

While the two men talked, the little girl stood beside Mr. Lindsay, with her hand still in his, with a grave, trustful, wondering look. Leone, smiling at her, was getting closer. Mr. Lindsay seemed to remember her then and looked down at her.

"Well, Patricia, what about you while I'm looking after my business?" He smiled then at the other children. "Think you can find something to do with all these kids here?"

Leone looked up at him and her blue eyes pleaded brightly in her eagerness. "I guess they's plenty of them to look after her," Mr. Sieverson said shyly, but still grinning. "They can entertain her," Mrs. Sieverson put in. She could do the baking without Leone this morning, she thought rapidly, but feeling hurried and anxious.

"You going to play with them for a while, are you?" Mr. Lindsay felt responsible for Patricia. All the same, he wanted her off his mind for a while until he had finished his business. "I don't know whether—"

"Oh, Leone'll look after her," Mrs. Sieverson assured him; and Mr. Sieverson repeated, "Sure! She'll be all right with Leone."

Leone came up now, smiling eagerly and with a sweetness that transformed her thin freckled face. She shook back the wisps of uneven, tow-colored hair. She took the little girl's hand protectingly and confidingly in her hot palm that had a gleam of dusty perspiration along the life-line and the heart-line. The tiny hand felt like a soft warm bit of silk—or a flower.

"That's right! Uncle Dave won't be gone long. Don't take her out where it's too hot, kids, you know she isn't used to things the way you are."

"No, you be careful," Mrs. Sieverson warned them.

"Will you go with Leone?" The little girl did not say that she would or wouldn't, but she was courteous and did not draw back. "You'll be all right! *You'll* have a good time! Oh, I guess Uncle Dave didn't tell these kids who you were, did he? This is Patricia."

"Can you say that?" Mrs. Sieverson asked—doubting if *she* could.

Vila drew shyly back, with one shoulder higher than the other; but Leone laughed in delight. "I can say it!" She nodded. She squeezed Patricia's hand.

"You can say it, can you? All right, then. Well now, you kids can show this little girl what good times you can have on the farm. That so? All right then, Henry."

Mrs. Sieverson went into the house to get back to her baking. She had a lot to do today. She wasn't at all worried about leaving their little visitor so long as Leone was with her. But she turned to call back to the children, who were still silently grouped about Patricia in the driveway:

"You better stay in the yard with her. Mr. Lindsay won't like it if she gets her dress dirty. Leone! You hear me?"

"I heard. Do you want to come into the yard, Patricia? You do, don't you?" Leone asked coaxingly.

Patricia went soberly with her. Her eyes, gray, with threads of violet in the clear iris, were looking all about silently. Her little hand lay quiet but with confidence in Leone's. The other children followed, the boys lagging behind, but coming all the same.

"There now! Here's just the nicest shady place, and Patricia can sit here, can't she, and just be so nice?" Leone placed Patricia in the round patterned shade of an apple tree, and spread out her linen dress, making it perfectly even all around, and carefully drew out her little legs straight in front of her with the shiny black slippers close together. "There!" she said proudly. "See?"

She sat down on one side of Patricia, and then Vila shyly, and with a sidelong confiding smile, sat down on the other. The boys hung back together.

"Leone!" Mrs. Sieverson called from the house. "Ain't you got something to entertain her with? Why don't you get your dolls?"

"Do you want to see our dolls, Patricia?"

So far, Patricia had been consenting but silent. "You go in and get them, Vila," Leone ordered; and when Vila whined, "I don't want to!" she said, "Yes, you have to. I can't leave her. I have to take care of her. Don't I, Patricia?" But when Vila came back with the scanty assortment of dolls, Patricia looked at them, and then reached out her hand for the funny cloth boy doll in the knitted sweater suit. The boys laughed proudly, and looked at each other, the way they had done when the swan in the park at Swea City took the piece of sandwich they put on the water for it. "Isn't that doll cute, Patricia?" Leone begged eagerly.

Patricia touched its black embroidered eyes, and its red embroidered lips—done in outline stitch—and then looked up at the eager, watching children and smiled with that gleam of mischief.

The boys laughed again. They all came around closer. "That's mine," Vila said softly. She reached over and touched the big stuffed cloth doll, with the hair colored yellow and the cheeks bright red, that was smooth along the top and bottom sides like a fish, but crisp along the edges from the seams. Patricia took it and looked at it. She looked at every one of their dolls—there were five, one of them was a six-inch bisque doll from the ten-cent store—and then smiled again.

"I'll bet you have nice dolls at home, haven't you, Patricia?" Leone said in generous worship. "I'll bet you've got lots nicer dolls than we have."

Patricia spoke for the first time. The children listened, with bright eager eyes wide open, to each soft little word.

"I have fifteen dolls."

Marvin said: "Gee!"

"Have you got them named?" Vila leaned over the grass toward Patricia, and then quickly hitched herself back, frightened at the sound of her own voice asking the question.

"Oh, yes, I always name my dolls," Patricia assured them.

"My dolls have beautiful names. They're all the names of the great actresses and singers." And she began gravely to repeat them. "Geraldine Farrar; and Maria Jeritza; and Eva Le-Gallienne; and Amelita Galli-Curchi—"

While she was saying them, the boys looked at each other over her head, their eyes glinting, their mouths stretched into grins of smothered amusement; until Clyde broke into giggles.

Leone was indignant. "Those are *lovely* names! I think Patricia was just wonderful to think of them!"

Vila stretched across the grass again. She touched the cloth doll and drew back her fingers as quickly as if it were hot. "Her name's Dor'thy," she whispered.

After Patricia's gracious acceptance of the dolls, the children wanted to show her all the treasures they had—even those they had never told any one else about. Everything, they felt, would receive a kind of glory from her approval. They liked to repeat her name now. "Patricia." "She wants to see the little pigs. Don't you, Patricia?" "Aw, she does not! Do you, Patricia? She wants to see what I've got to make a radio." Patricia looked from one to the other with her violet-gray eyes, and let the others answer for her. But after a while, she said with a cool, gentle, royal decision:

"No. I don't want to go anywhere. I want to stay right here in this round shade."

The children were highly delighted. They began to bring their treasures to her. Vila had run off to the edge of the garden and dug up two glass precious stones she had buried there, but when she came back to Patricia, she was too shy to show them and kept them hidden in her hot little hand that got sticky and black from the earth clinging to them. The boys were getting quite bold. Marvin said:

"I bet you never saw a mouse nest, Patricia."

"Patricia doesn't care anything about that," Leone said impatiently. "I wish you boys would go off somewhere, anyway, and let us look after Patricia."

"I can show it to you, Patricia."

"*She* doesn't want to see that!"

"Yes, I do," Patricia assured them with an innocent courtesy that made Clyde giggle again.

The boys ran off to the woodshed to get it. It was all made of wound-about string and little bits of paper and a soft kind of woolly down. Patricia examined it with her large grave eyes. She reached out one finger toward it delicately, and drew the finger back. She looked up at the boys.

"What is it?" she breathed.

"A mouse nest," Marvin said nonchalantly.

He held it carefully in his brown sturdy hands, partly to keep it together, but more because he liked to have Patricia's soft little fingers come near his. They were as smooth as silk, and rosy at the tips as the pointed petals of the dog-tooth violets he had found near the little creek in the woods, when he was out there one day last April, all alone. A happy shiver went over him at the thought of their touching him, silvery and cool.

"Do the mouses—*mices*—live in it?"

"Sure! They did before we took it away."

"Oh, but can't they live in it any more? What will the mices do?"

"Gee! What can they do?" Marvin swaggered. Clyde giggled.

Her pink mouth opened into a distressed O. She looked from one to the other for help, and the violet in her eyes deepened. "But they won't have anywhere to live! You must put it back." She was very serious.

"Shoot! Why, they're run off somewheres else by this time!"

What did it matter about mice anyhow? Gee, they were something to get rid of! Why did she suppose pop kept all those cats and fed 'em, if it wasn't to get rid of the mice? But she looked so distressed that Leone, with an angry glance at the boys, assured her hastily, leaning over and hugging her:

"No, they haven't, Patricia! Boys just like to say things like that."

"Aw, gee—!"

"But what will the mices *do?*"

"The boys'll put the nest back, and then the mice'll come there," Leone warmly promised her. She didn't care if it wasn't true.

The boys had never heard anything so funny in their lives. Gee whiz! They despised her for such ignorance, and could hardly keep from laughing, and yet they felt uneasily ashamed of themselves for they didn't quite know what. They had just wanted to bring her the mouse nest to make her interested, and then to show her, too, that they weren't afraid of things most people didn't want to touch. But they seemed to be out of favor. They hung around while the girls talked a lot of silly talk, and laid all the dolls out in the grass in front of them.

"I'll bet you've got awful pretty clothes for your dolls, haven't you, Patricia?"

Patricia didn't like to say, or to talk about her dolls, because she didn't really think that these dolls' dresses were one bit pretty. Leone went on questioning her, with naïve admiration, and Vila listened with her eyes glistening.

"I'll bet you've been into lots of big stores, Patricia. Did this dress you've got on come from a big store?"

They both bent and examined the creamy shining linen with its coarse silky weave and the large roughened threads that Vila scarcely dared to touch with her fingers all dirty from the precious stones. Patricia graciously let them touch and see until, gently but with a final dignity, she drew the cloth out of their fingers.

"Now you mustn't touch me any more."

The boys giggled again at this, admiring, but feeling abashed.

A striped kitten came suddenly into sight at a little distance—became motionless, saw them—and flattened and slid under the cover of the plants in the garden. Patricia gave a little cry. Her face bloomed into brightness.

"Oh! Do you have a kitty?"

"A cat! Gee!" They all laughed. "*One* cat! I bet we got seventeen."

"Really seventeen kitties? Did your father buy them all for you?"

"Buy them!" The boys shouted with laughter. "Gee, you don't buy cats!"

"Oh, you do," Patricia told them, shocked. "They cost twenty-five dollars, the kitties that sit in the window in the shop."

"Twenty-five dollars! Pay twenty-five dollars for a *cat!*" Cats, when you had to drown half of 'em and couldn't hardly give the others away! The boys were hilarious with laughter over such ignorance.

Leone couldn't help know that Patricia was ignorant, too. But she gave the boys a hurt, indignant, silencing look—it was mean of them to laugh at Patricia when she didn't know! Anyway, she was so little. Leone put her arm around Patricia in warm protection.

"But they do!" Patricia's eyes were large and tearful and her soft little lips were quivering. It was dreadful to have these children not believe her, and she couldn't understand it. "Some of them cost a hundred dollars!"

"Oh, gee—!" the boys began.

"Maybe some of them *do*," Leone said quickly. "You don't know everything in the world, Marvin Sieverson." She knew, of course, that cats couldn't—but then, she wasn't going to *have* the boys make fun of Patricia. "Come on now, Patricia," she pleaded. "We'll go and see our kitties. Shall we?"

The boys watched anxiously. They didn't want Patricia to be mad at them. They wanted to take her out to the barn and have her look at everything.

She considered. Her eyes were still large and mournful and a very dark violet. At last she nodded her head, held out her hands trustingly to Leone to be helped from the grass, smoothed down her skirts—and the whole tribe went running off together.

Patricia had to climb up the steep stairs into the haymow one step at a time. She felt along the rough sides carefully with her little hands. The boys would have liked to help her and were too bashful, but all the time, Leone was just behind her, telling her, "Don't you be afraid. Leone's right here, Patricia. Leone won't let you fall." When they got up into the haymow, Patricia was almost frightened at first, it was so big, and there were such shadows. A long beam of sunlight fell dimly and dustily golden from the high window in the peak, across the great beams, and the piled hay, and widening over the great stretch of wooden floor.

"Haven't you ever been up in a haymow before?" Clyde demanded.

"Of course she hasn't," Leone answered indignantly.

Patricia looked around at them and her face was pale with awed excitement. "It's like the church!" she breathed.

"Gee, a *hay*-mow!"

Still, it really was. Even their voices, and the way they walked, sounded different up here. The boys were tickled and a little embarrassed that Patricia had thought of that.

"Is this where the kitties live?"

"The little ones do. Where are the little bitty ones, Marvin?"

"*I* know!" both the boys shouted. They leaped up into the sliding mounds of hay, calling back, "Come on if you want to see, Patricia!"

"I'll help you, Patricia," Leone encouraged her.

She boosted, and got Patricia up onto the hay pile, and helped her flounder along with her feet plunging into uncertain holes, and the long spears of hay scratching at her bare legs above the half socks, and the dust making her eyes smart. Then Patricia began to laugh. She liked it!

"Here they are!" the boys shouted.

A bevy of half-grown cats suddenly fled down the hay like shadows. "No, no!" Patricia screamed when the boys tried valiantly to catch a little black cat by its tail. Leone was assuring her, "Never mind, they won't hurt the kitties, Patricia."

"Look here! Come here!" the boys were calling.

Patricia was almost afraid to go. The boys had found the nest of little kittens. They had got hold of the soft, mousy, wriggling things and were holding them up for her to see. Fascinated, she went nearer. The little kittens had pink skin fluffed over with the finest fur, big round heads and little snubby ears, and blue eyes barely open.

"Oh . . ." She looked up at Leone with her pink lips pursed.

She loved the little kittens, but she was afraid of them. "Oh, but they aren't kitties! They don't look like kitties."

The boys were highly amused. "What do they look like?" Marvin demanded. "What do you think they are? Cows? Horses?"

She said tremulously, "No, I *know* cows are big. But their heads look the way little baby cow heads do in the pictures. They do."

"I think they do, too," Leone asserted stoutly. She coaxed, "Touch them, Patricia. They won't hurt you."

The boys grinned at the way Patricia put out her fingers and drew them back. How could these little bits of kittens hurt her? Didn't she know they couldn't bite yet? Their little teeny teeth couldn't do anything but nibble. It was fun to feel them. Marvin caught up the white one and held it out to her, and they all kept urging her. He hoped her fingers would touch his. She cringed back, her mouth pursed in v onder.

"Oh, but they have such funny tails!"

"No, they ain't. They got tails like all cats got."

"Oh no, Marvin. In the show, the kitties had tails so big, and they waved them—just like the big plumes on men's hats, riding on horses."

The boys doubled up with laughter. "Who'd put cats in a show?"

"Oh, but they are!" Patricia looked at them in distress.

"Why shouldn't they be?" Leone demanded.

Of course she knew why, as well as the boys did. Nobody would pay to see a cat! Patricia had meant the tigers. She was so little she didn't know the difference. The boys were not to tease her, though! Clyde was giggling. Gee, if she didn't have the funniest notions!

At last they got her to touch the kitten. She did it first with just the pink tip of one finger—then it felt so soft, so little and fluffy, with tiny whiskers like fine silk threads, that she reached out her hands. Marvin felt the brush of her fingers, as if a cobweb had blown across his hand, and a shiver of joy and pain went down his backbone. Patricia laughed in delight, and looked from one to the other of the children with her large shining eyes, to share her wonder.

"Take it!" Marvin urged.

"Oh no, I wouldn't!"

"Why not? Go on and take it!"

She shook her head.

"She doesn't have to if she doesn't want to," Leone said warmly.

"Yes, she does!" Marvin thrust the kitten into her hands. She gave a little shriek and squeezed it by its soft belly, while the weak pinkish legs wavered and clawed out of her grasp.

"I'm going to drop it!"

"No, you won't!"

Its fluffiness filled her with ecstasy. "Oh, see its claws! They look like little bits of shavings from mother's pearl beads!" The boys grinned in amusement and delight at each other. Vila laughed happily. "Oh, and inside its little ears! Just the way shells look inside—only these are *silk* shells!" The boys grinned broadly. She caught the kitten to her cheek and held it wildly wriggling. "Oh kitty, I love you! I want to have you to take home!"

"You can—you can have it," the children all urged her eagerly. Marvin said, "Gee, we got all kinds of cats, and that old gray one—" Clyde pinched him. "Shut up!" He grinned and blushed. Patricia laid the kitten gravely and reluctantly back in the rounded nest. She shook her head until the fluffy bell of shining hair trembled. She said solemnly, and as if she had forgotten that the others were there:

"No, I won't. Because all its other little sisters and brothers would be lonesome for it. And its mother would."

The boys stood grinning but they said nothing.

What were the kittens' names, Patricia asked. She was horrified that they had none. "Gee, we call 'em kitty." Marvin said; but Leone hastened to add, "Well, we call that one we have, Old Gray." Patricia told them:

"Oh, but they must have names! That's wicked. Nobody goes up to heaven to our Lord Jesus without a name!"

The boys just barely glanced at each other. They kept their red faces straight with agony. Then Marvin went pawing and rolling through the hay over to the other side of the pile where he buried his flushed face and snorted.

"I'm going to give every one a name," Patricia asserted solemnly.

"What are you going to name 'em, Patricia?" Leone and Vila were impressed.

"I'm going to give them jewel names. Because the cats make me think about things like jewels. This is what I'm going to call them. I'm going to name this one Pearl because it's white, and this bluey one Sapphire, and the other bluey one Turquoise, and this little pinky one Coral, and this one . . . Jade!"

"Aren't you going to name one Di'mond, Patricia?" Leone asked eagerly. Vila thought that, too.

"No." Patricia was very decided. "Cats don't look like diamonds. They look like colored jewels."

The boys giggled. Besides, that one she had named *Pearl*— gee, they had already looked at these kittens and they knew very well that one was a he-cat! If she wasn't funny!

Vila was looking at Patricia so intently that she trembled. Now she said, "Patricia's eyes are jewel eyes, too. They're—they're . . ." She didn't know how to say it, and yet she felt what she meant and wanted to say—felt it so that it hurt! The whites of Patricia's eyes gleamed, and a little blue spread out into them from the circles of the colored parts, and in these there were all sorts of threads of color woven together, the way they were inside the glass of marbles—bluish and violet-colored and gray, and a sort of golden—! All just as clear . . . ! Vila reached out and took Patricia's wrist, quickly and with shy ardor, but then she only smiled and couldn't think of anything to say . . . she would have been afraid to say it, anyway.

"Now she must see all our places!"

They went through the big barn. "Look here, Patricia!" "Patricia can't. She's looking at this." She looked at everything, but when they urged her, "Touch it! Go ahead!" she wouldn't quite do that. When they went out of the barn, they all took hands and ran pounding down the long slope of heavy boards and out into the farmyard. Patricia was afraid at first, and then shrieked with laughter, and wanted to do it over again.

"Now we mustn't do it any more," Leone said after the third time. "Her little face is all red. Let go her hand, Marvin! Now, darling, stand still, and Leone'll wipe off her little face."

They thought it was funny the way she ran when the chickens came near her. "Oh gee, if we had time we'd go down to the pond and show her the geese! Wouldn't she run if that old goose got after her!" Leone said, "Marvin Sieverson! We shan't go there."

But the very best place was the orchard. Even the boys were

not too wild and noisy there. Their feet made only soft swishing sounds when they went through the long grass. The boughs were loaded, some broken and sweeping the ground, and the sky was patterned with leaves.

"Patricia!" Marvin hinted, tempting her, holding out a little green apple.

Leone snatched it from his hand. "Why, Marvin Sieverson, shame on you! Do you want to make little Patricia sick?"

"Aw, gee!" He had just wanted to see if she would take it. He and Clyde had both been hunting through the grass for some apples that Patricia could really eat.

Only the yellow transparents were ripe. The large apples had a clear pale color against the leaves that were only slightly darker—mellow and clear at the same time, a light pure yellow-green through which the August sunshine seemed to pass. Patricia took the big yellow apple that Marvin picked for her and carried it all around with her. *"Eat* it, Patricia, why don't you?" But she wanted to hold it. "Oh, thank you!" she said very earnestly for every single thing the children gave her—the red dahlia, and the tiny bunch of sweet peas, the bluebird's feather. Whenever she saw a bird she stopped. She put her little silky hand on Leone's wrist. "Look!" "It's just a bird." She stood and watched with fascinated eyes until the bird was lost in the sky and she had to turn away dazzled with blue and gold.

"Do you wish you could stay here and belong to us, Patricia?" Leone asked her wistfully. "We'd play you were my little girl, wouldn't we?"

Patricia wished that she could stay. There were streaks of dust down the shining linen dress and on the soft little arms, a damp parting in the lovely wave of the bangs, and around her mouth there was a faint stain of red from the juicy plums the boys had brought her to suck. Oh yes, the country, she said, was *nice!* She looked about with shining innocent eyes of wonder. She loved the animals. In the city, she told them, animals weren't happy. There were the beautiful green birds in the shop—just the color, almost, of these apple-tree leaves!—but her father wouldn't buy them for her because he didn't believe in keeping things in cages; and he wouldn't get her the big gray dog because it wasn't right to take dogs out on chains.

"Oh, if I lived in the country—" she cried—"do you know what I'd do? I'd just run around and run around—"

"You'd play with *me,* wouldn't you, Patricia?" Marvin cut in jealously.

"I'd play—"

"Children!"

The grown people were calling them. Disaster showed on the children's faces. "Oh, we don't want Patricia to go home!" There were so many things still that they hadn't shown her. But Mr. Lindsay came into the orchard calling out jovially:

"Well! Here she is! Ready to go home now with Uncle Dave?" He took it for granted that she was. He took her reluctant little hand and the other children trailed after them. When they reached the farmyard, he said: "See what's going with us!"

Patricia looked in awe and wonderment. "What is it?" she breathed.

"Don't you know what that is?"

Mr. and Mrs. Sieverson, standing back, both laughed. The children, too, were grinning.

Patricia ventured . . . "A baby cow!"

Then they all laughed to think that she had known.

"That's what it is, all right! But don't you know what baby

cows are called? Calf! That's a calf! Well sir, do you want this little calf to go with us?"

Patricia didn't know whether or not Uncle Dave meant that for a joke. But the little calf was so sweet—she loved it so terribly the instant she saw it—that she couldn't help risking that and begging, "Oh, yes!" Its head really was shaped like the tiny kittens'! But its eyes were very large, and colored a soft deep brown under a surface of rounded brightness, so gentle and so sad too, that it seemed to her as if the color showed in each eye under a big tear. The calf turned its head toward her. Its frail legs bent forward, to prop it up. Its coat looked like cream spilled over with shining tar. There were curls, like the curly knots showing in freshly planed wood; and the shining ends of the fur looked as if they had curled because the whole coat had just been licked by the mother.

"Oh yes, Uncle Dave! Is it going with us?"

"It's going to be our back seat passenger. If the boss permits?"

It made Mr. Sieverson laugh—feel tickled!—to see how the thought of riding to town with that calf pleased the little girl. But he said dutifully to Mr. Lindsay:

"Now, if that calf's going to be any nuisance to you—"

"No, no. As long as I've got the old car, put it in. Tie it up."

Patricia saw the rope then in Mr. Sieverson's hand. She cried, "Oh, not *tie* the little calf!"

"Sure," Mr. Sieverson said, grinning kindly at her. "You don't want it to jump out, do you?"

She looked at Uncle Dave for confirmation of that. He said:

"Sure! Calves won't go riding any other way."

The two boys laughed.

Patricia stood back close to Leone, but not saying anything

more. She looked frightened. Mr. Sieverson said, with some feeling of reassuring her still more:

"You don't want to let this calf get loose, or you won't get any of it!"

She didn't understand that.

"Get any of it to eat. This calf's going to make veal."

"Eat it!" She cried in horror; and she earnestly put him right. "Oh, no, I wouldn't *eat* it." Mr. Sieverson was joking.

"Why, sure!" he said. "Don't you eat good veal? You're going to take this calf to the butcher."

"Oh, no!" He meant that! Patricia was suddenly wild with crying. They all stood back, shocked, never expecting such a storm as this. "Oh, no! The little calf isn't going to be killed! I won't! I won't! no!" She put out her hands blindly and turned from one to the other for help. Mr. Sieverson didn't know what to do. She turned to him and beat the air with her little fists, shrieking, "Oh, you're *wicked!*"

He couldn't stand that. His face got red. Even if she was just a child, he demanded, "Don't you eat veal?"

"No! No!" Patricia shrieked.

"What then?" he demanded.

She had to look at him. Her little pink mouth was open and her bright eyes drowned. She quavered, "Other kinds of meat . . . I'll eat chicken," and turned piteously to Uncle Dave.

Mr. Sieverson didn't like to be called "wicked" by any one. The injustice, when he had just been trying to be nice to this little girl, too, hurt him. His wife murmured, "Well, now, Henry—!" But he insisted. "Don't chicken have to be killed before you can eat it?"

But even Mr. Sieverson, although he was in the right of it,

felt ashamed when he saw the little thing cry. Mrs. Sieverson gave him a look, stroked Patricia's hair, and said, "They won't take the calf." Mr. Lindsay hastened to promise. "No, no. Of course we won't take the calf." They were all trying now to reassure her. Vila was crying too. The boys were pleading, "Patricia!" although they didn't know just what they would say to her in comfort if they got her to look at them. "No, no, it isn't going. It won't have to be tied up. See, he's put away the rope." The two men settled the thing with a look above her head. Patricia looked up at last, with piteous drowned eyes, as dark as wet violets. She broke away from all of them, and running to the calf—fearful of touching things as she was—she threw her arms in protection around its neck and stared fiercely at the shamefaced people.

"Oh no, we couldn't take it!" Mr. Lindsay muttered. He cleared his throat.

The children surrounded Patricia again. They were begging her not to cry. Her cheek was laid against the little calf's silky ear, and she was telling it, in her own mind: don't you care, don't you mind, precious little calf, I've saved you. She let herself be drawn away, but said "No!" when Mrs. Sieverson wanted to wipe the tears from her cheeks, and held up the little wet face trustingly for Leone to do it. That pleased all the Sieversons greatly.

"So now we can go! Hm?" Mr. Lindsay asked her.

She seemed to have forgiven them. She didn't want to look at Mr. Sieverson, but when she said good-by to Mrs. Sieverson, she touched her little skirts and made a courtesy. Clyde pinched Marvin to tell him to look. The children watched her with as great delight as they had watched the tightrope walker in the "show." Mr. Lindsay lifted her into the car. She smiled faintly at the children, but there were stains of tears on her pearly cheeks, and her eyes were still violet-dark.

"You children go get her something—apples or something," Mrs. Sieverson whispered.

"We have, mamma! We've got a whole lot of things for her."

They began piling presents into her lap. "Don't forget your little feather, Patricia!" Marvin ran off to find something else. The wilting flowers, the apple, the six rosy plums, the bluebird's feather, she carefully took again. Marvin came panting back with his new game of "Round the World by Aeroplane." But Mr. Lindsay wouldn't let him give her that.

"No, no, my boy! You keep your game. She's got more things at home now than she can ever play with."

Now she seemed happy and appeased. The children crowded close to the side of the car and pleaded, "Come out again, won't you, Patricia?" Vila whispered in her shy voice, "I'll take care of Pearl and Samphire and those others, Patricia." Marvin said fiercely, "If any tom-cat comes 'round, I'll—" and ground and gnashed his teeth and made fiercely appropriate motions. Leone gave him a look for making her think about the tom-cat! But Patricia was still smiling and happy and hadn't understood. Now in her relief, and in the flurry of going, she was more eager and talkative then she had been all afternoon. She promised everything they asked.

"I will. I will, Leone. I will, Marvin. Thank you for all the beautiful things."

In the midst of it, Mr. Lindsay leaned over to say in a low tone to Mr. Sieverson, a little ashamed, "Well, somebody else'll take that in for you, Henry, if you can't go."

"Sure. That's all right, Mr. Lindsay."

"Well now, my little girl, tell them all good-by."

"Good-by." "Good-by, Patricia!" They called and waved madly to her, all standing back together. She answered them. At the very last minute, just as the car was going out into the driveway, she leaned out with her shining hair mussed and blowing in the breeze and cried:

"Good-by, calf! I forgot to say good-by to you."

Marvin laughed in delight, and then Clyde echoed him.

Mr. Sieverson stood looking after the car. That "wicked" still rankled. He said, as if very much put out, "Well now, I'll have to find another way of getting this calf in or else take it myself before night." Then he said, as if ashamed, "Gosh! I don't know. I almost hate to take it. That little thing put up such a fuss." He couldn't help adding, "She was a pretty little kid, wasn't she?"

Mrs. Sieverson did not answer at once. Then she said in an expressionless tone, "Well . . . maybe you better take the other one, then."

He looked at her and seemed to want to assent. Then he cried: "Oh, no! We can't do that. This is the one we'd picked on." He looked angry, and yet in his light blue eyes under the shock of lightish hair there was a hurt, puzzled look. "Oh well," he muttered. "Folks can't be foolish!" If ever folks were to start thinking of *such* things . . .

He went forward resolutely, saying "Hi! Stand still, there!" as he took hold of the calf. His wife stood back watching him and saying nothing. The calf turned, bolted for a little way, and then let him take hold of it again. It did not seem to know whether to be afraid of him or not. Its eyes looked up into his. In the large eyes of dark mute brown and the small eyes of light blue, there was much the same reluctant bewilderment in some far depths. But the man knew a little of what he was after, and the calf did not know what was to come.

"Come on here!" Mr. Sieverson said sharply.

He put the rope around the calf's neck.

Experience

ELIZABETH was in her room. She knew that "the folks" worried about her when she sat there alone. Once in a while her mother came to the door, usually on some pretext. "Dad and I are going to pick the berries. Don't you want to come out with us, Elizabeth?" She nearly always said no. She would rather be alone, living over, in sweet, wounding detail, now this and now that moment with Harold. But then she would get to thinking of them out there talking about her in low voices, how dad stepped carefully about the house with a solemn face, and mother's painful little efforts to be ordinary and cheerful; and she would have to go down.

Everything about "the folks" hurt her, too. Sometimes she went into their bedroom and looked at the wedding photograph on the wall. When she was a child, she used to ask wonderingly, "Was this you, Mamma? Was this really Papa?" she didn't think it looked like them at all. And she was quite impressed.

Then later, that first summer when she was at home from college, when Margie was visiting her, she took Margie in and they giggled together over the way dad's hair was curled, and the way they both stood there against a background of charcoal clouds. The *clothes!*

"Just look at mother's pishy knot!"

With eyes of horrified laughter, they counted all the little satin ruffles on mother's dress.

"Look how the skirt hikes up in the front, though! Women all wore corsets that stuck out in front. They didn't have garters fastened to them, or something. Look at that little curl over dad's left eyebrow! Isn't it sweet? Look at dad's ringlets!"

Mother heard them and met them just as they were escaping into the hall.

"What are you girls finding to amuse you so?"

They looked at each other—Margie a little scared—and giggled.

"I just wanted Marge to see how sweet you and dad looked when you got married."

"Oh, was that it?"

Mother laughed. She made fun of the picture, too. But she went on into the room and Elizabeth saw her standing in front of it with half-smiling, remote expression, and then turn away.

How could she ever have thought of it like that? Now she stole in all by herself; and the look of those two young faces with the rounded cheeks and serious, innocent eyes hurt her so that her throat ached. They had been *young*. She thought of all that had happened to them since that picture was taken, and she didn't see how they could bear it. Their first baby had died. Elizabeth used to feel important saying to the other children, "I had a little sister that died before I was born." She felt very pleased when mother told her to gather flowers to decorate the little sister's grave on Memorial Day, because the family had a lot where she could put flowers; and then she remembered how she had come dashing into the house with her bouquet—"Look, Mamma! Look what I've picked!"—and how through the open kitchen doorway she had seen mamma with her head on papa's shoulder and papa kissing her.

Why were they doing that? she had wondered.

She heard her mother now at the foot of the stairs.

"Elizabeth! Dad and I are going to drive out in the country and get a chicken. Won't you come along?"

She waited a moment, scarcely breathing. She couldn't bear to hurt them by refusing . . . but when she thought of the wedding picture she knew she couldn't stand the sight of their faces, to have to realize that they could get old and die.

"I guess not."

A pause.

"What are you doing, darling?"

"Just reading."

She waited, rigid, and heard them drive away.

She stole into the bedroom again and looked into the innocent eyes in the picture. How pretty they were—both of them! Yes, dad too, with those silly ringlets, and those nice dark eyes. It seemed terrible to her that they must lose their beauty.

She used to tease mother about buying that "complete beauty program" from the woman with hennaed hair who was going around selling toilet articles. When she or Charles took snapshots, mother always tried to get out of them. "What do you want *me* in it for?" Charles and Elizabeth thought she was silly. But now it seemed to Elizabeth that she understood only too well how mother glanced at the mirror and quickly away.

She looked around the bedroom with its white curtains and its lowered shades. It used to be just "the folks' room" to her. Now it was breathing with strange half-secrets and open intimations all around her. She saw the big bed where she used to sleep with mother when she was ill. She saw the closet where they kept their clothes, and the worn familiar intimacy of their toilet things on the dresser. Had they been happy with each other, as she and Harold had been once? She seemed to feel

piling upon her all their years and years of being together . . .
until she realized all at once, all over again, with new blinding
pain, what she had lost.

Oh, Harold, Harold . . . she couldn't stand it. She ran into
her own room, flung herself across the bed, cried and cried.

After an unchartered time, she lay still in that drained apathy
after tears that she had come to know. She saw her own wrists
flung lax on the counterpane. Now she could think about
Harold again. She knew that her mother and father wished
she wouldn't "brood"; but they did not understand the torturing consolation of going over and over her brief drama of happiness. She hadn't forgotten it, anyway, in this awful darkness
that had followed. That would be the most terrible thing of
all, if she began to forget. Then her heart would have to close.

Yes, but if she kept it open, to feel the happiness, then she
would have to feel the rest, too. . . . She would have to feel
again, like blows on her open heart, every cruel detail of
Harold's suffering, and the awful blank fact of his death.

It couldn't be. That terrible struggling unbelief had to come
all over her again. Something like that couldn't happen to them,
to Harold and Elizabeth—not to *her,* to Elizabeth, whose life
was always ringed about in a kind of sanctity of fortune. It
couldn't be over so soon. Harold couldn't have died. It couldn't
be true that she was here at home, submerged in the hot leafi-
ness of mid-summer, with nothing of that whole wonderful
spring but a few memories.

Lying drearily on her bed, she thought of her grandmother
when she had lived in the big bedroom downstairs. Grandma
used not to hear when Charles and Elizabeth spoke to her. Day
after day, she used to sit there with nothing but her thoughts.
Why was grandma so funny?—Charles and Elizabeth used

to ask. Elizabeth understood it now. . . . Oh, but how could
grandma have endured it to live on, after nearly every one she
cared for was gone? How could anybody endure things?

They would hurt too much. Now it even hurt her to see
the roses fall. She couldn't bear to look at the rose-bush in
front of the house because she knew how all the yellow petals
were going to lie scattered. She didn't even want mother to
plant her fall flowers. She had seen things happen before, but
she had been outside of them. It was that first morning after
she and Harold had been together—it was then that she had
come awake in her room at Mrs. Grover's to feel her heart wide
open like the apple-blossoms outside the window. When she
had walked to the schoolhouse with the other teachers, stopping
to make little runs into yards as they passed to smell the fruit
blossoms—"E-*liz*-abeth!" the girls were scandalized—she had
felt as if she were suddenly a part of the whole blossoming
world. In the schoolhouse all the windows were open and warm
air was blowing through. On her shiny desk she had found a
big bunch of tulips that an adoring child had brought her . . .
and she remembered how, crowding them all lightly into her
hands, she had looked deep down into the very centers where
yellow pollen had shaken and powdered the bloom. . . .

Elizabeth got slowly off the bed. She sat on the floor beside
the window and looked out into the heavy green of the leaves
across the street.

A big brown dog came loping along. He stopped and sniffed
at some paper on the street. A man came past, and the dog
stopped, quivered, and gave a clumsy jump and a hopeful,
eager, pitiful yelp. Elizabeth shrank back from the window.
She knew that the dog was a stray. She knew how the man had
given him a quick push down, without looking, and gone

straight on. She knew . . . and yet she didn't take him. She crouched down and put her hands over her eyes. When she looked again, he was gone.

Now she almost wished that she had gone with mother and dad. She couldn't tell them why it was she hated to go any-where. But it was not merely because she was "brooding." She had consented to go just once to a party. Mother said that if she didn't the girls would think it was because she had gone away to college. But she suffered so terribly all through the chatter that she thought she would have to say she was sick and come home. She felt as if Veronica Porter's birthmark were printed on her own cheek. She understood the nervous, high-keyed laughter of girls who were beginning to be afraid; and she knew what lay under Mae Garner's subtle, secret smile. When mother had entertained the Aid, it was just the same. Elizabeth passed the napkins and the cream and sugar; and then she had to run upstairs to hide from the marred faces of all those women . . . old Mrs. Kaster in from the country with her furtive glance of a dark little slave; big fat Mrs. Hitten-miller with her worn hands spread on her billowing stomach; thin little white-haired Mrs. Ritchie with the starved brilliant eyes that gave away her life with that awful Mr. Ritchie. . . .

There was a knock at the back door.

"You folks want any melons?"

"No. . . . Yes, I'll take one," Elizabeth said hastily.

She was ashamed as she hurried back upstairs for her pocket-book. Dad had bought some melons, and she knew these didn't look very good. But she couldn't stand the sight of that totter-ing old man with the two or three loose tusks in his open drib-bling mouth rimmed around with old white stubble—not unless she at least took one of his melons. She shuddered. People could actually get to be that way. She saw him go out to his wagon. The heavy trees and the rich green lawn beyond the kitchen door seemed darkened to hold all the old things dying and sinking into them.

Elizabeth was afraid to look out of the window. She might see something like that dog again. Her Hardy book was lying face down on the dresser. But she was even afraid to read. It was as if she entered now into the very center of the long, difficult, solemn phrases and couldn't get away from the irresistible, inevitable wear of their bitter truth.

But she couldn't sit here, either. She got up restlessly, washed, powdered, and went out of the house.

She went hastily down the front walk to get away from the sight of the house behind her. The broken laths in the lattice below the porch, the spreading look of the yellow rose-bushes that grandma had planted, the open door of the garage that used to be the old barn, made her realize how, slowly, the stability of the household was crumbling. Last winter dad and mother had been alone.

She looked with a kind of horror at all the houses. An old couple lived in this place that she was passing. She had seen them, on these summer evenings, sitting together on the narrow, sunken porch closed in with vines and plants that had an earthy odor. Soon, one or the other would be dead. Then the one left behind would live alone for a little while. There was a crippled man in this white house. Elizabeth was used to seeing him from the time she was a child, but she hadn't thought to ask dad or mother how it had happened. Now it was as if she could feel the distant shock of the sudden accident long ago and then the slow, maimed years and years of creeping through the richness of life and taking, a little here, a little there, whatever was left to him. . . .

She stopped. All at once she felt herself standing in the midst of the whole town. She felt it all around her . . . the streets under the summer trees where cars flashed out of the driveways of the bright new houses where life was all happening now, flowers in bloom, and children's playthings scattered on the walks—and coming slowly after, an old horse patiently jogging to the end of its days; the business section where the stores lasted a while and then changed hands; the aging houses on the edge of town before you came to the cemetery dark with evergreens; fields and woods all about it blooming and fading with the seasons; and the little river that moved slowly to join a bigger river flowing slowly to the Gulf, that finally met and merged with the sea.

What could people do? She could close her eyes and harden herself. Then she would forget—as mother told her—and after a while begin again. But if she really forgot, she would have to deny all the knowledge that opened up the depth of existence . . . and if she kept that, if she remembered, how could she wholly trust herself again? To stop feeling made everything useless. And yet, to see and feel like this would be annihilation. . . . She was being torn apart and scattered through all the pain there was. . . .

She turned blindly and escaped into a side street that ended in a pasture where a few big oak trees stood. There was a sense of staidness about the few white houses with old-fashioned flowers. The lawns were watered, perennials were planted, and the houses, when they faded, were painted the same white again.

This was the street where Miss Gurney lived. Elizabeth saw

the plain white house with a sense of relief. She remembered how, when she was a little girl, and felt lonely—when she had quarreled with her chum, or got a poor mark in arithmetic— she used to go for consolation to see Miss Gurney.

She couldn't talk to mother. Mother cared for her too much. It hurt mother so to see her child unhappy that she would lie about the way the world was, and in the end could only plead, "Don't cry!" People who had never known were of no use, and she couldn't bear to look at those who had known too much. Miss Gurney's house held the only refuge.

Elizabeth moved through a neat pattern of shade to the clean white steps. The tinkle of the bell, faint but clear, marked time for a moment; and the quiet freshness of the lawn kept the shade and sunlight still.

There was a reassuring sense of custom in having Miss Gurney, just as always, open the door, and say in a tone pleased and yet not surprised:

"Why, Elizabeth!"

She liked to have her add, too:

"I'll have to take you into the kitchen. Do you mind? I'm baking a cake for the supper the ladies are giving."

"Oh, no. I always liked to be in your kitchen."

She could take a faint sense of melancholy pleasure in sitting down in the low, cane-seated chair where she always used to sit, and in looking around and seeing that the room looked just the same. There were six glasses of dark red jelly on the window-sill. It was even quieter than it used to be. Miss Gurney, large and fresh in her black and white apron, with her strong face framed in iron-gray hair, was briskly creaming the butter and sugar.

"Well, Elizabeth," she said, "I haven't seen you for a good

while. What have you been doing with yourself this summer?"

"Oh . . . nothing much."

Elizabeth herself flushed faintly at the concealing reticence of her tone. She had come wanting to talk to Miss Gurney; but there was something in this atmosphere of cheerful, sustained quiet, within which Miss Gurney's brisk activities were going on, that she dared not break. The white sash curtains shut her in with her untouched childhood; and she could only hear the dwindling rattle of a wagon outside in the street.

"Well," Miss Gurney said, "I expect you've been busy like the rest of us."

She did not know whether she was hurt or reassured by the friendly, acceptant lack of comprehension. No one but mother and dad knew what had happened to her. Even they didn't really know. There was a terrible shame in suffering, as if one were picked out from all the world. But she felt, as always, a consolation when she saw Miss Gurney's strong arms at work. People sent for Miss Gurney when something was wrong. She was kind and helpful, but she was brisk and cool; as if there were something in her not concerned; as if—Elizabeth thought, and the thought was like a cold breath coming over her—she could help other people with everything, because she had never started living for herself.

"Here, Elizabeth, you're pretty good at beating eggs, aren't you? Seems to me I remember you are."

"I'll try."

Elizabeth got up. The temporary relief of the small, brisk action helped her to mark time a little while longer with ordinary talk.

"What kind of cake is it going to be?"

"The regulation old kind. Chocolate frosting."

"Do they always make you bake cakes?"

"Always."

Elizabeth laughed. She clung to any intimation of the refuge of continuity.

"Yes, Elizabeth, if all the cakes I've baked for suppers in this town were put end to end, they'd reach into California and the frosting melt in the Pacific ocean. Wish they'd take me out there," Miss Gurney said.

"Do you really want to go?"

"Well, I've always had kind of a hankering to see it."

"I don't want you to," Elizabeth said, in a low, quick tone.

"Don't want me to?"

"No. I always want you to be in this house."

Miss Gurney flushed with pleasure that had a queer touch of girlish shyness. She laughed. But she said a little ruefully, as she opened the oven door and tested the heat:

"It's where I'm likely to be, I guess, Elizabeth."

Elizabeth surrendered her bowl of beaten eggs. Now, as she looked about the kitchen while she stood waiting, she saw even that in a different light. Yes, they were the same things, but it was as if she couldn't keep herself from realizing now where the things had come from. The low rocking chair had been Miss Gurney's mother's. The clock with the octagonal face must have belonged to the old housekeeping days. A brown coat, that had been Miss Gurney's father's, hung on a nail beside the door. The evidences of the life of the household stood out now like visible marks and were not going to let her escape their significance.

"How are your father and mother?" Miss Gurney asked.

"All right, I guess."

"You guess?"

"Well, all right as far as I know."

"What's the matter with 'em?"

"Nothing." Elizabeth looked down. She wanted to keep her voice from shaking. "Only they look older to me this summer. I never noticed it before."

"Well, Elizabeth, we all have to get older."

Elizabeth looked up in quick protest. She rebelled against, and yet envied, the cheerful acceptance of the tone. Was there nothing to do but accept and act cheerful?—she wanted to ask. Were you helpless under what life did to you?

Miss Gurney said suddenly:

"You knew father was gone?"

"No!"

"Yes, he died last winter."

Elizabeth, startled, realized that there was a different quietness in the house. Then this was what it meant! There were no little grunting moans and shifting sounds from the bedroom where for years old Mr. Gurney, injured by a fall, had sat in his big rocker beside the window. Indeed, it seemed to Elizabeth that he had always sat there.

"Yes," Miss Gurney repeated soberly, "father died last winter, sitting in his chair, just fifteen years to the day since mother passed away. It doesn't seem as if they could both be gone."

And then more cheerfully, with recovered briskness, she added:

"Well, I miss him. But it's better. It was ten years since he was hurt."

"Only that long?" Elizabeth breathed.

"Isn't that long enough, child?"

"I mean . . . I can't seem to remember him any other way."

And Elizabeth sat, quiescent but resentful, under what she knew was coming, must be coming, words that would break forever the illusion of peace in this old white house and spoil even the refuge of this kitchen.

"I suppose not," Miss Gurney agreed. "But it was very different before that. Father was a very active man. He was old, but he chopped his own wood, and drove the team . . . you don't remember that?"

Elizabeth shook her head.

"Yes," Miss Gurney mused, "he sat in that chair for ten years. He was ninety-one when he died."

The words, the time, year by year, sank into Elizabeth. In the midst of these years, the little moans and sounds she used to hear from that shadowed bedroom—meaningless then—took on a significance of protesting pain all the more terrible because it was barely articulate.

"How did it happen?"

Miss Gurney said, "Well, he was getting into the wagon. I suppose he was stiff with cold. He'd been working around the place. Anyway, he slipped, and the wheels went over his body. Broke both legs. He was too old for them to mend. He never could get around again."

Yes, Elizabeth realized now that the faint sense of difference in the house, troubling her even while she held it off, was just the deepening of its quiet. And there was something like pain, only wider and bleaker, in the quiet itself—something that seemed to be an echo to their voices, to Miss Gurney's matter-of-fact voice as she went on.

"Yes, he was helpless ten years, and mother before that. You don't remember my mother, Elizabeth. She died when you were a little girl. But it was a queer thing—yes, sir, I've often thought

of that—that mother should have been crippled by an accident,
too. She was picking some apples, and either the branch broke
with her, or the stepladder slipped out from under her feet—
anyway, she was crippled for the rest of her life. It was a pretty
hard ending for folks that had been so active and worked so
hard."

Elizabeth said:

"Did you take care of them both, Miss Gurney?"

"I was the only one to do it, Elizabeth."

Miss Gurney broke off what might have been a sigh, perhaps only a breath, to open the oven door. Elizabeth sat staring
at her. Then even this quiet household was not set apart! It had
to take its place with the others, all changing, within the loop
of the moving river! It was quiet . . . but what help was there
in a quietness that was only what was left over when the worst
was done? She was going to ask Miss Gurney if she minded
being there alone.

But looking at that strong face, with the eyes averted and the
lips compressed, she suddenly knew the answer too keenly to
hear it. She saw that active, cheerful life within the silent house
as a diminishing, perhaps unconscious waiting for what had
never come, and now never would. And yet Miss Gurney could
do things. All at once, the words that she had come here to
speak rose uncontrollably to Elizabeth's lips.

"Miss Gurney—when things happen to people, how can they
stand to go on living? Why don't they simply die?"

She waited not daring to breathe.

Miss Gurney said, after a moment, poking at her cake with
a broom straw, "Well, Elizabeth, I guess they just have to learn
to take things as they come."

"Yes, but then . . . *how* do they? I don't see how."

Miss Gurney gave an abrupt laugh, although her face was sober.

"Well, they just learn to, I guess. Because they have to."

In the lonely quiet of that house—a faint crackle of fire in the stove, a rustle of leaves outside—Elizabeth seemed to feel, at a far distance, her own suffering sinking slowly into the darkness of trees and ground that had held everything before it.

But was that all the answer? She stared at Miss Gurney with eyes wide open and dark with pain in her young, quivering face. A remoteness came over the strong, averted face of the older woman. It was as if she dared not meet the living pain in Elizabeth's eyes with its absence in her own. Elizabeth saw that look. Then the answer was worse than none! She would not have it. And she squeezed her hands tightly together, clinging to her suffering . . . as if, when its freshness was gone, it would be the one thing lost forever.

Mrs. Kemper

"Isn't she a bedraggled-looking piece?" That was what Belle Farmer, fat and coarsely vigorous, sitting in the local Beaute Shoppe and having her bobbed gray hair marcelled, said when Mrs. Kemper went past. It was what other people thought but were not brutal enough to say. To state such things was, perhaps, the chief usefulness of Belle Farmer in the community.

It did describe Mrs. Kemper exactly! But she lived in a good house, a white-painted frame house just outside town, with mowed lawn and flowers and a bird-bath. In the living room, she had silk draperies and tapestry-covered furniture, just as in town. The Kempers had enough so that Mr. Kemper could hire his farming done. They were not counted among the country people. Mr. Kemper was a director in one of the banks, and they were good members of the Congregational church. They had sent their two boys to college.

And besides these material advantages, Mrs. Kemper was an Easterner, her speech had a refined softening of the r's that sounded like culture, and she had taught in the high-school before she married Mr. Kemper. As a matter of course, she had been taken into the principal study club. She was always counted among "the ladies" in this little town. Her personality was protected against primitive comment from any one but a Belle Farmer or a stranger.

She seemed to accept the full protection of her circumstances. In the club she occasionally put or seconded a motion of her

146

own accord. She was one of the first to welcome new church attendants, and she brought the arrival of strangers in town to the attention of the minister and his wife. She patronized Essie Whittie, a half-wit and the town's one object of charity, like the other ladies. She did all these things with a certain poise, as if she had told herself that her position gave her the right and the obligation.

And yet she did them with a nervous obliqueness, too. When she made a call, even upon the minister's wife over whom— because she and Mr. Kemper were such well-paying members —she felt a bit of rightful although respectful authority, she rocked too much, one foot always pushing at the floor, and her sallow hands fumbling at the chair arms. When she rose to put a motion in the club, she never got quite away from her chair, never took her hand from the back, and in her voice there was a determination to assert her rightful place prevailing resentfully over a fearful timidity. At first, talking to strangers, although her voice was refined and controlled, she did not look at them; and when she did, with a quick sort of inadvertency or that same determination, both turned away ashamed.

With Essie Whittie, her relations were the most painful of all. A pretense had to be maintained of Mrs. Kemper as patroness and Essie the humble and grateful beneficiary. And yet it was as if Mrs. Kemper was a fraud in that rôle, and both of them knew it. Nervousness fluttered the refinement of her voice, although she sat with great dignity. Other ladies were at their blandest and most assured with Essie. But Mrs. Kemper feared that primitive quality. It took off her protection with a crude contemptuousness and left her a bedraggled-looking piece.

When she entertained the club, the ladies said how nice it was out here in the country. She smiled, with that painful

assumption of poise that always diffused an atmosphere of shame
about her. Yes, they thought it was nice, she said nervously.
She and Mr. Kemper had thought of moving to town, but they
really preferred this. She tried to accept praise for the improve-
ments, the furniture and the curtains, with a conviction she
could never make quite real. When they praised the refreshments and envied her the country cream, they were all made
uneasy by the sense of that pained sickishness underlying her
manner. It was as if these things did not really belong to Mrs.
Kemper and she could not quite claim credit for them. The
guests felt as if they had made a mistake somewhere.

Only when they admired her phlox, her manner brightened.
Her other flowers were only so-so—"did pretty well." But she
had a genuine knack at raising phlox, and for the warmly fragrant, tufted masses of white and rose and magenta bloom, her
smile did for the moment take a pleased credit. "Mrs. Kemper
has nice phlox," the ladies occasionally said to each other, and
with a relieved gratification, as if they were glad to be able to
say that much, at least.

After the ladies were gone, the living room was warm and
disordered and the kitchen full of the best thin dishes, with
genteel débris of cake crumbs and melted pink ice cream. An
afterglow of hospitality spread through the house in the long
low slants of country sunlight that fell now through the west
windows. Mrs. Kemper paused in the living room, momenta-
rily warmed and enlivened, deceived by the polite thanks of the
good-bys and the gratification of entertaining into feeling herself one of the ladies. Mrs. Butters, who helped out for all the
principal families, was washing dishes in the sunny kitchen.
"Well, I think your angel cake turned out real good, Mrs.
Kemper," she said. Mrs. Kemper tried to talk with Mrs. Butters

about the refreshments and the house, but always with that furtive uncertainty, the same that she felt with Essie Whittie . . . as if Mrs. Butters were going to see through her somehow or other.

"Well, I guess here comes somebody wants a little of these refreshments too!" Mrs. Butters said heartily when Mr. Kemper came to the kitchen door. "You better set down, Mr. Kemper, before it's all et up. I don't know, though," she added, "whether you deserve any of these good things for not getting back while any of the ladies was here."

Mr. Kemper seemed to be surprised by Mrs. Butters' good-natured attack, but to enjoy it. Mrs. Kemper became more uncertain and subdued when he entered, and she lost the dignity of her hostess attitude. They could cook him a supper, she said, fry him some eggs—

"My goodness, a man that couldn't be satisfied with good things like this!" Mrs. Butters cried. She knew how the other families did on club days.

And yet there was something in just having Mrs. Butters, in making the arrangements and paying her and sending her home with angel cake, as the other ladies did. After she had left, the talk died out in the kitchen.

"Are you having enough, Arthur?"

"Hm? Oh yes, plenty."

She went into the living room, stood a moment at the screened door, and then went out on to the lawn where she idled and wandered. She looked across the pleasant slope of their land, green as far as she could see, and bright under the evening light—the elm trees tall and leafy, and on the other side the plain and useful dignity of the big barns—looked with a timid wistfulness;—hurt and resentful, too, as if she wished she dared really claim it all.

She was never sure of herself on her own ground. She was never certain that she had been given the right to take this home-like pleasantness into her heart. She averted her eyes with that veiled and sickened fear, and turned back to the neat refuge of her garden. She touched with her fingers the rough stone warmth of the bird bath, walked over the fresh grass, and stood beside the phlox. She touched these almost with authority, brushing off a cobweb and disentangling two flower masses—they were hers, they did well for her. She bent and smelled the warm fragrance, . . . and then she stood, her face lifted and averted, her figure still against the sky of early evening—it was all so quiet, so peaceful and yet living, the green fields and green pastures stretching away, and two moths here in the garden hovering over the sweetness of the phlox. If she only dared enter into the heart of the place!

She went back into the living room. Mr. Kemper was sitting there. He was trying to get something to suit him on the radio. There was a wavering about her figure in the doorway; she overcame it and entered the room. He looked up; then, between cracklings of the static, asked her:

"Well, did it go off all right?"

In her careful, refined speech, with a tinge of shy gratitude, she told him that it did. But he did not go on to talk to her, or to let her talk. He turned off the radio, went through the kitchen and out of the house. She dared never feel quite sure that he did not leave a room because she came into it—although his manner was friendly enough, if bleak, and he had never hinted at such a thing. She did things to the room—arranged the ornaments on the table, examined a rent in a cushion cover—claiming it in that way, and unaware of the timidity of her manner;

unaware most of the time of the reason for her halting approach
to everything and everybody, for what underlay and spoiled
all her attempts at sociability and dignity.

It was quiet at home with the boys both gone. Mrs. Kemper
dreaded the silent evenings with her husband. Perhaps he
dreaded them, too.

She went into the downstairs bedroom where the ladies had
left their hats. But she avoided the reflection of herself in the
wide mirror in the evening light. She would not actually take
into her consciousness the thin figure in the nicely made summer dress of good material—not actually accept as herself the
sunken chest and protruding stomach, the thin and sallow neck
and sallow face and faded hair, to realize that she had been allowed to sink into this dim disguise.

Yet Mrs. Kemper was not so meek as she looked. The ladies
in the club had found that out once or twice. She had her sense
of dignity. She felt the claims of her refinement and competence
and intelligence that could never quite take their due. She was
resentful now, standing beside the bedroom window and looking out at a bed of tiger lilies, resentful that a never resolved
fear kept her from owning this that was hers.

She wandered through the house. It was too late to see to
read, too early to turn on the lights. Her footsteps through the
empty house had a restless loneliness.

It was darker upstairs. The doors of the boys' rooms were
closed. Charles was married and in business for himself. Wilbur
was through school and working in Chicago—engaged, his
parents thought, although Wilbur hadn't said anything; they
weren't sure. Mrs. Kemper went on into her own room. She
loved her sons, but never closely. She was undemonstrative with
them. Something had always kept her a little apart from them,

as if she dared not quite claim them, too. And they were fond of her, but she was in the background.

In her bedroom the light was dim. It gave a strangeness to the familiar furniture . . . so that after entering the room she seemed to forget just what she had come to do, and stood there. . . .

Sunk into the silence, into the dim light, it seemed as if her self-consciousness was lost and all the old half-forgotten—yet never forgotten—things had their chance to rise and possess her. Her throat and her breast ached with them. She had to remember the lovely figure of her husband's sweetheart, the girl he had been in love with, and whom she could never be quite sure that he had forgotten—she had to see it as it was in the photograph, the breast so rounded and small in the tightness of the taffeta basque, and the round throat, round chin, dark eyes under the fringe of dark hair.

She had to remember all that old history. Some of it was only hearsay to her—the illness and the death, the very personality of Arthur's sweetheart . . . but with irresistible painstaking, she must go over again all the details of it. She herself had come from the East and was teaching in the high school; and she had been living with her aunt next door to Arthur Kemper; and Arthur had started going with her, and then one night he had asked her to marry him. She had to live again through the tentative delight, the halt and the long sickening uncertainty.

He had asked her to marry him. When she thought of it, that night after he had asked her, a happiness seemed to grow and grow in her until it was just about to bloom . . . but it could not, chilled by the fear that he did not love her, did not really want her, had only taken her out of weariness because the other girl was dead. The staying and crushing of the bloom hurt her, so that even now she moved her head a little in pain.

But anger invaded her again. He had married her. He had taken her. They had two sons. She was his wife. She was Mrs. Kemper. Why need she feel this way?—Again she must go over, with that same painstaking minuteness, the evidences that still kept her fear uncertainty. After the wedding, when they were alone together for a moment, he had put his arm around her and said, "Well, I guess it's us two now, Caroline." And when she was so sick, after Wilbur was born, she remembered that one glimpse of him standing uncertain and awkward in his concern, and then driving off twenty miles through the cold for another doctor. And when she had been sick again, just a few years ago, and the doctor here didn't seem to be helping her, he had said himself, "Well, I guess I'll have to take you up to Rochester." And he had kissed her sometimes, even in these last years, of his own accord—when Charles was married (the night after that), and when they got news that her father was dead. And then once Mr. Wellington had said, "I tell you, we fellows that married good wives are lucky," and Mr. Kemper had agreed: "That's so, all right." And he was good to her, gave her all she needed, had wanted himself to refurnish the house, and seemed to be satisfied here. . . . She went over every one of these things to get the full savor out of them. They convinced—almost—of course he cared for her. But there was something needed to complete them. He had never once said, "I love you."

Again, over the timid sweetness of these memories, there flooded the whole of her fear and her resentment. She could never ask. She feared to end the fear, lest she be dispossessed finally and altogether. Even in this dusk, she must keep her eyes averted from the faded, drooping image in the mirror—the pale eyes sought for reassurance but could not ask it, the thin breasts beseeched it and sagged in humility, the hands trembled and could not reach, . . . and without the word, the eyes had never dared to brighten, or the breasts to bloom, the hands had wavered and clenched uncertainly and never dared to touch. She dared not claim her sons because she could never be sure that love had conceived them. She dared not take her place among the women who had received the certain consecration of that crown. When she looked at the Parkins girl, and Mollie Regus, outlaws now both of them, an awful envy seared her; for although she bore the title, they had been taken in desire. She dared not look a low and primitive creature like Essie Whittie in the eye.

What was she doing in this room? It was a strange place. She could not claim its terrible intimacy that only increased her solitude. Lonely and restless once more, avoiding the sight of the mirror, of the bed with its smooth counterpane, she went downstairs and out on the lawn again.

There she had the pleasant sight of the house and the fields and the barn. The feelings of the bedroom were only imaginings. She thought: Why, I have a nice home, two sons, a good husband—all she had ever dreamed of having. . . . She tried to make that statement end the uncertainty. She tried to take the pleasantness of the farm-yard in the summer evening light into her heart and let her heart rest in its peace.

But then she began wandering again. She had forgotten for a moment what she was thinking . . . she paused near the phlox, and touched the bloom. But even that she did not take into her hands. Yes, she had a good home, two sons, a good husband . . . but she could never take possession of them. All her own treasures were sunk within herself, within this drooping pallor, and could never be loosened—brightness, laughter, tenderness, bloom . . . she had been a shy girl, prim, and not very pretty, sensitive under the primness . . . yet she felt that all this was sunk within her, and that she could not possess even herself without the key that had never been laid in her hand.

She wrung her hands with a little secret gesture. Then she moved to the house through her uncertainty.

The next day Mr. and Mrs. Kemper drove into town. Mrs. Kemper went into Dodd's Dry Goods to do some shopping. She went timidly through the doorway, in a dim dread; then with dignity enforced over her reluctance, she went up to the counter and asked to see some goods. She had a right, she was Mrs. Kemper, every one knew that she had means—and who was this clerk but Gertie Evans, a spinster, brittle and bleached? She would insist on the kind of goods she wanted. Other ladies came in. They spoke to her about the church. She was pleased with her purchase. . . . But going out of the store, she turned her eyes away from having to meet her dim and drooping reflection in the window glass, and hurried, shoulders bent, feet moving nervously—the aversion was only a habit, she had forgotten why she felt it, as usually she did forget. The sunshine was pleasant out there on the street and their car was waiting.

People spoke to her. She was Mrs. Kemper. But Mrs. Hallie Davis, looking down from her Beaute Shoppe, frowned impatiently, resenting that nervous manner and sunken figure— remembering what Belle Farmer had said, and wondering why she need look like such a bedraggled piece: a woman who had a nice home, and a good husband, some one to look after her, and not a real trouble in the world.

The Man of the Family

Floyd Oberholzer was just opening up the drug-store when
Gerald came.

"Hello, Gerald. Want something?"

"I come to start in working."

"This morning?" Floyd was startled. "Why, school can't be
over yet, is it? What is this—Wednesday?"

"Yes, but we got done with our tests yesterday, all but arithmetic, and I didn't have to take that."

"Oh, you didn't have to take that?" Floyd repeated vaguely.
"Well, you come into the store and we'll see what there is for
you to do."

Gerald followed him into the drug-store.

Floyd looked around somewhat helplessly. It was only a few
months since he and Lois had bought this little business in In-
dependenceville. They knew what to do themselves, but it was
a different matter setting some one else to work. They hadn't
expected Gerald so soon, or wanted him. Two or three months
ago, he had come into the store to ask if he couldn't have a job,
and because they hated to turn the kid away—it wasn't very
long after the accident in which his father had been killed—
Floyd had told him: "Well, you come around when school's
out. Maybe we can find something then." And now he was
here.

"Well, you're starting in early," Floyd said to him. "You've
beat my wife—she isn't in the store yet. Well, I don't know,

Gerald—I guess you might as well sweep out, the first thing."
He remembered then that Lois had swept the store before they
closed last night; the boys had left so many cigarette stubs
around. But he guessed it could stand it again. It would keep
Gerald busy while Floyd decided what to have him do.

"All right," Gerald answered soberly. "Where do you keep
your broom?"

"Right out there in the back, Gerald. See—I'll show you.
Then you'll know where it is."

Gerald started in to sweep the wooden floor with awkward,
scowling concentration. His back was stooped and intent. He
took long hard strokes, trying to do a good job of it. Floyd
looked at him, and then turned and went scuttling up the stairs.

"Hey—Lois!" he called softly.

" 'Smatter, pop?"

Lois, still in her bungalow apron, came to the door of the
kitchen. The Oberholzers were living over the drug-store.

"Say, that kid's here."

"What kid?"

"Gerald Rayburn. He's come to start in working. Seems
awful anxious to begin. What in the dickens shall I have
him do?"

"You're a fine boss!" Lois began to laugh. "What's he doing
now—standing in the middle of the floor and sucking his
thumb?"

"I've got him sweeping."

"Why, I swept last night, you idiot!"

"Well, I know you did, but I forgot it. I didn't want to tell
him to stand around. He goes at it like a little beaver. You
ought to watch him. Oh, I suppose the kid *is* anxious to start
in earning."

Lois didn't know what to say.

"You come down," said Floyd, "and tell him about the soda-fountain. That's your end of the business."

"Oh, it is, is it? All right, I'll come down and give the boss's orders since he doesn't know what they are himself," she replied with mock commiseration, and pinched Floyd's ear.

"Well, gosh, I didn't expect that kid the minute school let out! Most kids aren't that anxious to go to work. Isn't this the day they have the school picnic? Why, sure—that's why we got that pop."

He started down the stairs and then went back to the next-to-the-top step and stood frowning uncertainly.

"Think we can really use him, Lois?"

"Well, I guess we've got him, anyway!"

"I know we'll have to have somebody, but he's such a kid. I don't know—"

Lois said hastily: "Oh well, let's try him. You told him he could come. I feel so sorry for that family."

"Well, so do I. But then— Well, all right—"

Floyd left it at that, and scuttled down the stairs again. Lois went back to the kitchen which she herself had painted blue and white, with figured curtains, changing it from the gloomy old hole that the Tewkesburys had left it, to a gay new room. She hated to leave this beloved little place to go and help Floyd in the store. Now that they had hired just a little boy to help them for the summer, she supposed she would have to be downstairs most of the time. She almost wished she hadn't told Floyd to keep Gerald. Well, if Gerald couldn't do the work, he'd have to go, that was all.

"All right, Gerald," Floyd went into the store saying loudly and cheerfully. "Finished that? Well, then, I guess you'd better—" His eyes, quickly roving, caught sight of the magazine rack. "I guess you'd better straighten up those magazines. Folks take 'em out and read 'em all through and then put 'em back."

"All right."

Floyd whistled as he took the long gray cambric covers off the tables in the middle of the room, where boxes of gilt-edged correspondence cards and leather-bound copies of the works of Edgar Guest had to be displayed until the graduating exercises were over. Gerald went at his work with such silent concentration that it almost embarrassed Floyd.

"What do you want I should do next?"

"Oh, well . . . Guess maybe I better show you about these cigarettes and tobacco. That's probably what they'll be after first. I'll show you how we've got things marked."

"All right."

Lois came down. Floyd gave her an expressive look and nodded toward Gerald.

"He's right at it!" Certainly the boy seemed to be trying hard. His freckled face with the crop of red hair was surly with concentration. Floyd couldn't help remembering that he was just a kid and too young to be starting in to work in earnest. He was quite willing to give up his charge and let Lois initiate him into the mysteries of the new white soda-fountain which they had installed in place of the cracked, lugubrious onyx splendor of the earlier day. Gerald stood silently beside Lois, bashfully aware of her bobbed hair and her plump white arms, answering dutifully: "Yes, ma'am."

"You can watch me this morning, Gerald, and run some errands, maybe. Wash up the glasses. Do the dirty work—how's that?"

"Yes, ma'am."

He was a little clumsy, partly out of bashfulness, but so serious and determined that Lois thought: "Goodness, I wonder if it'll last!" She wanted to give him all the help he needed, but she didn't quite know what to make of his surly little face. He hated to ask her questions, and several times she had to say, "Oh, not like that, Gerald!"

"Gee, that was an awful thing to happen to that family!" Floyd said to Lois in the back room of the store, where he had gone to look for a special package of hog medicine ordered by old Gus Reinbeck. "I think this kid kind of realizes, don't you?"

"Have they got anything, do you suppose?"

"A little insurance, they say, and that house, but not much more than to keep them until this boy can start earning."

"The mother can earn something herself, I should think," Lois said rather defiantly. *She* worked.

"Yes, but with three kids to look after. . . . And anyway, what is there for a woman to do in a burg like this except take in washing?"

"Well, maybe."

Back door and front of the store were open, and through the shimmery blackness of the back screen the garden was green and fresh. A tin cup hung on an old-fashioned pump under the vines. Gerald looked longingly at the boards of the platform, wet with spilled water. There was city water in the soda-fountain, but the pump looked so much cooler out there.

"Run out and get a drink if you want to, Gerald," Lois told him. "I always go out there for my water. It's fun to work the pump." Boys never could see a pump or a drinking fountain or even a hydrant without being consumed with thirst, she knew. Lois liked boys. Gerald made her think of her kid brother. It

was a shame he had to go to work. She wanted to reassure him
somehow, to rumple his red hair or pat his shoulder. But she
must remember that they were hiring him. They couldn't af-
ford to keep him out of pity. Besides, he seemed determined
to evade all personal advances and stuck doggedly to work.
Maybe the kid was miserable at missing that picnic.

It was getting hot in town. Cars began to rattle and whir
down the street, and in a few moments Louie Grossman's big
red truck drove up to the side door of the drug store.

"Hey, Floyd! Got the pop?"

"Got the pop? You bet I've got the pop. You want it now?"

"Sure do, if it's goin' on this picnic."

"All right, sir! Want to come and help me take it out,
Gerald?"

"All right."

Gerald went with Floyd into the back room of the store,
bright and cool and scattered with light from the green leaves
outside. He tugged at one end of the big pop case, and helped
Floyd carry it outside and shove it into the truck.

"Now, another one, Gerald."

"All right."

"Well, the kids oughtn't to get thirsty to-day," Floyd said.

"No, they sure got plenty. What are you doing, Gerald?"
Louie asked. "Ain't you going to the picnic?"

"I got to work," Gerald answered.

He went back into the store. The two men looked after him.

"He workin' for you now, Floyd?"

"Guess so. It looks like it. He came this morning."

"Goes at it pretty good, don't he?"

"Yes, he seems to be willing. He's pretty young, but then . . .
Where they going for the picnic to-day, Louie?"

"Out to Bailey's Creek. You ever been there?"

"Not yet. Mighty pretty place, I guess," he added.

"Yes, but it ain't much of a road."

"Well, don't tip 'em out, Louie."

"No, I'll try and keep the old bus in her tracks."

Louie started the noisy engine of the big truck. It went roaring up the street between green lawns and white houses and pink peonies, to where the school children, boys in freshly ironed blouses and girls in summery dresses, waited in a flock under the elms of the school-yard . . . then out, spinning down the graveled highway between freshly planted fields, turning into the little woods road, narrow and rutted, where the children had to bend their heads under the switch of honey locusts that left small white petals in their sun-warmed hair . . . on into the depths of green woods through the heart of which the shining creek was flowing. . . .

Lois had come to the doorway to watch the truck leave.

"I wouldn't mind going to a picnic myself on a day like this," she murmured.

When she went back into the store, she looked curiously at Gerald. It gave her a guilty feeling, wholly unreasonable, to have him at work in their store to-day when it was a holiday for all the other children. But he had come of his own accord. They hadn't told him to do it.

"Did your sisters go on the picnic, Gerald?" she asked.

"Yes, *they* went," he answered, rather slightingly.

"How many have you, Gerald? Just Juanita and Betty?"

"Yes, ma'am."

"And you're the only boy?"

"Yes, ma'am."

"You could have started in to-morrow just as well, Gerald."

He did not answer.

The bright morning grew hotter and hotter, until to enter the
drug-store from the glaring cement outside was like going into
a cool, clean-scented cavern. The regular set of loafers drifted
in, asked for tobacco, and stayed, sitting on the white-topped
stools at the soda fountain and trying to be facetious with
Gerald. "Well, you got a new clerk?" every one who came in
demanded. It was a new joke every time. In an interval of no
customers, Lois stooped down and drew out a pale green bottle
frosted over with cold moisture from the case under the counter. It was still a treat to her to think she owned a store.

"I'm going to try some of this new lime stuff," she said. "See
how it tastes. Don't you want the other straw, Gerald?"

"No, I guess not," he answered bashfully.

There was a glint of longing and reluctance in his eyes. But
Lois thought: Maybe I oughtn't to start offering him things and
being too easy with him. After all, Floyd was paying him to
help them, and it wasn't her fault that his father had been killed.
They were doing the best they could for him by letting him
have a job. When, later, she decided to try one of those
chocolates Floyd had ordered from a new traveling man, she
turned her back while she nibbled it and wiped her fingers on
the scrap of oiled paper in which it had been wrapped. Running the business all by themselves was still an adventure to
the young Oberholzers; but even now they had run up against
the fact more than once that it wasn't just a game. They had
halfway discovered the meaning of that term—"If you want to
do business—" Lois couldn't pick out from the traveling man's
stock the delicately scented toilet waters that she herself liked,
but had to choose the red and green brands with big gaudy

flowers on the labels that the girls here in town would buy—
the kind that "went." She had had to freeze out old Bart Bailey
who came in every morning to read the paper and the detective
magazines he had no money to buy, and left dirty thumb marks
on all the pages.

Noon came with the shriek of the whistle from the power-
house, with the noise of cars being started and of the men driving home to dinner.

"When does your mamma expect you home for dinner,
Gerald?" Lois asked.

"Oh, I guess it don't matter," Gerald mumbled bashfully.

"Didn't you tell her when you'd come?"

"No, ma'am."

They let him go; but if they kept him in the store, he would
have to go later and let them have their dinner at noon. That
was one reason why they wanted help. He was back in good
time. "Well, didn't take *you* long to eat your dinner!" Floyd said.
But maybe it wasn't a good thing to act surprised at his prompt-
ness. It would wear off soon enough, if they could infer anything from their experiences with Marcelle Johnston, who had
pretended to work for them for three weeks in the winter.

At intervals during the afternoon, Floyd and Lois re-
ported to each other. "We're going to have an awful time teaching him to make a decent sundae. He doesn't catch on any too
fast, but he seems to be willing to do whatever you tell him."
Whether they wanted to keep him or not, it was evident that
he meant to stay. He wanted the job. His surly little freckled
face scarcely relaxed into a smile even when there was a dog
fight outside and Miss Angie Robinson's little poodle sent that
big hound of Ole Swanson's off yelping. He went at whatever
he was told to do with dogged earnestness, although he didn't

see things for himself. He said "Yes, ma'am" with sober respect; but he would ask: "What's the price of this here kind of to-bacco, Lois?" and say to customers: "No, Floyd ain't in just now, he went over to the depot." As the afternoon wore along, his freckled face grew flushed.

"Does it seem like a long day, Gerald?" Lois asked him once. He admitted: "Kind of. Not so very."

Late in the afternoon, the picnic trucks came rattling into town with all the children disheveled and shouting. A few mo-ments afterwards, a group of girls came bursting into the store. Their bright-colored summer dresses were wrinkled, their bobs were wildly rumpled, their tired eyes were shining.

"Oh gee, but we're thirsty! We're just dying! Oh, look at Gerald Rayburn! Are you working in here, Gerald?"

"Yes, didn't you know he was?" his young sister Juanita asked. "We want six bottles of pop, Gerald," she ordered airily.

"Have you got any money?"

"Yes, I have!"

"Where'd you get it then?" he demanded suspiciously.

"None of your business, Mr. Smarty! I guess it's not yours, is it?"

A bright pink flared up in Juanita's cheeks. Her eyes sparkled angrily. She was a pretty child, with red hair, like Gerald's, blazing out in a fuzzy aureole around her freckled face. She flounced down into one of the white chairs. "We want a table, don't we, kids? We don't want to sit at the fountain, like the boys." When Gerald brought the six cold red bottles carefully toppling on the tray, she lifted her little chin and disdained to look at him.

"You needn't think because I'm working here, you can come in and order what you want," he told her.

"Shut up!" she whispered furiously.

Her eyes were brighter still with tears. Mamma had given her the nickel for helping with the ironing yesterday afternoon instead of going off with the girls. She had given it to her for ironing Julie Bronson's pink chemise, with all the lace, so beautifully. It was none of Gerald's business what she did with it! She said to the other girls, with flashing eyes and quivering lips:

"He thinks he's so smart now just because he's starting in to work and Betty and I aren't. You'd just think he *owned* us to hear the way he talks. I don't care. I guess he isn't the only one who does anything. I guess I do lots of things. I'd like to see Gerald Rayburn ever wash the dishes!"

She stuck two straws into her bottle of strawberry pop and sucked it all up defiantly. Maybe she ought to have saved her nickel, but Gerald had no right trying to boss her in front of all the girls.

He told her, when she was leaving the store:

"You needn't go running around now, you can go home and help mamma."

"You keep still!" She threw her nickel down with a ring on the white counter of the soda fountain. "I guess you aren't my boss *yet!*"

"That's all right, I know what I'm talking about."

"That's right, Gerald," old Hod Brumskill shouted, with humorous approval. "You make the women folks mind you. Ain't that so, boys?"

"You tell 'em it's so!"

They laughed loudly; and then, clustered together with their arms on the glass counter, that had a sign in red letters "Do not lean!", they tore open their packages of bitter-scented tobacco

and began to talk in lowered voices about the Rayburn family:
how it had been "left," how it got along, about the tragic death
of Frank Rayburn, still disputing over the minutiae of that
event which they had never yet been able to settle, although
nearly a year had passed since the thing happened. "Well, I
never could understand how a fella like that, that was used to
climbin' all over everywhere, come to fall off that ladder like
that . . ." "Why he just kinda stepped backwardlike—I s'pose
he forgot maybe where he was at . . ." "Some says the ladder
broke and let him down." "Naw, the ladder didn't *break.*"
"Well, was it true he'd been out drinkin' the night before?
That's how I heard it." "Naw, he hadn't been out drinkin' the
night before." "Well, I can't figger out . . ." "Why, he just kinda
stepped backwards . . ." It was terrible, they all agreed with
solemn faces, to think that poor little woman should have been
left with those three children, although there was dispute again
about how much they had been left with. Some said they "had
something," some said they "had nothing." She was a nice
woman. Yes, and she was a good-looking woman, too. . . . And
then they drew closer together, and one of them said something
about "Art Fox," and their voices broke into a laugh and a
snicker.

Gerald was washing glasses at the soda-fountain. His freckled
face flushed a dull red, and when they snickered he looked over
at them furiously. He had a notion of what they were saying.
When they passed him, leaving the store, they praised him
loudly and self-consciously.

"Well, Gerald, you're all right, ain't you? Takin' right
a-hold!"

"You bet he's all right."

"Well, Gerald's the man now, ain't that so, Gerald! He's

the one."

"That's right."

The six o'clock whistle blew.

Gerald looked about hesitatingly for Floyd. Finally he went out to the back room of the store to find him.

"Shall I go now? The whistle blew."

"Yes, sure, you go along now, Gerald. I wasn't paying any attention."

Floyd was busy over some boxes on the floor. Gerald hesitated. His face was red. He wanted to ask if he had "done all right." But he was ashamed. Finally he blurted:

"Do you want I should come back to-morrow morning?"

Floyd was still busy over the boxes. Gerald waited.

"Yes, you come back in the morning, Gerald," Floyd answered cheerfully.

Gerald got out of the store as fast as he could. How bright the street seemed outside, and how fresh the air was! He felt as if he had been smelling camphor and perfumes all his life. He had a job! It seemed to him that every one must know. He wanted people to ask him what he had been doing, it made him feel proud and important; although when Mr. Baird, the minister, who had been in the store earlier in the day, greeted him with: "Well, is the day's work over, young man?" he was suddenly too bashful to do more than grunt in answer. He walked soberly down the main street, and broke into a run as he cut across the corner.

His feet burned. It was hard to stand all day like that, although he had told Lois he didn't mind it. He grew hot all over when he thought of the mistakes he had made. But the ache that had seemed lodged in his chest somewhere, ever since the day when his father was buried and all the relatives had told him: "Well, you'll have to look after your mamma now, Gerald, won't you?"—when his mother cried and clung to him that night—that ache was strangely eased. He was earning money. He could take care of his mother. It humiliated him that his mother should have to be doing the washing for other people, although it was only some of their neighbors; but she wouldn't have to do it always. He had not heard more than a few words of what those men in the drug-store were saying. But at the thought—the very suspicion of it—his mind felt hot and sore. If they'd been saying anything about his mother, they'd be sorry for it. He'd—he didn't know just what—but anyway, they'd better look out!

The new little semi-bungalow house looked bleak and desolate. It had been that way ever since his father died. No new flowers had been planted this spring, the clothes-line hadn't been fixed, the garage for the car they had been going to get this summer stood unpainted just as his father had left it last fall. But they would have things again. The relatives needn't say anything; he guessed he could take care of his own mother without their telling him. He loved her, but it was none of their business to know it.

She was standing in the doorway. Gerald evaded her kiss, ducked away from her and went tramping out to the kitchen. He was afraid she was going to make a fuss.

"I gotta wash my hands," he told her importantly.

She followed him and stood looking at him, pitiful and proud.

"Why don't you go up to the bathroom, sweetheart?"

"I druther wash down here."

It was what his father had done when he came home from work.

"Are you ready for supper?" she pleaded.

"You bet."

She touched his face, he couldn't avoid that. But he got into the dining room as fast as he could and sat down with satisfaction. There were all the things that he liked—hot biscuits, and jelly, and strawberries. He demanded coffee, and his mother gave it to him. Betty's little mouth puckered up and her eyes were round with amazement.

"You don't let *us* have coffee," she said.

"Well, brother's been working. He has to have it."

The two little girls chattered eagerly about the school picnic. Gerald stuck to the business of eating. He had never been so hungry; hot biscuits had never tasted so good. He replied briefly to his mother's fond questions about what he had been doing all day.

"Were Floyd and his wife good to you? Did they show you what to do?"

"Yeah, they were all right."

"Did you know how to wait on people?"

"Sure."

"Didn't it seem terribly long to you?"

"Naw."

"Well, you want to eat a good supper."

It was over now, and he didn't want to talk about it. He wished she'd let him alone.

The one cooky left on the plate was given to Gerald. Betty followed her mother into the kitchen, weeping and complaining. She was the baby, and the extra pieces of everything were for her.

"I don't see why you gave it to Gerald, mamma. You didn't even make him give me half."

"Well, darling, listen—when men have been working they get hungrier than women and little girls do, and then we have to let them have what they want to eat. We don't get so hungry."

"*I* was hungry."

"Were you, pet?" Her mother laughed, half commiseratingly. "Then you eat this strawberry mamma puts into your little mouth."

"I don't want a strawberry. I had enough strawberries. And I was working," Betty insisted. "I put on all the knives and forks. I *was* working, mamma."

"Were you? Well, you were helping. You're a nice little helper."

"Before I'd make a fuss about an old cooky!" Juanita said scornfully.

She flashed a quick indignant glance at Gerald, remembering how he had talked to her in the drug-store. Let him have everything in the house to eat if he wanted it, and if mamma wanted to give it to him! But there was an obscure justice that silenced her even while it made her resentful. Well, she wouldn't be here all her life. She'd get married some day—and then she'd do as she pleased.

Gerald went out and sat on the steps of the porch. This was the time of day when his father always used to come out here and look at the paper. Gerald was ashamed of having eaten the cooky. He thought it belonged to him, but let that baby Betty have it! He would after this. He didn't know when he had had such a good supper. He watched Bobbie Parker's yard across the street so that he could shout across at Bobby the instant he came outdoors. Maybe they could go over and see those turtles Bobbie's uncle had in his back-yard. It would be fun to see if they could really be taught tricks. He could hear the girls complaining about the dishes. "It's your turn to-night." "It isn't!" Gee whizz, if they couldn't even do a little thing like washing dishes!

The evening came on cool and bright. Gerald stayed on the porch steps, although Bobby didn't appear in the yard. What he had really meant to do was to ask Bobby about the picnic, and try to find out, without saying it in so many words, whether any other boy had hung around Arlene Fedderson. He didn't care, anyway. He had thought about it in the store all the time, but it didn't matter so much now. His mother was the one he had to look after. Again he felt a fine, tired glow of satisfaction. He had put in a good day's work, all right.

Then he blushed. He remembered those men at the drugstore. Here was that old Art Fox coming up the walk with a pailful of strawberries! Well, if he thought he was coming here with those berries, he could just go away again.

"H'lo, Gerald," Art Fox called out cheerfully. He was a good-natured man, a widower, with a red sunburned face and grayish hair and mustache. He lived about a block away from the Rayburns, in a good-sized house. Gerald had always thought he was a nice man, because he never said any more than " 'Lo, boys!" when the boys ran across his lawn playing run-sheep-run.

"H'lo," Gerald answered briefly.

"Your ma around anywhere?"

"I don't know."

Art Fox halted. "Oh, well . . . She ain't gone out anywhere, has she?"

"I guess she has."

What did it matter whether that was true or not? Art Fox

had no business coming here. He felt a sense of pain and out-rage.

"That's too bad. I thought I'd drop around and see if you folks couldn't use a few strawberries. I got a bunch of 'em ripe —too many for an old fellow to eat by himself," he added with a mild attempt at jocularity. "Didn't know as you folks had any."

"We got some."

"That so? Well, I guess you can use a few more, can't you?"

"No, we got all we want."

"That so? Well, if you got all you need . . ." Art Fox stood there awkwardly for a moment. "Well, I guess I'll have to try to dump these on somebody else."

Gerald was silent.

"Your ma be home pretty soon, will she?"

"No, she ain't here."

"That so? Well . . . good-by, then."

Gerald said nothing. He could feel his heart thumping. He looked away. Art Fox was going down the walk with the straw-berries newly washed and freshly red in the bright tin pail. Just as he turned the corner, Mrs. Rayburn came to the door.

"I thought I heard somebody. Have they gone? Was any-body here, Gerald?"

"Art Fox." Gerald did not turn around.

"Oh!" His mother seemed a little flustered. "What did he want? Has he gone away?" she asked.

"He brought some of his strawberries."

"Why, Gerald, why didn't you call me?"

" 'Cause I told him we didn't want 'em. We got some of our own."

"Why, *Gerald* . . ."

"Well, we don't want him around here," Gerald said roughly.

He stared straight ahead at a little bird hopping about on the lawn, fighting down the childish tears that made his throat ache and his eyes burn. That sense of pain and outrage swelled in his heart. He thought of the unfinished garage standing bare and desolate in the back-yard—his father's old coat still hanging in the kitchen entry. If his mother couldn't take care of herself, he'd do it for her. He was the man of the house now. Art Fox could stay at home where he belonged. This was *their* home. She was *his* mother. Above that ache of unmanly tears he felt a hard exultance. They wouldn't laugh any more in the drug-store. They wouldn't talk about her.

She looked flushed and disconcerted. She stood in the doorway looking at Gerald. The back of his red head was like his father's. So was the set of his sturdy shoulders. She looked at them with an unwilling respect that turned slowly to resentment. All these last few weeks, a secret girlish pleasure had been growing up in her heart most surprisingly out of the blackness of her grief and loneliness. She knew that she was admired. She had thought it hidden from every one. At times she had laughed and called herself a fool; and at times her eyes were dreamy and a warmth settled softly about her. Now it was shamed and trampled. . . .

She started to say something to Gerald. But she stopped, as she had always stopped with Frank. She felt her anger melting helplessly away from her. He was so proud of working for her. He was so proud of his strength. He was only a little boy, after all—her little boy, sitting small and pitiful and unapproachable in the twilight.

She turned, her face suddenly quivering, went back into the hot darkness of the empty house, and sat down there alone.

Charlotte's Marriage

G RACE VANCAMP had said from the first that she was going
to look up Charlotte when she went to California.

"Oh, let Charlotte Evans alone!" Roy told her.

"Why, I'm just going to look her up! It'd be funny if I didn't.
She's one of my oldest friends."

"Yeah," Roy muttered. He knew Grace's "old friends."

But anyway, he wouldn't be along.

Grace had that visit to Charlotte in mind all the time that
she was out in California. She stayed in LaJolla which proved
to be exactly the right place, for she met awfully nice people,
several artists among them, and she could drive down into
Mexico and have a little wine and lose a little money at roulette.
She loved roulette—her mother would have died if she had
known Grace ever gambled! Oh, of course, there was the beach
too, and the sunset that everybody pretended to be so crazy
about. She had plenty to do that winter besides wonder about
Charlotte, you would have thought—unless you had known
Grace as well as Roy did. But once let curiosity about a certain
person get into her mind and hell itself couldn't make her let go.

She was much too adroit, however, to go straight to see
Charlotte. Grace didn't like to do things that way. It was more
fun to work the thing out under cover of something else. She
had that trip more or less in mind all winter. She led Major
Raleigh up to proposing a long drive; and then, pretending she
wanted to see the redwoods beyond, worked the plan around

until she was sure the drive would take them through Wood-lands.

Now why did she go to all that trouble? Grace wondered about it herself that night. She looked around at the pretty Spanish apartment, that was costing a lot more than Roy thought she ought to spend. It had all the things that she just simply must have—not because of the things themselves; people were always pretending to find something deep and mysterious in old furniture and dishes and things; but because her hungry sense of values told her that she couldn't be right without them. A little carved mission balcony of brown wood opened out from the flat white wall, and she had all the semi-Spanish modern colors of white and yellow and wood-brown and blue, and the kind of view of the sea that every one seemed to be after. She knew very well that Charlotte had nothing like this. How could she? Charlotte and Ken had left with almost nothing. And yet Grace couldn't be satisfied without seeing exactly what Charlotte *did* have. She liked Charlotte. She admired her. But—besides being curious about any women, her cook, girls in beauty shops, a woman whom she saw at a tea; aching until she had burrowed her way into the secret of their personal lives and held it up against her own—she had certain old grudges against Charlotte that were not in the least Charlotte's fault. Grace was always perfectly candid in admitting these things to herself in spite of her deviousness in getting satisfaction. It was all that made Roy forgive her.

"What have you got against Charlotte Evans?" one might imagine him asking—and Grace answering quite candidly:

"Nothing. Except that she was always the most popular girl in our class, and then my grandmother was always talking about what a dear little girl she was when we were kids."

You could say until you were black in the face that there wasn't anything particularly pretty about Charlotte Evans. It didn't make a bit of difference. Grace remembered when they were children, and her grandmother had made such a fuss when Charlotte came to the house. "The sweetest little girl." Why? Grace, looking eagerly into the big walnut-framed mirror in her grandmother's bedroom, and comparing her thin little face with Charlotte's, couldn't really see why Charlotte should get all the praise. Grace knew there was always a mysterious reserve in her grandmother's fondness for Grace herself. But at that time Charlotte was just a little girl with a round face and blue eyes wide apart and two perfectly smooth dove-brown braids. But there was something—smiling dents at the corners of her lips, a little tilt to the corners of the eyes . . . and then there was something about the way Charlotte spoke and acted . . .

"Distinction." Grace had heard that once. That was really what Charlotte had.

And Grace knew perfectly well that it was just what she didn't have herself. Even her yellow silk sports suit, yellow stockings and white sandals, white hat, smoothly parted hair and earrings, couldn't give it to her; or the dash of crimson on her thin lips.

But even without that old rivalry, Grace couldn't have rested until she had ferreted out just how Charlotte and Ken were getting along.

Grace was excited over the trip and pleased with the party. It made a good appearance in the long low car with the gay red wheels. Both Mrs. MacArthur and Mrs. Dupont had the proper look of wealth and authority; but Mrs. MacArthur was big-bosomed and considerably older than Grace, and Mrs. Dupont was small and over-refined, so that neither of them gave her any real competition with the Major. She could take gratification in the company of Major Raleigh himself, well-dressed, with wind-reddened face and clipped white mustache. And she felt happily that she herself in the front seat beside him, in the yellow knit silk and the white hat, was definitely the most striking of the party.

But the Major was curious to understand why Grace was so determined to go through Woodlands. Just a little California town, he said. People used to go there, but didn't much any more. She must have an interest there.

"No," Grace said. "I'll tell you. It's an old friend from home."

"Man?"

"No, woman. Believe it or not!"

"And you're really so anxious to see her?"

"Oh, it's not friendship! It's curiosity."

The Major was pleased at that. It carried out his theory that all women hated each other. He liked audacity, too, in women —good looking women—and when it didn't seem to be directed toward him and to endanger his pleasant state of widower. Grace VanCamp made it known that she had an adequate husband at home. He didn't mind the slight touch of intrigue, either. It pleased him to help women put through their little games—to arbitrarily range himself on their side. He promised Grace they'd manage to stop for an hour or so in Woodlands.

The trip was made in late winter—a beautiful time, the Major thought. Grace tried to look as if she felt it too when they all exclaimed over the golden hills and the rocks gray in the sun; but what really pleased her was the lordly roll of the big car through little towns. She was glad it was a nice day, and that the landscape was pretty and not just flat, but Woodlands was her real interest in the trip. The Major—amused, and to have some subject for raillery—asked about this friend of hers.

"Charlotte?"

Charlotte! That was a pretty old name.

"Makes me think of crinolines," Grace said. "Charlotte Eyre. Or Jane Somebody. Some old novel, anyway."

"Are you making insinuations, young lady, about my years?"

Even Charlotte's old-fashioned name seemed to be interesting, Grace thought rebelliously; besides getting her that legacy from that queer old aunt. Who cared about "Grace"? She hated her parents for calling her Grace. "A good name" was as much as anybody could say for it.

"Well, are you going to take me with you to call on Charlotte?"

No, Grace said coolly, she wasn't.

Wanted to see for herself, did she? And what did Charlotte look like?

"Oh, rather good looking," Grace answered nonchalantly. "Used to be, anyway."

"Miaow!"

Well, Grace said shrugging her shoulders, maybe was now. But she'd had enough to make any woman lose her looks. And without quite meaning to do it, hating her own tongue that she knew was hung in the middle, just as Roy said, Grace began to expatiate on Charlotte's marriage.

"She's married the most awful man. Or at any rate, a flop. Doesn't even try to make a living, and had to get out of town."

Grace was ashamed of herself as she said it. What made her? She was always doing things like that and then feeling sick inside. She knew Ken wasn't as bad as that. She saw his face while she was talking, a pleasant face with nice brown eyes. But she went right on.

"All the Robinsons hated to have her do it. Charlotte comes of a wonderful family. Everybody thinks it's a shame."

Why was she talking like that? Of course, Ken had made a failure. . . . But Grace thought of Ken as he had been in college, in his thick white sweater with the big red D, coming down the street under the autumn trees. She would have given anything for just one date with him. He was the hero of the school where Grace had gone just one year, not because she cared about going to college, but because Charlotte Robinson went there. "Ken and Charlotte." And then, when he'd visited at home that summer, all the crowd had been crazy over Charlotte's man. He played football and basketball, was good in track, he was handsome and he could sing. It absolutely crowned Charlotte's distinction, bringing home with her the pick of the land. They were just the right ones for each other, all the crowd said exultantly. The Robinsons were pleased to death. Grace knew that. Mr. Robinson talked all over town about taking Ken into his business.

"And they had an enormous wedding!"

Grace laughed.

Nevertheless, old-fashioned and simple as it might seem now, one of the occasions of her life had been Charlotte Robinson's wedding. Before that, she had always thought church weddings the thing, but this—perhaps because it was Charlotte's—had eclipsed them. She could see now the spills of sunlight and dapples of shade on the great wide Robinson lawn, where boys with bare heads, and girls with light dresses and wide-brimmed hats, were idyllically wandering. There was just something about it . . . she remembered yet the blush pink of the roses in the heat, beside great bushes of which Ken and Charlotte had stood to be married.

"Hasn't turned out so well?" the Major said with easy cynicism.

"Scarcely!"

And then, to make up for all she had said, Grace began to praise Charlotte hectically.

"She's just a grand girl. Don't look at me like that. I mean it. I've been wild, honestly, about Charlotte all my life. Used to want to have all my clothes made like hers! She was terrifically popular. And now just think of being thrown away on Ken Evans! It's amazing that it's lasted as long as it has. *Every* one wished Charlotte would get rid of him."

Ugh, what a sickening mixture of candor and falsehood! Grace despised herself. Despised the Major if he believed it. Even the humiliatingly true little bit about copying the clothes —she had, people used to laugh at her for it, once there had been something in the high school annual—but it couldn't make up. Why did she say that last thing? It had been like a turning of the fates, making them side at last with Grace, that Charlotte's marriage—her enviable, perfect marriage—had turned out like that! Grace couldn't really believe it yet. And she herself had the perfectly good husband! She dreamed about it sometimes, and it was all mixed up—hadn't really happened.

"Well," the Major said heavily, "all the fine fellows fall for the lemons and vice versa. Law of life."

Grace was so preoccupied that it was a moment before she thought to say vivaciously:

"Why, Major Raleigh! When I've told you over and *over* what a perfectly grand husband I have."

But she heard his satisfied little chuckle.

Now they were coming into Woodlands. Grace's eyes were

avid and bright under the white sports hat. So this was all it was!—a little California town of the older sort, slightly shabby, lots of houses with the kind of porches that showed they had been built by middle westerners. In fact, an old winter resort, where elderly couples from home used to come and take rooms in some big frame house with palms outside, called The Whittier or The McClellan.

"Good heavens! To come *here,* with the whole coast to choose from!"

Santa Barbara and Los Angeles and LaJolla—even Pasadena. It didn't cost much. She believed that was it. And yet she couldn't get over the suspicion that because Charlotte was living here there must be something mysteriously superior about the place.

"Are we stopping here?" Mrs. MacArthur cried.

The Major gave a wink at Grace. "Sub-generator needs oiling," he said solemnly.

"Oh, dear!" cried Mrs. MacArthur. She took it in good faith.

"Sorry, ladies. Have to amuse ourselves for an hour or so. Mrs. VanCamp says she has an errand. Now I propose that we three have a good old-fashioned dish of ice cream and then stroll about the town."

What a silly business!—making this mystery of it. Still, Grace liked it, and the Major was in high delight.

Charlotte was watering the garden. She liked to do that when Ken was at work and the children were in school. She always felt as if she got back, in some mysterious way, her old free self when she was out in the midst of the flowers . . . the Charlotte who, at home, in the red brick house with the white pillars, used to run lightly out to the lawn early in the morning, when only

Tom and Annie were up in their vine-shaded rooms above the stables, and go browsing around among the wet blue iris and the roses. This garden was still strange. Still, when she touched the big winter roses, she could catch the spicy breath of the briar rose at home in the summer heat. But all her anxieties lay quiet in her mind under the soothing of the sunshine.

She stood still, the old-fashioned garden hose in her hand, the sun making rainbows through the falling water. The town taxi was driving up. Charlotte stifled an impulse to steal away. She was always afraid that some one from home might find her out here, and she was ashamed of the feeling.

Yes, it was stopping. A woman in a yellow sports suit was getting out. Charlotte saw the lovely clothes—the soft white of the hat, the rich gleam of the sun on the yellow silk. It made her angrily aware of her old blue linen dress. Those were *her* clothes, the way *she* ought to dress. But she hated that feeling. It was just what Ken was afraid of, and what she always denied . . . yes, and the denial was true, too, true in a deeper sense, and the thought of Ken's pain if he knew of that feeling hurt her as if it had been her own. She forced herself proudly through the first instinctive reluctance and went to the house.

"Charlotte!"

"Grace!"

Grace kissed her dramatically. Good heavens—Grace Van-Camp! Of all the people on earth, she didn't want Grace VanCamp to come. She was ashamed when she remembered how more than nice to her Grace had always been . . . except when they were little, then Grace used to be horrid . . . yet she always had the feeling that there was something under all this kindness—couldn't help remembering the kind of little girl Grace had been . . . Charlotte loathed suspicions.

"Why, Grace, I didn't dream of seeing you!"

"Didn't you know I was in California? I couldn't leave without seeing you. If I hadn't known you must be tied with the children, I would have made you come over and visit me at La-Jolla."

"I didn't know you were in LaJolla."

"Oh, yes. A *dar*-ling little apartment. The grandest view of the sea."

"Shall we go inside?" Charlotte said.

She tingled with reluctance when she gave that invitation. What did it matter if Grace saw how they were living? She wasn't making any pretenses, certainly. The situation was so far beyond that, such considerations had almost dropped out of sight. But when she saw Grace, whom she had always known at home, she remembered her own pretty white house with the green door. She remembered luncheon with "the girls" at the Country Club on the wide porch under the gay orange and green sunshades, overlooking the thick green stretch of the golf course where some of the husbands were playing. It seemed that she simply couldn't be here. It made her aware of every bit of shabbiness about the cheap little old-fashioned bungalow with the white paint getting dingy, the horrid rented furniture in the living room that no more belonged to her, Charlotte . . .

And yet she didn't really care. That was the funny part of it. It was just that Grace would think she *did* care.

"I'm so glad to *see* you!" Grace cried vivaciously.

She went on to tell how she was driving through with Major Raleigh's party.

"Do you know him, Charlotte? I thought you might have run into him. Owns a lot of aviation business, you know."

Charlotte's lip curled a trifle as she thought how very likely she was to meet Major Raleigh or Major Anybody! The party sounded very gay, driving so easily around the country. But Charlotte suffered with the feeling that it was not sincere, that Grace was always playing up to her somehow. The party didn't really tempt her much. She knew she wouldn't care for the people. It was what people expected of her that hurt her, not the thing itself.

Grace, still talkative and animated, was telling her all about things at home. Perhaps it was only Charlotte's sensitiveness that made her suspect double motives and feel that Grace's sharp eyes were taking in everything under the brim of the white hat.

"Oh, hadn't you heard about the Dixons? I thought surely your mother had written you!"

"I don't think so," Charlotte said.

And for some time after she was in such a haze of pain as she thought of her parents that she lost half of what Grace was saying. How could they have done it? Would she ever do a thing like that to her own children? And yet these were her parents, the papa and mamma of her childhood. And it was to get away from her parents that she and Ken had left.

She remembered that light-hearted old existence . . . for a moment thought of herself as Charlotte Robinson again, and all that had happened later than her college days was unreal. Her father—his heavy figure, dominant but kindly voice, the sun on his gray hair as he stood on the lawn looking at the roses . . . her mother, the dainty figure with the flossy waved white hair moving like a little aging princess through all the rich comforts of the big rooms. . . . She had never supposed she could break with her father and mother. And yet, when she thought of how they had treated Ken—! Papa loved them as long as he could do everything for them. He hadn't let Ken make a move for himself in the business . . . and when Ken left it, he had laughed in the horridest way, an incredible way, and predicted his failure, wanted to make Ken fail, said Ken had lost his chance and could never come back to him again. . . .

"And what, then, does Ethel Dixon do but start up an af-*fair,* my dear, with this man! I found out all about it."

Ethel Dixon. It was just as if Charlotte had never known an Ethel Dixon, that whole way of living seemed so far away. . . .

That was what hurt the worst of all—that her father had been right. Ken didn't have business brains. He couldn't make a go of it. What of it? She wanted to break out fiercely. Was that all there was to existence? Ken—as if anybody else knew what he was, his intelligence, his fairness, his absolute kindness with the children, their love . . . It had taken a long time to draw her away from her father's way of looking at things, from all that her parents considered necessities; it had almost broken Ken, almost broken their marriage. . . . But just having Grace here, some one from home, brought it all back and made the break incredible—made her think of her father and mother and what they had been to her when she was a child. . . .

But the other was the truth, too. It had actually come to the point when she had to choose between her parents and her husband. She couldn't accept anything from her father after the way he had talked to Ken. She would rather live out here, on the little Aunt Charlotte had left her, on nothing if need be. She wasn't dependent on the old comforts, she had amazingly shown them, amazingly even to herself.

But it hurt even more that mother, her dear little devoted mother, had taken father's side—as it hurt mother that she had taken Ken's. . . .

"And so, my dear, that was the way it ended!"

Charlotte hadn't the faintest idea how.

But Grace was off on another tack.

"What grand flowers!"

The calla lilies. She *would* pick the biggest. "Yes, we have wonderful flowers here."

"I remember—" enthusiastically—"what a wonderful garden you always had at home. Oh, your mother's having the whole garden done over! Pool and everything. That woman that designs those darling pools. I want Roy to get hold of her, too. But you know that, of course!"

Charlotte was noncommittal. But she was amused in a way. When Grace used to praise the garden, her eyes were always looking at anything but the flowers themselves—studying what Charlotte had on, or the way her hair was cut. Lots of people detested Grace VanCamp. But there was something about her that always made Charlotte feel sorry for her. Now, in spite of the beautiful sports clothes, and Major Raleigh's party, they seemed all at once to be back in the old relationship.

"Where are the children, Charlotte? In school? My dear, isn't it awful? Have you been able to find a decent private school? You know, Roy and I can't bear to send Alan away yet. But we're afraid we'll have to. You know, the Miss Fenners are really getting awfully old. But there isn't anywhere else. What do *you* do?"

Charlotte felt amused again. "We send them to public school," she said. Did the looks of the house suggest that the children were being educated in Europe? And as if she and Grace hadn't gone to high school together!

"Oh, really, Charlotte? I wonder if you aren't right! Roy always says that Alan would be better off in the public school."

Roy, Roy, Roy. Grace brought him in most insistently. How anxious she was to get back to Roy—although she a-*dored* California, didn't see how she could ever stand those winters again. How wonderful Roy was, how he wanted to have her enjoy herself. But still more how Roy had missed her, how she felt she must go back again.

"But I'm so restless, Charlotte. I can't just stay somewhere and be contented, the way you do."

Well, there was that redeeming touch of candor about Grace! But at the same time her bright eyes were taking in the shabby room and boring into Charlotte.

"You're looking grand, Charlotte."

"Oh, do you think I am?"

"Well, perhaps you're a little thin."

Charlotte gave a slight laugh. She knew very well how thin she was—she had moments, when she came suddenly face to face with the mirror, when she felt an angry desperation because her looks were slipping away from her and there was nothing to be done about it. And yet in a sense it didn't matter. She couldn't spend all her time thinking about herself. She had cast in her lot with Ken and the children. She would lose her looks sometime, anyway.

"Oh, and tell me! *How* is Ken?"

That was the question that Charlotte had been expecting. She said lightly. "He's quite well."

All through Grace's visit, she had been preparing herself against this question.

"Really? I'm so glad. He looked so badly when you left, Charlotte." Grace was very solemn and earnest. "He isn't here, I suppose? It would be too much luck to find both of you."

"No, he went out a little while ago."

Grace VanCamp could worm almost anything out of anybody; but she was not to know—nobody at home was to know —what Ken was doing. Charlotte was aware of what people at home would think if they heard Ken was working in a store downtown. They would all pity Charlotte. But simply at the mention of Ken's name by Grace, an outsider, her allegiance to Ken, so much deeper these last few years since they had been out here together, since they had been through so much that was grinding and painful, came over her in a rush and blotted out everything. Oh, she knew what people would think of it! She supposed she couldn't expect any one outside to understand. But she didn't care what Ken did if it would only help him to get back his self-respect and happiness. Charlotte felt a terrible resentment and pain. Why must she defend the inner trouble and sweetness of her life against her old playmate as against the bitterest enemy? Against her own father and mother!

"And you like it out here?" Grace asked. "Both of you?"

"Oh yes, I think we do."

"And you really think it's better for Ken?"

"Much better."

"I think it's so *lovely* you can be out here together and that Ken's contented. I wish Roy could come with me. But he thinks he must stick to business! You know how Roy is."

Charlotte smiled. She fully understood the sting. But there was a queer wistfulness in Grace's tone that she half understood, too. Roy VanCamp was a decent fellow. But no one had supposed, when Grace married him, it was exactly in an outburst of romance. In fact, Charlotte suddenly seemed able to draw upon a depth of dispassionate understanding that comprehended the whole of her relationship with Grace.

How strange! Life was painful, and yet most interesting to contemplate. Because after all, according to the ideas of most of the world, it was Grace's marriage that had turned out to be the success! Roy VanCamp was making money, as much, at least, as most of his friends. Grace and Roy kept their proper position in the town. And she, Charlotte Robinson, was out here in a little town in California and her husband was working in a store. That, as most people would see it, was the outcome of "one of the most popular and charming weddings our city has ever seen." Charlotte could see how it would all look to Grace. It would sound like a tragedy to her mother. In a way, it *was* a tragedy. . . . The day of her marriage, the laughter and tears and roses, and she and Ken standing in front of the sweetbriar bush. . . .

This was what it had meant. That bright June day . . . and earlier, the spring night at college as they crossed the wet grass under the big trees, the moment alone in her room when she said to herself that the grandest man in school had asked her to marry him—she remembered her wild, trembling joy, her amazed humility. They were always going to be "Charlotte and Ken." . . . It had meant dropping her old ambitions, leaving all she had, taking his failure into her, putting her pride in his goodness into him, letting it mold her own life and body. When she saw some one out of the old life again, she knew what she was—her thin face, the lines about her mouth and the hollows under her eyes. But she felt something different, too, something worn and capable and sustaining about her hands. A sweetness and solace of which she had never dreamed in that first trembling happiness had sunk into her and, perhaps, molded her too. No matter what they had lost or dropped overboard, she and Ken had kept their allegiance to each other and a breath of its first freshness.

And yet all the same, in spite of her reluctance and the cringe of her pride, she was glad to see Grace. There was an aching, unappeased something in her that was hungry for anything from home. Over all the old life, painful as it had become to her, there was a sweetness of the past that had a depth beyond happiness.

But it *was* a past to her.

"Well, Charlotte, I'll tell your mother I saw you. She misses you terribly. And I'm so *sorry* I didn't see Ken."

Charlotte suffered, but she smiled with a slight touch of irony. How much did Grace know, and how much was said to hurt? Grace cried in one of her rushes of candor:

"Yon don't know, Charlotte Evans, how I've always admired you. Honestly! I was always so jealous because my grandmother liked you when we were little girls. She liked you better than she did me."

"Oh, no, Grace!"

"Oh yes, she did! Aren't you ever coming back?"

Charlotte smiled and shook her head.

"Don't you want to come, Charlotte?"

"No, I don't think I do."

"You tell Ken I don't forgive him, all the same, if he doesn't bring you back. Every time I pass your old house, I think you ought to be in it."

Grace kept looking into Charlotte's eyes as if she couldn't get away. It made Charlotte uncomfortable. Again it made her feel unreasonably sorry for Grace.

Just as Grace got into the taxi, Charlotte saw Ellen, the young English girl who sometimes stayed with the children, coming.

"Oh, Mrs. Evans!"

She was going to hear all Ellen's troubles again. Grace's last vision was of Charlotte and the distraught young girl going into that little house together.

The Major said:

"Well, find your friend?"

"Yes, I found her."

"Things as bad as you hoped?" He chuckled.

"Worse!"

Grace launched out into an animated description. But she was dissatisfied under the forced vivacity. All at once she became silent. The Major glanced at her, and then put his attention on his driving, with a pleasing thought of the unaccountability of women.

Getting out of the taxi loudly panting in front of that little house, Grace in her smart clothes had felt proud, relieved and assured. And then when she had seen Charlotte—! No matter what there might be about Roy that she wanted to criticize— and there had always been plenty—certainly as things had turned out, she could congratulate herself. She could have the satisfaction of thinking "Poor Charlotte!"; and the envy that gnawed at her—making her eyes restless, thinning her lips— should have been appeased. She had everything now that Charlotte didn't. She had seen for herself!

But at the involuntary mention of her grandmother, the old uncertainty and dissatisfaction had to come up again, a teasing perception of values she could never quite grasp. Before she left, she had that same old feeling that Charlotte was looking at her and being kind to her, as if she knew something that Grace didn't.

Grace tried angrily to shake off this feeling. Why, think of

Charlotte—thin, faded, in an old blue linen dress that Grace wouldn't have worn for a *house* dress, probably hadn't had any new clothes since she came out here, gray threads in her hair. Certainly no stranger looking at her would ever think of how good looking she had been. Grace wished she *had* taken Major Raleigh; heard him say, "Is *that* your good looking Charlotte?"

Or was she, as Roy told her, just bound to be dissatisfied?

She thought of that queer-looking girl that had come up to the house just as she was leaving, and her tone—"Oh, Mrs. Evans!" People—servants, every one—used to go to her grandmother like that. Grace thought her grandmother had had a horrible life, too, raising all those children after grandfather had died. Why was it? Grace had tried being terribly nice once to one of the maids. But the girl's face was simply closed up when she talked to her. She supposed *that* girl would have talked to Charlotte.

"Ah, now we're reaching them!" the Major said in a tone of satisfaction.

Grace looked out of the car. She saw a lot of big trees again. Now the rest of the trip would be a bore until they reached the Inn, and she would have to pretend she was enjoying it.

And the winter was almost over. She ought to have gone home before this. She knew Charlotte had thought it queer that she could leave Alan for a whole winter. She had seen that same look on other people's faces. Well, goodness, she couldn't be just tied to Roy and Alan all the time! She couldn't just stick around home. She had never yet had the—something, she didn't know how to express it—that she had always felt she must find somewhere, and that would start her out being happy for the rest of her life. Oh God, how she hated to go back! Not because she was more unhappy at home than anywhere else, but just because . . . oh well, what was there? When she had first married Roy, she had loved going into shops and giving her name: "Mrs. VanCamp." Then she had felt satisfactorily married. But marriage hadn't seemed to be much else, as far as she could see, but Roy always trying to make her go *his* way, and Grace holding out for her own way.

The Major glanced shrewdly at her.

"You don't seem to have enjoyed your visit much," he told her. "With your dear old friend."

"Well, when I found her living like that—!" Grace got hold of her animation with an iron hand. But she couldn't seem to keep it up. "Only . . . oh, I don't know! But I was just thinking—what *is* anything, anyway?"

"Oh, tut, tut!" the Major said gently. "Look out at the trees and refresh your soul."

"Aren't they *grand!*" Grace cried.

But she still wondered why Charlotte had seemed to be patronizing her again.

She glanced mechanically at the big trees.

A Great Mollie

MOLLIE SCHUMACHER drove into the yard of the Bell farm. At first she thought there was no one about, it was so quiet. The garage doors were closed, however, and Frank always left them standing open when he took out the car.

She shut off the engine. But she kept on sitting in the car with her hands on the worn steering wheel, so comfortable that she hated to get out. She noticed how dry the September sunshine made everything look. The heavy pale grain of the grindstone was warm in the sun. Milk had been spilled at the corner of the corn crib where the cats were fed. It made a whitish stain on the bare ground and flies were thick above it. There was a look of country peace about the old red barn. The loft window was open, and shaggy, dusty hay stuck out. In the open wooded pasture behind the barn, the oaks had that dry look, too, in the sunshine.

Summer was almost over again! Mollie felt a thrust of fear. Summer, no matter how hard any one worked, was an interlude. It didn't really matter. But just as soon as that first crispness came into the air, it was different. The handle of the pump burned with cold when she went out to the vine-covered stoop to get the water before breakfast . . . again she was impatient because they kept on living in that old-fashioned house at the edge of town where they couldn't even have city water or a furnace—things everybody had nowadays! In the summer, it was pleasant enough, with the flowers, and the birds for which

Charlie had made a dozen queer little houses of bark and boards. But the cold spurred her ambition. When frost came, you had to decide things. It might come any time, now. It would get harder and harder to start the Ford. It would be too cold to drive in an open car. Her summer work would be over.

Nearly over . . . These days when she started out early, eager to get away from the puttering routine of home; packed her bag of samples; called back impatiently that they could expect her when they saw her; and then, after long dallying with the starter and heated attempts at cranking, heard joyously the loud steady noise of the engine, sprang in quickly before it had a chance to die down, and at last was out on the open road. . . .

She had been grumbling all summer about the annoyances —having to fool with this old car; getting caught in the rain somewhere out in the country and driving home over slippery roads; her goods not coming on time. But she had an affection for the Ford, which she had bought second hand at a sale in the country—although she got so furious at it sometimes that she called it every name she could think of. "You damned hell-fired old SKATE!" once she had sobbed at it.

But when it was running well, when the road stretched long and smooth, when the fields were fresh and the sky was blue, when the engine hummed noisily and the fenders rattled, she squeezed the steering wheel with both hands and felt that she loved the old rattletrap. She was so happy that she sang. She drove on and on and on, trying new roads, pretending that it was because she was enterprising and was looking for new customers. When she came to a patch of woods where it was shady, she stopped the car, took out from her handbag the sandwich of homemade bread and summer sausage she had stolen into the kitchen to make when Luisa wasn't around, and ate it luxuriously. She liked to sell things and to dicker.

"Hoo hoo!" Mollie called.

Mate came to the door at last in an old bungalow apron.

"Well, look who's here!"

"I thought you folks must be all asleep."

"I was lying down. I don't know, I've felt kind of bum ever since I had those teeth out. I ought to get my ironing done to-day, there's some pieces I need, but—come on in, Mollie, what you standing outside for?"

"Wait. I want to get some things out of the car."

Mollie ran out and opened the back of the car.

"Land, you do pick up the most things! Where'd you get all that junk?" Mate demanded, in amusement.

"Oh, I don't know," Mollie said, laughing and blushing, half sheepish and half proud, like a child caught in some game of its own. "I see things when I'm driving around, and folks give me things. Gosh, Mate, I don't know where it all does come from! But I always seem to come home with the old bus loaded."

She had some seed corn that Henry Fuchs had given her to try out, and a bag of crab apples, a jackknife she had found in the road, a few hazelnuts she had picked to see whether they were ripe, a pail of honey, a spray of sumach, and half a dozen melons.

"Where'd you get the melons?" Mate demanded.

"Oh, some girls back here on the road had a stand and were selling them. I always like to take something home to Lu and Charlie. Here, I want you and Frank to try one of these."

"Oh, no; we'll have melons of our own before long."

"Oh, take this one—it's supposed to be a new kind. Go ahead, Mate."

"Well, but I hate to."

Mollie followed Mate into the parlor and sat down with a luxurious sigh, in the cool room shaded by pine trees. She took off her hat and wiped her face and neck until they were red. Her hair felt stiff with dust.

"You're sweating like a man," Mate observed.

"I have to work like a man, I can tell you."

"Ain't it awful hard work for you, going around with that Ford?"

"Oh, well, I can do it!" Mollie boasted. She laughed, and her eyes sparkled. "I came across a fellow in the road—couldn't get his car started, so I got out and tinkered around with it a while—and I don't know just what I'd done to it, but the darn thing started up the minute I turned on the gas! You ought to have seen that fellow's face!"

"You ought to have been a man," Mate said, admiring, yet disapproving.

She looked at Mollie.

Mollie was big all over, and Frank always said, when she helped him lift anything, that her arms were as strong as his. Her reddish brown hair grew rough and thick and slightly curling, and below the dusty roots was a tiny gleam of perspiration. There were dark hairs on her upper lip and chin. Her lips were full and vital, and her nose had a bold outline. But her brown eyes were childlike. They had an ingenuous glow in the coarse vigor of her tanned face. There was something defenseless in their warm darkness. When she was pleased, or touched, they misted over.

"I expect I look like thunder by now," Mollie said, uncomfortably. "Well, who could keep fixed up, running around the country, and doing the things I do?"

"You're all right," Mate lied politely. Really, she was disapproving of Mollie's dusty shoes and her blue gingham dress with big hoops of perspiration under the arms and the hem of a dark brown slip showing at the back. "You've got a smudge, though, on your neck."

"Oh, well, when I get home I'll have a good scrubbing. I start out clean, Mate, but gosh, I can't keep that way! Who can, that runs a Ford? Anyway, I caught an old biddie for Lena Toogood, when I was there, that she couldn't catch, and I had to chase that female devil all over the landscape."

Mate did not answer. She had always disapproved of Mollie for not thinking more about her clothes, although—when they were off together after nuts or elderberries—she depended upon Mollie to shake the trees and find a way of getting over fences. Mate herself had never learned to drive their car and had to wait to go to town until Frank could take her. She regarded the car as beyond both her management and her comprehension, just as she did some of the farm implements—and this although she had been brought up on a farm, had known how to milk since she was an infant, and would have no help with either her stove or her washing machine.

Mollie opened her sample bag.

"I brought along that underwear I thought'd be nice for Frank," she said. "And then I got your corselette, in the other bag. I think this is the nicest thing yet I've struck for men. Look here."

She held up a winter weight union suit, eying it with proud satisfaction and discussing all its good points in detail, while its pathetic legs dangled.

"I don't know," Mate said, dubiously. "Frank's never worn that kind."

"Best of reasons for wearing it now!" Mollie said vigorously. It always made her impatient that the people around here were so afraid to try new things, which were the very breath of life to her. "I know what Frank wears—those old clumsy two piece things, still! It's not that I'm so anxious to sell, Mate, but I'd like Frank to try a good handy piece of goods like this and get rid of those old contraptions. I want the people around here to take up new things once in a while! Now, I'll tell you, I'm going to leave this sample here, and as soon as it gets cold, I want Frank to try this, and if he don't like it, all right; I'll take it back—give it to somebody for Christmas, or let Charlie wear it."

"I don't think we ought to take your sample," Mate demurred.

"Oh fudge! Season's ending, anyway."

"Did you say you brought my corselette?"

"You bet!"

Mollie talked while she fitted it. "I had another nice suit of men's summer underwear, but I sold it to a fellow I met on the road. That was a funny sale! I passed him, and I saw he was walking, so I says, 'Want a ride?' He says, 'Sure!' We got to talking. He told me he was a lightning insurance man. His car broke down and he was walking out to see Bert Gulley. He asked what I was selling, and I told him I had the best line of men's underwear he'd ever seen. I says, 'Don't you want to look at some of it?' and he says, 'Sure,' and I stopped the car and got out my samples, and he bought that one—it was just his size. He told me he'd get me a job selling insurance if I wanted it!" Mollie gave an eager, delighted laugh. "I bet I could make a go of it, too!"

"Aren't you afraid to ask strange men like that to ride with you?" Mate asked, in horror.

"Afraid! What of? Think they're going to run off with me?"

"They might rob you."

"Oh fudge! And all they'd get from me—!"

"Well, I think it's awful risky."

"That don't bother me any. I like it! Oh, anyway, I can't pass somebody walking along in the heat while I'm riding and not at least offer the fellow a chance to ride if he wants it. I had a tramp one day—I took him as far as the creamery."

"Weren't you scared to have him in the car?"

"No, he was a real nice fellow! He'd been bumming around out in California, and he told me a whole lot about raising honey from onion blossoms—I'd like to try that! I learn all kinds of things from these bugs I pick up on the road."

Mollie laughed delightedly again, and rocked strenuously. It was fun to horrify Mate—and then it was so cool in here, and she wasn't anxious to get home where they all disapproved of her "going around selling things."

"You better stay for dinner," Mate urged.

"Oh gee, I can't, Mate! I've got to get on. I spent half the morning chasing that old biddie for Lene. Say, though, if you'll let me do a little of that ironing for you—"

"Oh, I couldn't let you do that! You've got your own work."

"Oh, come on, Mate, I'll be glad to do it for you. It'll give me a change. I can just as well help you out a little while I'm stopping here."

There was no resisting Mollie when she was determined to do something for you, Mate knew. So Mollie was soon hard at work with the electric iron in Mate's back kitchen. Mollie always worked harder at anything that wasn't her own work, and wasn't what she was supposed to be doing.

Frank Bell came into the house shortly before noon.

"I thought I saw a car out here that didn't belong! Hello, Mollie," he said, heartily. "How you was?"

"Fine, boy! How's yourself?"

He stuck out his hand and grinned. "Want to shake with a nigger?"

Mollie said, "Sure, you bet I do, yours aren't much worse'n mine."

"Well, us fellows that handle engines can't keep tony, can we?" Frank asked. He shook Mollie's hand with jocular vigor until Mate squealed:

"Frank, let go, you're hurting her!"

He retorted, "Aw, Mollie's not hurt so easy as all that. I'm working up her strength so she can crank that Ford."

"Well, you aren't going to set down in any of these chairs in those clothes you've got on now."

"Oh, I ain't!" Frank retorted jubilantly. He waved his blackened hands at her until she ducked and squealed again. "Say, what's that melon I see out in the kitchen?"

"That's Mollie's."

"No, it isn't," Mollie said, eagerly. "I brought it for you folks. Come on, let's have a taste of it."

"Now? Before dinner?"

"Sure!" Frank said, heartily. "Mushmelons, any time."

"I'm not going to have Frank Bell sitting down here in this room and eating melons in those awful clothes."

"Aw, say, I can't change my clothes every time I step in and out of the house!" Frank began, indignantly.

"He can eat outdoors," Mollie broke in. "Come on, Frank, you do get treated pretty mean. I got some more in the Ford. You come out mit."

They ran away from Mate's expostulations, and Mollie rummaged through the miscellany in the back of the Ford until she'd found a nice little melon for Frank. "Here, boy! How's this?" He stood, eating it happily, letting the juice drip into the road and caring nothing for his black hands.

"Gosh, look at the plunder!" he said, marveling. "Here, Mollie—want a bite?"

"Sure, I'll take a bite."

He broke off a dripping hunk of melon, orange-tinted and coolly juicy in its pale green rind. Mate stood on the back porch watching them in disapproval. They were spoiling their dinners. Frank and Mollie were like a pair of kids when they got together. Mate was glad to have Mollie stay, though, in spite of the extra work any company made. Mollie livened things up, and took a hand at helping with all kinds of work. Frank went back to finish his job with the machinery, and Mollie washed luxuriously in the cool soft water at Mate's sink. She was going to stay for dinner after all.

"I oughtn't to. But the morning's gone anyway—gosh, I don't know where to! Well, I got some of that ironing out of the way for you, Mate."

Mate's being so particular was all right when it came to a meal. Frank came in, scrubbed and with his hair wet, in a pair of clean, faded blue overalls. Mollie loved to eat in company. It wasn't the meal, she always said, but the sociability. Still, Mollie could get away with a pretty good meal, too, as Frank Bell had often noticed with amusement.

"Well, Mollie!" he began. "Business pretty good?"

"Took in fifteen dollars' worth last Friday!" Mollie boasted.

"Zat so! How much you taken in to-day?"

"Oh, not so much to-day—so far: I don't know what I may do this afternoon," Mollie said, easily. "I haven't stopped many places. Kind of got stuck. Well, Lena Toogood was chasing around after an old biddie, and I stopped and caught it for her, and I don't know—did some more things."

"She ought to save you a good order for that!"

"She ordered fifty cents' worth, I guess. One pair of cotton stockings."

"Well, that was pretty good for Lena."

Mollie ate with gusto of mashed potatoes, pork, and gravy. She had picked a big stiff bouquet of zinnias for the table, and it made her happy to look at the bright, gaudy colors.

"Well, if you can take in fifteen dollars' worth in one day," Frank told her, "I expect you'll go on selling union suits and stockings."

"No, that's only pick-up work."

"You've got the car, and I should think you could get all around the country here, and do a lot of business. Work up a good trade. I always thought you were a good salesman, Mollie."

"No, it's almost over. No, sir, what I want," Mollie said vigorously, and scowling, "is real work, something that'll call out the best there is in me. Oh, it's fun to sell stuff for a while . . . but *that's* what I'm after—something big!"

"Yes, something big . . ." Frank began, dubiously.

But she went straight on: "This is nothing! This is something I can do with one hand. What fun is it to make money that way? No, *this* isn't what I'm after."

Her face glowed darkly and her eyes sparkled. Frank was impressed, as he always was when he talked with Mollie face to face. She was a strong woman, all right, and a mighty capable one in lots of ways, about as much so as a man. But he asked facetiously:

"What do you want to do? Some more vi'lets?"

Those "vi'lets" . . . That was the trouble with Mollie: always wanting to get into some fancy kind of business that nobody'd ever heard of; not contented with straight buying and selling. That showed that she was a woman. He got rid of his respect and got back his amusement, which suited him much better . . . but still with a little uneasy feeling that Mollie might make a go of one of those crazy businesses some day: she could do things.

"That all fell through," Mollie answered him, robustly.

"What was the trouble? Couldn't you and Artie get together? Thought you and him was all ready to go down South and make your fortunes!"

"We might have, too," Mollie answered, looking back over the plan with a reminiscent glow—her schemes were always radiant to her in anticipation and alluring in retrospect. "There's something in it for the fellow that takes a-hold. No, the trouble was, Art got cold feet, and the Missus, I guess, got 'em first—heard about the snakes down South and was afraid to go down there."

She wanted to turn it off, but Frank was started on it now and wouldn't let it go. He asked, mulling over his amusement: "What was you and Artie going to do with the vi'lets when you'd raised 'em? Going to take 'em into town and stand and sell 'em to the visitors on the street corners? Say, Art Gilbert would have made a cute flower boy!"

Mate was listening to all of this nonsense without a smile, with her hand on the handle of the coffee pot, ready to fill the cups again, if anybody wanted coffee.

"Pass Mollie the meat, Frank. She's out of everything. You better tend to your knitting here instead of talking about vi'lets," she said, with a dry coldness. Mollie's schemes neither impressed her nor gave her any amusement. If Mollie had any real sense about things, she'd marry some farmer around here —a widower, somebody who needed a good, strong wife and would be glad to have her; her friends would help her look around for somebody—or else she'd make up her mind to settle down where she was, with Luisa and Charlie, and attend to things at home.

"Well, I still think it's a good plan for the fellow that can work it," Mollie affirmed, stoutly. "Why shouldn't people raise violets as well as raise potatoes?"

Frank was now highly amused. "Sure, and so was the goldfish a good plan!" he said. "What become of them? Last I heard you was chasing old man Davies all over town to try and rent his crick from him and set up a goldfish farm!"

"Well, now that was all—"

"And then once you was going to fence off half your place and raise skunks there and go into the fur business along with John Jacob Astor. Wouldn't you have a sweet place? Talk about the slaughter house! On summer nights—wow, pugh!" Frank laughed hilarious, and made appropriate gestures.

"Frank Bell, you're at the table! You act nice or leave," Matie said with frozen dignity.

Mollie was red, but she stood up under it. "That's all right, too, there *is* a fortune in that for the right fellow. I looked that up and I've got bulletins and reports to prove it."

"All I can say is—give me the pigpen!"

"Frank Bell!"

Frank saw, then, that he would have to behave for a while.

To show her disapproval of the whole conversation, Mate began to ask dutifully now about the other Schumachers.

"How are Luisa and Charlie getting along these days?"

The sparkle went out of Mollie's eyes and she looked scowling.

"Oh, the same as they always do! Lu don't have time from five o'clock in the morning to eight o'clock at night to pick all the grass by hand around the trees. Charlie goes back and forth to the office."

Mate, however, would not talk satirically about the two, whom she considered more sensible than Mollie because they stuck to home, although they weren't such good friends of hers.

"I suppose Luisa's got lots of sewing done this summer," she said, primly.

"Oh, yes, she's made over a lot of flour sacks into shirts and nightgowns that neither Charlie nor I will wear, and thinks she's accomplished a lot. Oh, yes, they're both the same as always: everything at our house is."

Mollie's face was dark as she stabbed her fork into her gooseberry pie, that had a sparkling crust of sugar upon the flaky, bubbled crust of dough. She said, defiantly:

"I may go away this winter!"

"Where to?" Mate demanded, with resentful skepticism.

"To Chicago," Mollie answered, pretending to be nonchalant.

"Chicago! What would you do there?"

Frank, a little remorseful for the way he had teased Mollie, and thinking that she had more ability than Mate would ever give her credit for, said, judiciously:

"Well, Chicago's got room for lots of people."

Mate looked as if Mollie had said the South Pole.

"I'm thinking about going there."

Mollie was too eager to unburden herself, however—too helplessly and expansively communicative—to keep up the barren triumph of mystification and reticence.

"Well, I s'pose you'll have a fit when you hear who—"

Then she told them about the letter from Dorrie Parker. No matter what people in White Oak had predicted, Dorrie had been getting on well, after all. She had been working in a beauty parlor, and now some *person* (Mollie went over that very hastily—she didn't want Frank and Mate to know that the person was a man) was going to help her to set herself up in business. She wanted Mollie to come to Chicago and go in with her.

"I'm not crazy about that business," Mollie said. "It always seems to me as if folks ought to have something better to do than just fool with their looks. But I'd kind of like to help out for Dorrie."

As Mollie had expected, Mate had "lots to say." While there was nothing absolutely definite against Dorrie Parker, her reputation had not been good and she had left White Oak under a cloud. There had been rumors of her carrying on with other men at the time of her divorce. Mollie Schumacher was about the only person who still heard from her. Dorrie had written, sentimentally, that Mollie was the only friend she'd ever had in White Oak. (Well, that wasn't true, but maybe it seemed so now.) She wanted to get Mollie out of there. Between them, they could work up a good business.

Frank Bell, however, was inclined to be on Mollie's side—perhaps it was just to oppose Matie.

"Dorrie Parker's a good worker," he declared. "Folks is patronizing those places now."

"Yes, the big fools!" Mollie put in, with a snort.

Frank said that Dorrie might have made a few mistakes, but she was a smart woman—knew where she was headed better than most women did. Mate listened, in silent indignation that he should defend Dorrie and urge Mollie on—she was scatterbrained enough without any urging—to desert her home and "go in with that woman."

"Well now, *that* sounds like a scheme that might work, Mollie," Frank said, in generous approval. "I'd rather polish up folks' fingernails, if I was to choose, than get up meals for skunks."

"Well, I think I'll do it," Mollie said, vigorously, "If only . . ."

"If only what?"

That warm mist filled her dark eyes.

"Oh, well . . . if it wasn't for Charlie and Lu. They needn't think they can stop me! But, I don't know . . . if they should really feel bad about it—if I thought they couldn't get along without me . . ."

The mist gathered into large tears. Frank was astounded. He saw no sense to that at all. With the quarrels that went on in that household, and Luisa doing all the housework anyway, and Charlie Schumacher such a mild soul he could get all the amusement he needed in life out of making those gimcrack bird-houses—! Mate thought it very proper, however, and something that Mollie ought to have been thinking of before.

"I don't know whether this pie's very good," she apologized. "I believe I got a little too much lard. Let me warm up your coffee, Mollie."

"Well, I oughtn't to—coffee upsets me—but then—"

"Oh, have some more!" Frank said. The ready mist had dried from Mollie's eyes. Frank felt happy and convivial. He said to Mate:

"Shall we treat wine?"

Mollie's coming was a fine excuse. Mate never touched Frank's wine. He went down into the cellar, found a bottle, and came in from the kitchen with the two miniature glasses almost slopping over with a deep red brightness that held all the warmth of the late summer—that was like the sparkle of dew in the morning and the grapes growing ripe on the fences and the dark velvety red of the blossom tufts on the sumach. Mollie liked to be a good fellow with Frank—and she liked the looks of the stuff, she said.

"This is my last year's grape. Time to drink it up and make some more. Well, Mollie—good luck!"

"Good luck, boy!" she responded heartily.

They drank.

Mollie, in spite of all the orders she'd meant to take that afternoon, didn't get away from the Bells' when dinner was over. Frank, when he'd had one glass of wine, had to have another; and then he thought about the cigars his cousin in Chicago had sent him for his birthday, and had to have one of those. The wine made him think about making more wine; and that made him remember his old cider press and how he had been wondering if he couldn't get the thing fixed up.

"You know, I'd forgot we even had it. Father used to run it every fall. But then, I don't know, guess it got out of kilter, and it got stuck into that old shed and I never saw it until I went out to look for something else."

("Yes, and you'd find plenty more things if you'd go through those sheds!" Mate put in.)

Mollie had to see the press. She liked to tinker as well as

Frank did.

"Come on, finish up that cigar, Frank; let's go out and have a look," she urged. "I can just take a squint at it before I go. Maybe we can get the thing to working."

She followed Frank out of the back door, calling back to Mate:

"Wait with those dishes, Mate, I'll be in to help you—now, don't you go and do them."

Mollie and Frank went off through the farmyard. The ground was dry and the air was warm and the sun was a glorious gold in the blue September sky. A string of cats, adult and half grown and mere little scampering infants, trailed after Frank. He made pets of the cats, and fed them.

"Oh, stop and give 'em their milk, Frank!" Mollie pleaded. Her eyes grew warm and humid. She had slapped Pete Heim in the face once for beating his old horse. "I can't hear the little beggars mee-owing like that. Here, kitty, come, kitty."

"You won't catch none of them!" Frank told her, with admiration for the adroit elusiveness of the cats. Mollie made a dive for them, and the whole tribe fled at once, with soft vanishing evasion—all but one little tiger with white mittens and round emerald eyes, who stood poised, with eyes glittering, until Mollie's fingers almost touched his whiskers . . . and then was gone, in one flattened furry dive, beneath the woodshed.

"Little villains! Confound 'em!" Mollie said, hotly. She adored cats, but they always ran from her.

Frank laughed uproariously. "You'll never get any o' *them,* Mollie! Not if they don't want you to. They're smart! . . . Well, here's where I dragged the press. I kind of gave it a looking over, but—I don't know, something's out o' whack—I ain't figured out what."

Mollie's eyes darkened into concentration. "Well, now, sir, we're going to find out what's the matter with this thing!"

Both began studying it, Mollie bending over it, and Frank crouching with knees bowed out. He had set the press outside the woodshed, and the pleasant sunshine of early autumn burned down glossily upon their heads as they conjectured and tinkered.

"Think it's this here that needs tightening?"

"I think it is, Frank. Then I think she'll run."

Mate came out when she had finished the dishes and stood watching them. She looked slightly satirical, but she had brought out a hat and a sunbonnet, and she said:

"You better put these on your heads if you're going to stay out here."

The dryness of her tone made them both feel guilty. Mollie exclaimed:

"Say! I wonder what's the time."

"It ain't late," Frank assured her. "Let's finish the job. Course, I hate to take you away from your canvassing—"

"Oh, well," she told him, robustly, "that ain't the only thing on earth. I'd like to see you get this thing to working."

It was late enough, when Mate told them the time. Frank said:

"Well, the afternoon's gone now, anyway, Mollie. Better stay on and have supper with us, and make a day of it."

"I can't!" Mollie cried, in a panic. "I was going to stop at all those places along the road this afternoon. I haven't sold a thing to-day but these cotton stockings and one of my own samples. Well . . . oh, well, why not go the whole hog!"

She threw away her afternoon with splendid recklessness. Her eyes sparkled and she was warm with sunshine and hap-

piness. She and Frank were like two children playing hooky
from school. They tinkered with the cider press for another
hour, coming at last to the conclusion that they couldn't make
it go, anyway.

"But I found out what was wrong with it!" Mollie boasted,
with a triumphant laugh. "I'll look for a bolt when I go through
town, and then Frank can make his cider."

Frank told her, seriously:

"I sure am grateful to you, Mollie. Hope I haven't taken too
much of your time."

She answered generously:

"Oh, shoot, Frank, forget it! It wasn't what I'd planned to
do, but I guess it was just as good as selling a few stockings.
You and Mate might just as well be enjoying some cider this
winter."

She glowed under Frank's praise of her mechanical prowess.

When they had finished with the press, he wanted to take
her to see his melons.

"Here's old Rastus! Why, what's the matter with him?"

"Oh, I don't know, he's hurt his paw some way," Frank
said.

"Rastus! Did the old boy hurt himself? Well, that won't
do!"

As soon as she reached the melon patch, Mollie sat down
on the bare, hot ground, and took the dog's paw in her hands.
The paw was swollen, and sand and burrs were tangled in the
coarse, black fur. Frank told her: "Oh, I guess it'll heal up,
Mollie," impatient to have her look at his melons. But that
wouldn't do, for Mollie. Here was something that called for
help, alive, and more absorbing than the cider press. She made
Rastus go back with them to the house, and then called for

warm water, a cloth, and a darning needle from Mate. Mate thought that was a dreadful fuss to make over a dog. Rastus yelped and snarled, so that Mate shrieked, "Be careful!" and even Frank was worried; but Mollie held him until she had got out the splinter.

"See there, what it was! No wonder! Now, old boy, just a minute—"

She laughed with triumph again. She forced Rastus to stay while she put salve on the wound and bound it up in her best surgical style. Frank laughed at her.

"How long do you think he'll keep that on?"

Still, he and Mate both, although they derided so much to-do over an animal, were glad to find out what was the matter with the dog and to have the splinter out.

"There now!" Mollie cried.

Mate was beginning to get the supper ready. Mollie remembered about the dishes—she was full of contrition and helpfulness.

"But there's always so much. If I'd done that, I couldn't have done the other things."

She insisted on gathering the eggs for Mate. Mate considered that a task: Mollie adored it. She hunted through old boxes with hay pushed into one corner, through folds of the harsh old dusty robe in the ancient cutter, through the mangers and the loft. She carried the eggs in a basket into the house through the low shafts of sunshine. The excitement of all her accomplishments was upon her still, of the praise and gratitude they had yielded her, and she sang, happily, and off the key.

"Well, I certainly didn't think when I stopped in here I was going to stay for supper! But I guess I've done a pretty good day's work of it, after all."

When Mollie came to leave, the glow and triumph of her visit were still upon her. She was taking more plunder with her: eggs, and a glass of fresh jelly, and an old rooster in a gunny sack mysteriously moving and plunging on the seat beside her.

"Now, you keep that sample, Mate," she was urging. "Frank, you try that suit when cold weather comes—you'll never wear anything else, I'll tell you that!"

"We sure are grateful, Mollie, for all the help you've given us—"

"Oh, shoot! Forget it!" But she glowed happily. "I think that press'll run now, Frank, when you get the bolt. Put some more of that salve on the dog's foot. He'll get some good out of it even if he does lick off most of it."

"Aren't you afraid to drive home alone at night?" Mate asked, fearfully.

"No! I enjoy it. There's nothing I like better in this world than to get off in this old car by myself, and get the wheel under my hands, and go it!" Mollie said, with shining eyes.

"Sure, you bet! That's the truth," Frank told her. "Mollie ain't one of these scared she-males that always think she's going to be run away with."

"You bet I'm not!"

She tried the starter, but it had a streak again, and wouldn't go.

"You crank it for her, Frank," Mate said anxiously.

Mollie cried:

"No, I'll crank the old beast, I'm used to it. Here, boy! Give me hold of that crank."

But Frank would not let her go. The car started, and Frank shouted at Mollie above the loud noise of the engine:

"Well, Mollie, we're glad you stopped. And we're sure grateful—"

"Now you forget it! If we can't do a few things for folks once in a while when we get the chance, why, what's the use? Well, I've had a fine day of it—and I'd like to know why that isn't just as good!"

"Sure!" Frank said heartily.

"You're going to get the engine heated," Mate told her.

"Well, good-by, folks!"

"Good-by, Mollie!"

She started with a suddenness that almost killed the engine —recovered, went on—and stuck her head out of the car, to Mate's horror, just as she was turning out of the driveway, to shout back to the dog:

"Good-by, old boy!"

Mate and Frank listened to the loud rattle of the car as it went on through the country stillness.

"Well, sir," Frank said with relish, and with a laugh, "she's a great Mollie!"

He thought over all Mollie's escapades, and the goldfish, and the violets, and laughed again.

"I bet she didn't do fifty cents' worth of business to-day. She'll have to hump when she gets to Chicago with Dorrie! Well, it's a good thing she's going, although I'll hate not to have her come around. Charlie and Luisa, you couldn't move with a derrick. If the town burned up, Charlie Schumacher wouldn't notice it as long as he could go on puttering with those bird houses."

"Well, I don't know what Mollie does so much more!"

"Fudge, Matie, she's got three times the get-up to her! Yes, sir, I'd like to see her to go to Chicago. Those girls haven't got a thing but that old place and what little salary Charlie gets. Now's Mollie's chance. Mollie may be left alone some day."

Frank felt satisfied. At last Mollie had a scheme that wasn't crazy. She was finally going to get to do something.

"She won't go," Mate said calmly.

"Why won't she?" Frank demanded belligerently.

The idea was a fine one. What was to stop Mollie this time?

"Because I know she won't."

Frank stopped to take this in. All at once he had a memory of the darkness of Mollie's eyes, warm and defenseless, and he seemed to see them mist with ready tears. Yes, sir, Mollie was a woman! After all, she was unaccountable. She could do anything for anybody but herself. Then Frank said, as if in defense of his own statements:

"Well, anyway, Mollie gets a darned good time out of it!"

Mate still had her look of small, calm, satisfied wisdom.

The last far-away rattle and hum of the car was lost, now, in the hugeness of the evening, and the crickets took up the sound in a thin, shrill, minor chorus.

Sunset Camp

MRS. GROBATY had the feeling that it must be time for getting up. Back home, it would be. But everything was different here. Even the hours of the day were changed. She couldn't get used to thinking that when it was six here it was eight back there. The light that came in through the drawn curtains of the cabin was different.

Mister was still sleeping and it wouldn't do to waken him. But she was growing more accustomed, now, to getting up first, and by herself. She drew up her legs, hoisted herself, and then crawled out cautiously over his feet. He still slept "on the outside." She stood and shivered a moment on the braided rug that she had made to cozy up the cabin. The floor was cold, but she scurried across it, grabbed up her clothes, and went into the kitchenette where she lighted the gas stove. It wouldn't do to light the fire in the other room until Mister was awake. Besides—although that, too, was only a gas heater —he liked to "make the fire" himself. He liked to keep a few little chores, as many as he was able to do.

At first the kitchenette was chilly. Let folks say what they would about the climate, the nights were certainly cold! Mist veiled a strange landscape of palms, mountains, and eucalyptus trees; and the few furnished kitchen utensils that hung above the stove were clammy. It was not much like the big kitchen with the warm range at home. She missed having her own things to work with.

Still, this was a pretty nice camp. She remembered some where they had stopped on their way out to California. They had water, and their own toilet and shower bath—not that either of them used the shower much; they couldn't get used to that way of bathing. It was nice to think that she didn't have to send Mister clear down town but could just step over to the store and get what she needed in the morning.

And the minute she got outside, she felt better. Maybe it was stirring around a bit. But it was nice here. She had to admit that. At first she couldn't get used to so many people. They had always had their own place at home. Now it was kind of pleasant seeing all the other cabins around her. It was exciting to have folks coming and going all the time. She didn't feel so lost and far away any more. The folks in the store knew her.

"Good morning, Mrs. Grobaty. What will you have?"

My, but there was nice fruit this morning! She and Mister were getting so they lived on fruit. At home, he always wanted just what they had on the place and needn't buy, plums or apples from their trees, or things she had put up for winter. Well, he had to buy things here, and she was glad of it! Oranges and figs and grape fruit—he said they grew out here, and they didn't cost much.

"I'll have a dozen of the oranges, I guess."

She talked to the man—told how Mister had slept—and even gave a kindly glance at the tiger cat that came purring around her skirt. She couldn't remember that Mister had been any hand for cats at home, although they used to have plenty of them around the barn; but he was getting kind of attached to this one. "I guess it won't hurt us to let kitty have a little milk," he said. Papa holding a cat! She would have to write that to the children. It was friendly, though, to have some animals around.

"Yes, you can come along if you want to."

Already the cars were whirring past on the road outside. Land, where were all those people going? But it wasn't long since she and Mister had been some of those people! That was a funny thought, maybe others wondered where *they* were going.

Yes, and she wondered sometimes herself. . . .

"Good morning—good-by!" some people were shouting.

Startled, she looked around. It was the Millers!

"You aren't leaving us!"

"Yes, we're going."

She hadn't thought *they* would go so soon. Here she had just been thinking she was used to the place, and it was changing! The Millers came from back home and they didn't seem to her like strangers. They lived in the very next county.

"Why, I thought you'd be here a good while yet."

"No," Mr. Miller said gayly, "we're off to-day."

My, but that was a shame. She didn't know what she'd do without them. She and Mrs. Miller talked, and tried to think of folks that both of them might know, and when Mister felt well enough, he and Mr. Miller pitched horseshoes. It didn't seem like she and Mister were so far off when they could talk to folks from the next county. But here were the Millers and all their things in the car, and she looking just as excited as he did. Yes, they were going on to L. A., they said. Had to see that before they went back. Might even, Mr. Miller thought, get down for a day into Mexico.

"Land!"

"Well, we ain't so far from there."

So it had been just this little while she had known them!

"Oh, we'll see you back home again. You and the Mister must come over to Oak Grove."

Mrs. Grobaty nodded. But she didn't know about that. Home? When would they ever get home? Maybe never. . . . Her eyes moistened, so that the Millers felt pretty bad for the moment to leave her; and when they had gone, and the dust had settled behind them, she felt almost as if she and Mister were deserted out here among strangers.

She might as well go back to the cabin. The tiger kitty followed. *"You're* not going away, at least," Mrs. Grobaty said. It belonged here. Cats were home bodies—that could be said for them; and it was a little consolation. It seemed as if everybody was leaving. Cars tooting and pulling out all around!— how could Mister keep on sleeping? She rebelled against this transient world, where a tiny while ago she had been feeling so much at home, with the cabins, and the bright geraniums, and the ragged eucalyptus trees. What was going to become of her and Mister? . . . And as she went down the path, she would not look off toward the mountains. Grass was what she wanted, and the old summer flowers, and the garden.

Those folks in Number 40, though, still seemed to be there. The man was out in front of the cabin. "Good mawnin', ma'am," he said. "It's nice to-day, hain't it?" She had thought they were awful queer folks, at first. But now it seemed friendly to have him speak to her.

"Well, I see you're still here."

"Yes, we ain't movin' on yet a while. How's the old man this mawnin'?"

What an awful way to speak of Mister!

But she could see that he meant well by it. "The old woman"

was what he called his wife. And they weren't old folks, either. They had a baby not more than a year old. Baby, children, dog, blankets, coffee pot, frying pans,—what a shiftless lot she had judged them, all packed into that rattletrap Ford, and with no idea of where they would land! Just goin' around a little, he had told her. Might stop somewhere if they liked it. But they'd keep on goin' while the weather was good. "If it hain't cold, what's the use of stoppin'?" She would have had no use for such folks back home.

But it pleased her to have him inquire about Mister. "I think he's a-lookin' better," the man said. He offered to do anything for her that she needed. "While he's a-feelin' so poorly." They were good-hearted folks, at least, even if their ways were so different. Children had come flocking out around him. Dirty! —land, to let them go like that! But there was a wildling, dark-eyed prettiness about them. The baby was cute. She guessed maybe all children were pretty.

She went into her cabin. The cat sat down on the steps and waited.

He wasn't quite awake yet, and she tiptoed across the floor. The little kitchenette was warmer. The clammy damp was drying off the pots and kettles. She felt like making some nice biscuit—felt like doing some real good cooking again. She had learned pretty well, now, to use the little one-burner oven they had bought, although at first she had thought she could never do anything with it. She would make some of those corn meal gems.

She did, and they turned out lovely. If only "he" would wake up now, and they could eat the things while they were good! At home, by this time, both of them would have been up two hours. She moved restlessly about the kitchenette. The sun was

up now, the mist was gone, the air was light and bright above
the mountains. The climate and the easy living seemed to have
put too much liveliness into her. She felt like pitching right
in and fixing up the cabin. Land, was that man never going
to wake up? Their nice breakfast would all be spoiled. Should
she call him? But when she looked into the shaded front
room, saw the slack but bony outline of his old body humped
under the covers, she hadn't the heart to wake him. And what
did the breakfast matter beside his rest! What was she getting
in such a stew about? Didn't they have the whole day before
them?

Still, she couldn't just sit down and twiddle her thumbs,
even if she didn't call Mister. She had to do something with
her nice cooking. She thought of those young folks in the
cabin next door. That little thing didn't look as if she knew
how to do much cooking. The friendliness of the funny man—
it was awful nice of him, offering like that to help her out, a
stranger—that unsolicited friendliness made her feel kindly
toward the whole camp. And then it was a little bit like home,
going over, with some of her nice baking, to the neighbors.

Noise and laughter came to her as she rapped on the door of
the next cabin. She guessed they hadn't heard her. She waited
a moment. How queer to be 'way out here—between the
mountains, the desert, and the sea! When she thought of the
Millers going back home, she wanted her elm trees and her
garden, the settled substantiality of her own house. But all the
same, it was nice to be out here. It was nice to have seen so
many strange things. Even the dusty, ragged eucalyptus grove
was kind of pretty in the sunshine. She might even come to
like these funny trees. Trees were trees wherever they were;
and there were more kinds of them in the world than she had

dreamed of. And these big bright geraniums. . . .

She rapped louder, this time thinking: Why don't they answer? There were queer scuffling noises, stifled laughter, then silence inside. What was going on, in there, she wondered?—and should she wait or go back home? She was about to retreat down the path when the door was cautiously opened. A boy's flushed face was looking out at her, and behind it she had a confused glimpse of a rumpled bed, disordered cabin, blankets on the floor, another boy, a tousled-haired girl in a man's coat just disappearing through the other door. . . .

"Excuse me . . . I just thought you folks might enjoy these gems."

For there seemed nothing to do, now, but offer the things she had come to bring them—make the offer and get away. But she was terribly flustered. What had she got into? Land! The boy was flustered, too. She heard some more smothered laughter.

"I thought your wife—traveling around . . . you folks might not have the chance to do much cooking . . ."

The girl came back through the doorway now, and paused, bright-eyed and uncertain. They seemed to realize now what her errand was. The boy's flushed face grew sheepish and friendly and the girl's bright eyes were wide and pleased, though all of them were still embarrassed. The other boy— if there was another, if there were still others,—was nowhere to be seen.

"Gee—I should say."

"Well, thank you—"

"If you can't use them—"

"I should say we can!"

"Well, I just thought—"

Now they took the gems, voluble with thanks, while she got

away as fast as she could. Land sakes! My goodness! What
kind of a bunch were they? She had never seen anything like
that before. And her scandalized mind recalled details—the
tumbled bed, the two pillows, those blankets on the floor!
Were there three of them or weren't there? Or even more!
She was certain she had seen that other boy. Were any of them
married, and which ones? The girl's short tousled hair, the
scanty little nightgown under that coat . . . she didn't believe
any of them were married! A bunch of crazy children just
running around the country . . .

Mrs. Grobaty was scandalized. Well, folks at home *would*
be! If such things were going on around this place—! She felt
all fluttered and upset. She wanted to wake Mister and tell him
they wouldn't stay here any more. The hundred little green-
painted cabins surrounding her were all hostile and mysterious.
She wanted to get home where she knew folks and knew just
what was what. . . . And off there were the strange blue
mountains, the stretches of desert land with the tumbled rocks
and the cruel cactus, and on the other side the unknown wilderness of the sea. . . .

Mister was waking up when she entered the cabin. She
heard him coughing and saw him hoisted in bed. She wanted
to go to him that moment. She felt she couldn't stand this any
longer. "Henry," she wanted to beg him, "let's go back home."
The Millers gone, nothing fixed, every one coming and going,
and that young bunch that she had just left. . . .

But he was going through his morning repertoire of coughing, wheezing, struggling. She had to sit on the edge of the
bed and wait. Her nerves were still all flustered. She felt as if
she would like to cry. He was absorbed in his illness. She
couldn't turn even to him. His drawn, struggling face was

remote from her. She felt utterly lonely and lost.

He was saying something to her. "Nellie . . ." He was beginning to call her that again. And she was beginning to think
of him as Henry. Her own name in his gasping voice was sweet.
All at once, it made her feel tender and different toward him.
Sitting there beside him, she had a dim remembrance, almost
too distant to be seized, of another time when they had been
in a strange place together. She didn't have the chance, now,
to remember it. He had turned to her, out of his remoteness,
and she had to help him. She fixed his pillows, brought him
water—and the realization of his age and frailty, his gaunt
face and his disheveled gray hair, overwhelmed her other
needs and suffused her loneliness with devotion. By the time
she was through with all she had to do for him, the other
feeling was gone.

"Are you better?"

He was spent and did not answer her. But after a moment,
in the midst of the tumbled bedclothes, she felt the shy, feeble,
trustful pressure of his hand.

"I guess I better fix us some breakfast, Henry. I'll be right
in the other room."

A few tears ran down her cheeks as she bustled about by herself out in the little kitchen. She knew—although she didn't
let herself think of it often—how far gone he was. What did
anything matter to her beside that? All the vigor her healthy
old body had left in it went out to support him. Why should
she worry about other folks? Now she could go back to that
memory—as she lighted the burner under the oven again,
heated up the cooled-off gems, opened the lid of the coffee pot.
It was just after they were married, when they had let the old
home in Pennsylvania, and gone out to Iowa . . . how strange

it had seemed, the trees so small, the houses so new, their farm
so big and rough and lonely—and she hadn't known any of
the folks. . . . Then she had depended upon Henry as the
only sure thing in a wilderness of the unknown. He used to
come into the house, sometimes, from his plowing, just to see
how she was getting along and let her know he wasn't far
away . . . she, a little slender homesick bride, away from her
home and all her people, and learning how to do everything at
once. . . . She squeezed out some of the oranges. Orange juice
was good for him. And why shouldn't they have it if it did
take more fruit? She was going to give it to him no matter
what he said. They were together all by themselves again. If
he needed to be out here, if it did him any good . . . They
didn't need to worry about any one but themselves.

"Nellie! Aren't you coming?"

He got up, after all, for breakfast. He had lighted the gas
and he even fixed up the bed a little—he had learned this
much, that it hurt her not to have things nice.

"Oh, you needn't have done that," she said.

She almost wished he had let the bed alone. She guessed she
could stand it—she'd kept house as she wanted to for enough
years. But with the cretonne curtains pushed back, the sun
coming in, the cabin was real pleasant.

"Muffins!" he said.

"They're corn meal gems. I don't know . . ."

She was going to say "how good they are warmed up again."
But she felt suddenly impatient with her own particular ways.
If he didn't make a fuss about it, why should she? The breakfast was pretty good anyway. Sunshine, light and brilliant,
came through the windows.

"That juice tasted kind o' good," he said.

That was certainly a concession for Mister! It had done him good to pay out a little money on this trip. He knew it—there was a shamefaced look about him as he said that. Was he actually, after all these years, going to let her manage her buying as she thought best? My land, it was almost worth coming out to California!

She got her work in the kitchenette briskly out of the way. Maybe it wasn't worth while fussing with gems. Maybe she'd just buy some of that ready fixed pancake flour instead of thinking she must fix up everything herself. She felt rebellious at her years of cooking—almost as when they were first on the farm, and she used to wish Henry would let everything go and take her into town to the social. If she told the children that, they'd say in triumph—"Mamma, you're getting skittish in your old age!" She would have to hedge and give them reasons, she had been the other way so long. She didn't want to admit that things could change. All she would acknowledge was that she felt better now than she had a little while ago.

When she got through, she looked around for Mister. She didn't want him to go doing too much— Oh, there he was, just out on the step! He was talking to that cat and petting it— thought she didn't hear him. "Was you waitin' for the old man to get up? How's the kitty this morning? Hm? How is it?"

She believed that cat really had been waiting for Henry. She wouldn't have admitted the fondness she herself had shown it earlier this morning. But she liked the sound of Henry's voice as he talked to it confidentially. Long as she'd lived with him, this was something she hadn't known about him.

"Millers left," she called to him.

"What?"

"Millers left. They're starting back home."

"That so?" No comment; but after a moment she heard him murmur to the cat, "Well, we're goin' to stay a while longer. Yes, sir. Don't get scared. We're going to stay a while with the kitty yet."

She thought, "Listen to that man!" But she didn't mind it. It made her smile to herself. Well, if that cat was any company . . .

When she thought about Henry again it was to realize that he had wandered off somewhere. It worried her. It was her business these days to keep an eye on him. She had to put down the magazine she was reading—the folks before them had left a lot of trash in the cabin—and go off in search. The air was so nice that, in spite of her worry, she couldn't seem to do anything but take her time. Then she saw him, sitting on one of the green-painted benches in that little sort of park-like in the center of the camp, talking to some man from goodness knew where. She thought she'd call at first—and then thought she wouldn't disturb him. After all, why shouldn't he do that as well as anything else?

She meant not to look at that fool magazine but a minute longer. It was nice and sunny in the cabin. She just sat there. It seemed funny to think she had felt so upset about being here just a little while ago. The camp had settled into the routine of the day. She looked out, once, to see what kind of a car that was coming. What did it say? Pennsylvania! Where she and Henry had first come from. . . . But that didn't seem to her like home now. "Ioway" did. The farms, the frame houses, the big corn fields, the elm trees and the oak groves—those were "back home." Those very places to which she had thought at first she could never be reconciled. Iowa had been just about as

strange to her once as this outlandish place was now—maybe
more so, it was hard to remember. Folks could get used to more
than they thought. The children that belonged to those queer
people were playing outside in the path. Yes, sir, that man
had been nice!—she didn't care. She thought of that young
lot in the next cabin. They were a crazy get-up. She couldn't
make them out. There was something funny. But even at the
moment, the boy's flush and the brightness of the girl's eyes
under the tousled hair had disarmed her. Not that she was
going to approve of such goings on!—but it wasn't just like it
was back home, either. There were lots of kinds of folks in the
world. Even those Indians she and Mister had seen, in those
mud houses . . . she remembered that woman, how really nice
she'd had it in that room with the funny fireplace—the little kids
were cute, she'd written Mabel—and the woman was kind o'
pretty, too, wearing beads, and those funny kind o' bed sock
things on her feet. She didn't know as she was called upon to
make up her mind about everybody. She eased her conscience,
with a secret rebellion, in that way. No matter what folks
back home might think. . . .

There was just a little square view of blue mountains from
the window. They didn't look so fierce to her from here. She
wanted to write Mabel about these big geraniums. The folks
who kept the camp were nice, they seemed to take a lot of pride
in it.

Well, as long as Mister felt like staying here . . . She didn't
know, after all, any good reason why they shouldn't. She had
admitted to her own mind—although she wouldn't admit it
openly—that there might be something in what the children
had always been telling her: You and papa take a trip. There
isn't anything to keep you. It's just that you think there is . . .

she had a loyal pang at the thought of the house, the windows nailed shut, maybe the garden going to seed . . . she guessed that couldn't get along so well!

But anyway, they were out here. They didn't have to think of the weather, the children, anything but just themselves. She didn't know for how long—maybe Henry . . . but as long as he and she were here together, she didn't know as anything else made so much difference, anyway. And in lots of ways, it was real nice. That young lot might be having a fine time gallivanting. But this was all right, for two old folks like Henry and herself.

She rocked, aware of the mountains, aware of the scarlet geraniums, and began to think what she could fix up for Henry this noon—something easy, but something they would both like. They might as well enjoy whatever they could.

Bᴇʀᴛ went flying over to get May Douglas to come and look at her table. It was all ready now, and she had to show it to some one. There was nobody at home who knew or cared about such things. Everything that she did there was done against indifference or opposition.

"May! Busy? Want to come and see the table now I've got it fixed?"

"Oh, yes!"

May was delighted. She left her ironing where it was and followed Bert with eager excitement. She was one of the people in Shell Spring who stuck up for Bert Statzer. She thought that Bert was a wonder.

"We'll go right through the kitchen. Smells kind of good, don't it? There! Do you like it?"

"Bert!"

May was fairly speechless. She gazed at the table with fervent, faded eyes. It seemed to her the most beautiful thing she had ever seen. She didn't see how Bert managed it!—how she ever thought of such things and how she learned to do them. Bert was just a genius, that was all.

"You really think it looks nice?"

Bert drank in May's admiration thirstily. She knew it didn't amount to much, that May would admire anything she did; but she had to get appreciation from somewhere.

"I think it's just too beautiful for words. You little marvel!"

She hugged Bert's thin, tense little form in fond worship. "I just don't see how you do it!" She sighed.

"Well, I'm glad you think it looks nice." Bert relaxed, with a long gratified sigh; but stiffened again to say to Maynard, who had tagged them into the dining room, "Be careful, Maynard! If you move one of those things—!"

May was looking at everything: the little fringed napkins of pink crepe, the tinted glass goblets that Bert had sent away for, the spray of sweet peas at every place, one pink and then the next one lavender, made of tissue paper—such a pretty idea! She had never seen any napkins like those. Bert went on talking excitedly.

"Well, if it's good enough for these folks, it'll be good enough for any one. I'll think that I've arrived, May!"

"I don't see how it can help—"

"Oh, but they're real big bugs. I've never had any one from Des Moines before. It scares me. This looks nice to us, but those people have all seen things—oh, my! Then, you know, they're going to have that famous writer with them. That's what I'm so excited about. If he likes it, then I thought maybe I could use his name. You know that'll help to get me known —if I can get his recommendation. Like those cold cream ads and everything—they're all doing that. Oh, I'm so excited, May! Feel my hands? Aren't they cold?"

"Why, you poor child!" May took Bert's tense, thin little hands and rubbed and fondled them. "You don't need to feel that way. I don't see how anybody could ask for anything nicer. If *this* isn't good enough for them—"

"Oh, I know, but people like that who have been places and seen things—! Well, I don't care, I've done the best I could. Maynard, look *out!*"

Bert's face was still gratified but screwed with worry. She knew how she really wanted things to look. She wanted flowered curtains instead of these old ones, and little painted tables instead of this big old thing . . . Of course, here was this stuck-in-the-mud little burg always holding her back, and her mother, and Arlie . . . Well, *she* didn't intend to be stuck in the mud, anyway! She had put up her sign where people could see it. "Hillside Inn." It made people in town laugh. They wanted to know where the "hillside" was. But she'd made a go of it so far, all the same.

She burst out: "The only trouble is mother!" And that was true. She couldn't do a thing with mother. Arlie would stay out—he didn't want folks like that to see him in his old working clothes—but mother thought she had to go in and entertain them, just the way she did with any one who came to the house. "I was so ashamed when those people from Cedar Rapids were here. The way mother came in! Now, of course May, I know mother's good as gold and means it the best in the world, but what do folks like that think of her? I can't get her to fix herself up or anything. She doesn't understand. 'Ach, well, if they don't like the way I look, then they can look at something they do like.' That's the way she is. She doesn't *see* things. She doesn't know one person from another —doesn't see why these people are any different from any others." May kept making little distressed murmurs. She did know how Mrs. Hohenschuh was. "Now, May, I went and bought a nice up-to-date dress for her, like people are wearing, when I was in Dubuque last. She'd look awfully nice in it if she'd wear it. But do you think she will? No, sir. Won't so much as put it on. 'Ach, I never wore anything like that. I'll stick to what I been wearing.' You don't know, May—" Bert's voice tightened into bitterness—"nobody does, they all talk about how good-hearted mother is, and everything like that, they don't know how stubborn she is. Honestly, if mother didn't want to move, I don't believe a motor-cycle running into her could budge her one inch! She's just hopeless."

"Oh well, Bert, it'll come out," May said soothingly.

"I suppose. But she gives these people who come here the wrong idea. I don't want them to think we're all like she is."

"Oh, well, I guess they won't think that about you!"

Bert felt encouraged after May's visit. It was nice to have somebody appreciate what she was trying to do, anyway! She was excited, flying around the kitchen, doing the last few things, watching out for Maynard so that he would keep his little suit clean. Where was mother?—she thought in exasperation. Oh, there!—out in the garden—*digging!* Why didn't she come in and get ready? Bert had no time now to run out after her. Bert snatched a look at the clock. Almost time for them to get here! Oh dear, but she did want everything just right. What was mother thinking of? Did she want to get caught looking like that? She was hopeless. "Maynard, if you don't keep away from that table—!" Bert thought she would go crazy.

Then mother came serenely waddling in.

"Want I should help?"

"Not at this late date!"

That was all Bert was going to say. But she couldn't hold in, even if it was more of a triumph to be simply cold and cutting and bitter; she had to let it all out.

"Here I am working, trying to get everything nice, with everything all fixed, and you don't care, you just go on with your old digging out there in the garden, and don't see or care!"

Mrs. Hohenschuh looked abashed. "Ach, well," she began; then she retorted: "Well, I ain't wanted around here. You wouldn't be satisfied anyway with things the way I'd do them. Ach, all this fuss! What are you making all this fuss about? All this business!"

She finished with an angry mutter, and went waddling off to the door. Bert didn't know whether she was going to change her clothes or not. Well, if she wanted them to catch her looking that way, if she didn't care, didn't know any better . . . Bert was left weak and trembling with anger. She flew about the kitchen, put a few more nuts on each plate of salad, with shaking fingers changed her old apron for the bright green smock she was going to wear to do the serving . . . it was what they were wearing; it was like the one she'd seen in the photograph of "Betty Lee's Tearoom" in the cooking magazine. . . .

She went into the dining room. The shining glasses twinkled up at her, the sweet peas were rosy and stiff, the dishes looked so nice, the little napkins were so pretty . . . was everything right? She had got ideas wherever she could, but was she sure? It had to be right! Everything was so lovely. Her anger and fear changed into a shining glory. The whole table dazzled before her eyes. She caught hold of Maynard who was tagging her. "Look, Maynard!" she cried. "Isn't our table pretty?" She snatched a kiss from him in her trembling happiness.

Then she heard a car outside on the road. The people were coming!

A large green car rolled up to the cement block that still stayed in the thick grass beside the road as a relic of horse and buggy days. Bert in her green smock stood waiting, a tense dynamic little person with her thin face and shining black eyes and short black hair threaded with early white. It seemed to her that it took the people a long time to get out of the car. She had time to wonder and to agonize over the place—the old frame house . . . she wished they could have it stuccoed . . . what would these people think? Then the people were out and coming up the walk, and she had just a confused, eager sight of two men and three women. . . .

One man was in advance. A large man with a rosy face and shell-rimmed glasses, smooth blackish-gray hair—he came toward her smiling. That must be the one who had ordered the dinner, the Des Moines man, Mr. Drayton.

"Mrs. Statzer?" Yes, that was who he was. "We heard you gave such good meals here that we thought we'd have to stop and try one of them."

Bert was so pleased and flattered that she scarcely heard his introductions—forgot the names just as soon as he mentioned them. She had been trying from the first to pick out the writer. It was that tall man, then, with the thick gray hair. She hadn't expected him to look like that, somehow. She wanted to show him that she knew who he was, even if most of the people here in town didn't. They hadn't known whom she had meant when she said Harry Whetstone was coming here. She held out her hand, alert and eager.

"Oh, this is the writer, is it? I certainly was honored when I heard we were going to entertain you. I haven't read any of your works yet, but I intend to—I don't get much time for reading . . ."

"No hurry, no hurry," the writer said with affable nonchalance.

She was looking, too, at the women. She hadn't got the

relationships between the women and men figured out yet. One looked older, one wore that smart little green dress and hat, and then there was that one who might be any age—where did *she* come in? They were looking around. "Isn't this lovely!" one of them was saying. What did they mean? Bert's brilliant eyes were watching them. She wondered what they thought of her sign. People in town made such fun of that sign. They were pointing to that terrible old brown tile in which mother had some geraniums planted. "Look, Harry! Isn't that lovely?" They couldn't really think it was *lovely*. Lovely had a different, suspicious meaning as these women used it. Bert's eyes were devouring the details of their clothes. She led them into the house. She was burning with anxiety, sensitiveness, eagerness. She knew how many things were wrong.

"I suppose you people would like to wash a little after your drive. We haven't any bathroom, I'm sorry to say, we want to have one, but this town is so slow, they've never piped the water out this far . . . But if you don't mind just washing in the old-fashioned washbowls—"

She hated that so. But they were nice about it. She was relieved.

"You know you're out in the country," she said with a nervous laugh, "and you have to take us the way you find us."

She ushered the women into her best bedroom, the guest room off the parlor. This was the one room in the house in which she could take some pride. She didn't mind showing them this room. She had fixed it up with furniture she had enameled herself, and white curtains with green ruffles, and she had put the stencil on the walls—all after the plan of the Model Bedroom she had seen in the household magazine for which she had taken subscriptions last winter.

"Now, if you'll just take off your hats and put them wherever you find a place—" She was eager and flustered. "I'm afraid I'll have to take you gentlemen upstairs."

"Well, now, can't we go out and give our hands a little shower bath under the pump?" Mr. Drayton asked genially.

Bert was horrified. He meant it for a joke, though. She was ashamed to take them up to her old room, full of horrid old dark furniture . . . was afraid, too, as she sped up the steep stairs ahead of them, although she knew it was all right, she had been up at four o'clock cleaning and getting the house ready. She banged the door of her mother's room shut as she went past. "Now I think you'll find everything—" She ran down.

The women were murmuring in the bedroom. She heard a soft laugh. She lingered in the front room, sensitive and alert, but she couldn't hear. The smartness of their clothes actually hurt her, showed her all sorts of unsuspected deficiencies in herself—although it pleased and gratified her too.

But when she went into the dining room and saw the table, she was exultant again. "If you'll excuse me," she called, "I'm afraid I'll have to be in the kitchen." They answered: "Oh, certainly!" She was in a flush of happiness. They were nice! Oh, dear. She had forgotten to ask the author to write in her visitors' book. Well, she would! And yet she was obscurely hurt and smarting. She wasn't sure they weren't laughing.

In the kitchen, she hustled about. Arlie had come in and was washing his hands at the wooden sink. "Well, are they here?" he asked. He didn't exactly like their coming, or to have Bert always fussing around with things like this—he didn't see why she wanted to do it—but then, he was all right, he kept out of the way. Bert was getting the roast chicken out of the oven. Roasted not fried. She thought that was what these people were used to. "People in the East never think of *frying* chicken." She remembered hearing Mrs. Elliott say that when she came home from the East. Bert wanted these people to be able to say they had eaten as good a meal here in the Hillside Inn as ever they had got in any city restaurant. She had taken recipes out of cooking magazines. She was so excited now that the ordeal was on that she felt herself working in a kind of tense calm. She could manage everything, nothing could upset her. She gave Arlie his dinner in the back kitchen. These people, with this famous author, were even a notch above those wealthy people from Dubuque whom she had served, and who had told Mr. Drayton about the place. If she could make *them* satisfied—!

"You can come in to dinner now."

There was a moment of quiet and formality as she seated them. They didn't exclaim like those Dubuque people. "Well, well, I didn't know we were going to find a first-class hotel here in Shell Spring!" the Dubuque man had cried. But then, these were a different kind of people. She served them, wondering if she oughtn't to have got in Donna Peterson to help her—but then, Donna wouldn't "know," and she wanted things right. She didn't talk as she was serving. She tried to remember what things should go to the right and what to the left. When she went out into the kitchen, she ordered Maynard to keep back. She was going to bring him in after the meal, all dressed up in his new little suit, and just introduce him. "This is my little boy Maynard." She had read somewhere that that was the way people did other places.

Through her preoccupation with the food and the serving —wondering if everything tasted just right—she heard snatches of the conversation. It was low-toned. The people seemed a little tired, maybe from that long drive. "Well, this is familiar." What did they mean by that? Did they like the little napkins or were they laughing at them? But those napkins were exactly the kind that were used in all the tearooms now! They must be right. "Standardization, I tell you. It gets into all corners." That meant nothing to Bert. They certainly must like these salads that May Douglas had said were simply too beautiful to be eaten. Nice salads were things people here in town didn't want to fuss with—"all those do-dads," mother said. The people were all affable and talking among themselves, and yet Bert could sense that the dinner didn't seem to be going just exactly as it should, and she couldn't see why. Her thin cheeks were flushed. In the kitchen, it was as if she were working in a vacuum, not in that shining flush of triumph she knew and craved. How fast everything was going—how soon this great dinner would be over!

Mrs. Hohenschuh had come into the kitchen from the back way. "Mother, you went and put on that old percale dress of yours, and I had that new one all laid out for you ready!" That seemed the crowning catastrophe. Bert suddenly began to tremble with anger. When she came into the kitchen the next time, she whispered furiously. "You aren't going to let those people see you in that! Since you had to go put it on, just to be stubborn, you can stay out of sight." How could she ever get anywhere with all this family to pull up after her? Mother looked like an old farm woman. Bert felt trembly and ready to cry and could scarcely bear to hear the quiet sound of the voices in the dining room.

The coffee cups were all set out on the little old sewing table that she was using for a serving table. She was going to serve her coffee with dessert, the right way. "Ach, let 'em have their coffee!" Mrs. Hohenschuh pleaded. She thought it was terrible to deprive people of coffee all through a meal. She didn't much mind Bert's reproaches, either. "Ach, Bert, she always gets so cross when she's got anything to do, I don't know." The old lady made off into the garden. But Bert knew how mother was. It would be a miracle if she let any people get away without talking to them—and probably telling them the whole family history!

Bert took in the fragrant coffee and the homemade ice cream. They *must* like that. They did, too. They were much more complimentary. The woman in the cute green dress (she didn't seem to be the author's wife, after all; that was the one that didn't look nearly so much like "somebody"—it surprised Bert) said very flatteringly: "What delicious ice cream! Did you make it yourself?" The older woman—that was Mrs. Drayton—smiled up at Bert. They all praised the ice cream. The talk was freer now. The author seemed to be saying the least of any of them, though. That seemed funny to Bert. Mr. Drayton was lots more talkative and full of fun—peppier. She bet he could write awfully good stories, better than the other one, if he just wanted to.

She was almost happy, when she happened to look out of the window and saw mother climbing up from the cellarway outside, lugging something—a bottle! Oh, for . . . Before she got any chance to get out to the kitchen, the old lady came shy but beaming into the room, with a great big bottle of that dandelion wine. Bert was in torment. As if these people cared for anything like that!

But there mother stood and there was nothing to do but introduce her. Bert suffered agony. It was all the worse, somehow, that they were being so polite and nice. "This is my mother." Mother began to beam at that. She loved to entertain people . . . that was all right, of course, but then she had never learned that people didn't do things the way she used to any more.

And mother was starting right in.

"Well, I thought it was mean you folks had to go all that time without your coffee, so I just brought you something else to drink." That awful old dandelion wine—mother was so proud of it! Bert hated it. "If you ain't afraid somebody's going to get after you—ach, it's all so funny these days—maybe you'll take a little drink of this wine. It's dandelion. I made it."

Bert couldn't stand it. She made for the kitchen. She sat down there, clenched her fists, and felt that she would actually fly to pieces.

The voices were louder in the dining room. She heard delighted laughter. Yes, now mother had some folks there, she had an audience, and she was just laying herself out for them —Bert knew how! She burned with humiliation. The whole thing was spoiled. How could anybody in this town try to do things the way they ought to be done?

Her mother came smiling out to the kitchen.

"Where are them little glasses gone?"

"Mother, why did you have to go in there with that stuff?"

"Ach, what are you fussing about? They like it."

After a while, Bert got up and began feverishly to get the messy plates cleaned off and stacked together. She couldn't eat a thing herself, not even good little crisp bits of chicken that were left. A lump in her throat was choking her. Mother had hold of them now. She heard them leave the dining room, and then the whole party trailed past the kitchen windows. Mother was waddling in the lead. She was going to take the whole bunch out and show them her flower beds.

Maynard was whining. "Are you going to take me in and introduce me, mother?"

Bert looked at him, cold and remote.

"No. I'm not going to introduce *any*-body."

They were all out in the garden. Mrs. Hohenschuh always thought it her duty as a hostess to take her guests out and show them everything she had. Here where she felt that she "had things nice," too—this place in town which she and Mr. Hohenschuh had bought when they moved in from the country —she could take real enjoyment with visitors . . . even if Bert did go on about the place and say how behind the times it was now. But it was a long time since she had got hold of any people as appreciative as these. Most folks came to see Bert. They only pretended to like the kind of things she had in her garden. These people were really enjoying it. Mrs. Hohenschuh expanded.

"Well, I don't know as there's anything you folks'll care much about looking at—" (she didn't mean that; she said it in a rich, comfortable tone)—"I only got the same old kind of flowers I've always had, they ain't any of these new-fangled kinds with fancy names here—"

"Oh, we adore seeing them!" the woman in the green dress cried enthusiastically.

Mrs. Hohenschuh beamed. "Well, I think they're pretty nice, they suit me, but there's lots of folks nowadays wants different things, I guess. Ja. Anyway, that don't worry me. I let 'em talk. I go on doing things the way I want to."

The people all laughed and she was gratified.

"Well, here's what I got! I put in all these things myself. Bert, she don't want to bother. She's got too many irons in the fire all the time."

"This is lovely!"

Mrs. Hohenschuh stood fat and beaming while they looked and wandered about. She thought her garden was pretty nice —ja, you bet she did! And these folks all seemed to think so too. Why, they was awful nice folks! Why had Bert got so fussed up over having them here for dinner? Why, they was real nice and common! That one in the green dress (she was older than she wanted to let on, too, Mrs. Hohenschuh shrewdly judged) did the most running around and palavering! but those other two, that husband and wife, enjoyed things just as much. The man in the glasses was *real* nice. Well, so was his wife, although she didn't have so much to say. But those other two, she kind of liked the best of the bunch. The woman was real sensible, the things she said and the questions she asked! and the man kind of trailed around after the others, and looked at things on his own account, the way Mrs. Hohenschuh liked to have folks do. That showed he wasn't putting it on, he was really enjoying himself.

Along with her answers and her explanations, Mrs. Hohenschuh managed to get in a good part of the family history. Bert had a fit when she told things like that; but Mrs. Hohenschuh never felt right until she'd . . . well, kind of given folks the facts and the right idea about the family. They'd hear it all anyway, so she might as well tell it herself.

"Have you had your garden long, Mrs. Hohenschuh?"

"Ja, ever since we moved into town. That's—how long is it a'ready?—ach, it's twenty years, I guess! Bert, she was only just in high school, then. That was partly why we come. The boys, they didn't get to finish, but Pa he said Bert was to get her diploma, he was going to see to it, she was always the smartest, anyway. Ja, how old was Bert then? She was seventeen, I guess. She's thirty-seven now. Ja, she's such a thin little sliver, I don't know, women seems to want to be that way now, but she's thirty-seven! Her and Arlie's been married twelve years a'ready —and then this here little fellow's all they've got! Ach, I don't know!"

As she talked, all in her deep comfortable voice rich with chuckles and drolleries of German inflection, she waddled about among the flower beds, pointing out this kind and that. "These? Moss roses, I call 'em. I guess that ain't the right name, some folks say not, but they grow just the same—ain't that so? Ja, the old lady Douglas over there, when she was living, she had to have the right names for all her plants, but I told her mine grew better'n hers did if I did call 'em wrong! Ach, these names I know 'em by, them are the ones I like to call 'em!" The moss roses in their flat matted bed on the hot earth were gay spots of scarlet and crimson and yellow and cerise and white. They made one of the women think of the colors in old-fashioned patchwork quilts, she said.

"She's got the real old honest-to-God peppermint! I haven't smelled any of that for years. Come here, Mary!"

"Peppermint? Ja! That I always have. That I like too."

The woman in the green dress came running and clutched the other younger woman. "Come here, Jean! I want to show you. The pump! Isn't that just right? And see here—all these little flower pots set out and slips started in them . . . just see, this foliage stuff, this old red and green funny leaf stuff, my grandmother used to have that. And look back there! One of those great big green wire flower stands that I suppose used to

stand in the bay window. Didn't you just *yearn* to take your
dolls promenading on that, and they wouldn't let you, because
you might spoil the plants? Isn't this *per*-fect?" Mrs. Hohenschuh had told them, "Ja, sure, you look around anywhere you
want to, what's the use of hiding what you got?" Charlie Drayton was enjoying the old lady's naïve revelations, but the other
man lounged about poking into the woodshed where the light
fell dim and dusty through a little square window high up
in the wall, and into a tool shed where pans of seeds were set
about in the midst of a clutter of ancient furniture. It was like
going back thirty years.

There was a little apple orchard at the side, grown up to tall
grass now; and there, on one of his silent excursions, he discovered a two-foot china troll plated down in a tiny hollow
with grass grown about his base as it binds in ancient tomb-
stones, and a little casual offering of fallen apples about his
chipped feet. He stood looking at it. The woman in the green
dress saw him and came running over.

"What have you found, Harry? *Oh!* Oh, isn't that *mar-
velous?* Oh, Mrs. Hohenschuh, we've found something simply
wonderful, won't you tell us what that is?"

Mrs. Hohenschuh wandered over. "That? Ach, is that old
thing still out there? Ja, it's funny, but then, I don't know . . .
Pa, he was the one that got that thing."

"It's German, isn't it?"

"Ja, it's German, all right. Pa, he come from the old country, he come over here when he was only eighteen years old, he
had just twenty dollars when he landed in this country. Ja, it's
German, is what it is. Pa, he always wanted to fix up the back
yard like the places he'd seen in the old country—that was why
he got this funny fellow, that was one reason we moved into

town when we did, because Pa wanted to fix up a place . . .
ja, and then we hadn't lived here but a year or two when Pa
got killed. He got run over, he was thinking of things the
way he always done, and didn't hear the train coming . . .
ja, that's the way of it!" But after a moment, while they all
stood about her soberly, she roused herself and went on. "Bert,
she always had a fit over that fellow. She was the one to put
him out of the front yard and lugged him out here. But I don't
know—" Mrs. Hohenschuh chuckled—"I always kind of liked
the little fellow. Maybe because Pa thought so much of him.
Well, I guess he's where she ain't likely to find him. She's too
busy inside there to fool around out here much. I'm the one
does that."

Slowly, Mrs. Hohenschuh in the lead, they trailed away
from the orchard. The troll, with his colors faded to dim faint
tints and curls chipped off his beard, stood smiling a one-sided
but jovial smile at the rotting apples about his broken feet
that had almost grown into the orchard ground.

Mrs. Hohenschuh picked some of each kind of flowers for
every person. "Hold on, now! You ain't got any of the pansies
yet." A circle of sticks set upright—little thin sticks with flak-
ing bark—enclosed the massed, butterfly colors of the pansies.
The tiger lilies grew in a straggling bunch tied with twine.
"Pick yourself some if you like 'em. Go ahead!" What else were
the flowers here for? "Here's a color you ain't got if you like
them zinnies, Mrs. . . . well, you'll have to excuse me. I can't
remember all you folkses' names." The sun shone down brightly
on the garden, bringing out the hot colors of the moss roses,
throwing clear antique shadows from the grape arbor, glinting
and losing itself in coolness in the thick wet grass around the
pump through which silent little streams of water soaked

slowly. They all had a drink before they went into the house. The sides of the glass were frosted with wet. The family story was twined with their wanderings among the little paths of the garden, tangled with the bright colors of the flowers, and brightened over with sunshine.

The house seemed cool when they went inside.

"Oh, you don't want to go yet! Come in and set awhile and let's finish our visit."

Mrs. Hohenschuh led them into the parlor.

"There's lots of things you ain't seen yet."

Mrs. Drayton was tired, even Mr. Drayton—although still genial—was ready to stop; but the other three seemed insatiable. Bert had heard her mother's invitation and burned with helpless shame. What else was mother going to show? And it was hopeless to try to lead her off now. Bert followed the others into the front room.

"I'll show you Pa's picture, Mr. . . . ach, that name's gone again! Well, I guess you know I mean you, don't you? Sure! That's right."

She got down that old faded purple plush album that held all the family pictures—Bert and the boys when they were youngsters, Mr. Hohenschuh when he first came to this country, wedding pictures of hired men. The two younger women sat eagerly close to her, the writer looked at all the pictures with a gravity that Bert couldn't fathom, Mr. Drayton laughed and made funny remarks about the clothes that pleased mother, and Mrs. Drayton looked at the pictures last with a pleased but tired smile; she wasn't quite in all the things the others were, Bert thought. "Ja, look at that one now! Ain't he funny-looking though? He was a cousin of mine. Ja, now they all look funny." Bert sat and suffered. Maynard sidled in. He couldn't give up the promise of being introduced. They were all nice to him. The author showed him a funny pin he had, carved by the Indians, and the women all smiled at him. But they went on making that fuss over mother.

When she had showed them the photographs, she had to let them see her other things: the shells and the "curios" that she prized so, and that she kept on a shelf in the bookcase. "Look here! Did you ever see anything like this before?" How could they act so pleased, unless they were just false and putting it on to get mother to make a fool of herself? Bert could have cried. That shell! Of course they'd seen shells. They'd been everywhere. Those old feathers from the tail of the peacock they used to have out on the farm, the cocoanut husk, that big long German pipe, the glass paper-weight with the snowfall inside. What else could she find to show them? They were asking about fancy work. Did she ever make the real old knitted lace? Ja, not so much knit' as crotchet', though—wait she'd show them! It would be just like her to ask them to all go up to her room with her and look through those terrible drawers —and if she did that! Bert was ready to kill herself. That room of mother's (and it wasn't any use talking to her about it, Bert couldn't make her do a *thing*) with dresses hanging on nails, and quilts piled up in the corner, drawers filled with junk—a perfect museum!

Well, they weren't paying any attention to her and Maynard anyway, so Bert went back to the dining room. She might as well finish with the table. . . . At least they were staying a long time and seemed to be enjoying themselves. In that way, she supposed the dinner was a success. But she couldn't understand them. It was she to whom they ought to be paying attention—she who appreciated them, and knew how different they

were, and wanted to be like them; they couldn't really mean
it when they made such a fuss over mother? Why should they?
They must be laughing at her. What on earth could they see in
all this old junk? It was so perverse and contrary and cruel
that she wanted to cry. All the very awfullest things in the
house—things *no*-body had any more! What kind of an idea
of the town would they get? She looked into the parlor, and
there was mother getting out all her old fancy work—that
terrible piece, that huge table spread, with horses and dogs and
cows and roosters crotcheted into it . . . and they were saying
"lovely"! She heard them.

"That dress. Isn't it perfect? The real thing."

"Oh, she's a jewel!"

"Lovely!"

They were going at last. They were very nice to Bert then.
The women sought her out in the dining room. "Such a wonderful dinner you gave us!"

"Well, I'm glad you liked it. I didn't know . . ."

She followed them into the parlor, feeling appeased and excited again, even though she seemed to scent a tactful patronage. But they were all complimenting her now, and she drank
in the praise, eagerly, but afraid to believe they meant it.

Mr. Drayton had taken her aside. "And what do we owe you
for this fine meal you gave us?" he asked her in a low, genial
tone.

"Well . . . a dollar apiece." Bert said firmly. She blushed,
but held her ground. She had heard that all the city tearooms
charged a dollar and a quarter now. Of course, she couldn't
ask quite as much as a city tearoom, that had everything just
up to snuff; but her dinner was good and she knew it, and

she was going to stick to business. He didn't seem to think that she was charging them too much, however. He counted out some bills and handed them right over to her. But when she came to look at them, there were too many—a five and an extra one!

"Oh, I can't—why, you've given me—"

He tapped her shoulder. "That's all right. Don't notice it. Doesn't begin to pay for the entertainment we've had here."

She still protested, flushed and happy, but he wouldn't listen to her; so she guessed there was nothing else for her to do. . . .

She hadn't forgotten about the visitor's book. She got it out now. All the tearooms in the East had those, Mrs. Elliott had said. She had seen several famous names in one place where she had eaten. It advertised the place; and then it was an honor, too, to think such people had eaten there. Bert was a little bashful but determined.

"I hope you don't mind before you go." She laid the new visitors' book, a notebook with black covers that she had bought at the drug-store, before the author. "I'd like to have you put your name in my book so other folks can see you've been here."

He didn't seem very much flattered about it, she thought, but anyway he wasn't going to refuse. How funny! She would have thought it would please folks to be asked to do things like that. The others teased him a little. "You can't escape 'em, Harry!" They seemed to think it was sort of a joke. Bert stood flushed, waiting and determined. She was satisfied when she saw, at the very beginning of her book, the small firm signature: "Harry Whetstone."

"How little you write!" she cried in amazement. It was funny for a man to write so small as that. "Now I want all the rest of you folks' names."

They protested.

"Yes I do. You're all along with him."

"Well, go on, girls. Sign yourselves," Mr. Drayton commanded.

They all signed. Mrs. Drayton blushed when she did it.

Bert wasn't through with the author yet. Before she let him go, she was going to get all she'd meant to get out of him.

"I wondered if you'd let me use your name, Mr. Whetstone."

He still had that funny, kind of bored way. His wife was really nicer.

"Say he ate with a large appetite, even mightier than usual," Mrs. Whetstone said.

But it seemed to Bert they were all amused.

She wanted to talk to the writer about his books. "You know I never met an author before," she said. "I've always been wanting to, because—" she flushed—"well, I've always wanted to write myself. I always thought I could if I just had the time to do it."

"Oh, don't," he assured her solemnly. But he wasn't as impressed as she had thought he would be. "It's much better to cook biscuits like those we devoured this noon. Infinitely better to make dandelion wine like your mother."

He was joking, of course. But Bert didn't quite like it. She had meant what she said, seriously. It was something she'd thought about all her life. He didn't seem to her a bit like an author.

Mrs. Hohenschuh came into the house, waddling and breathless.

"Dandelion wine!" she cried. "Ja, if you liked that, then you come back here and you'll get some of the wild grape I'm going to make this fall. You come and let *me* get you up a dinner. I'll give you some real genuine fried chicken and you won't have to wait all meal for your coffee."

They all laughed. They seemed to think that was *funny*.

She had been out in the garden again. She had dug up some plants, and wrapped them in newspapers and brought some slips for the women to take along and set out.

"You take these along with you. Oh sure, you go ahead!"

She parceled them out right and left and gave directions. The people went out to the car swamped with packages. They were thanking Mrs. Hohenschuh profusely, and promising to do just what she told them, laughing delightedly at everything she said. She went right up to the car with them, as she always did with people who were leaving. Bert stood back with the bills wadded up in her hot hand, and with Maynard beside her. They had complimented her on the dinner, and said nice things to her, done all that she had asked them: but she stood hungering for just the one thing they hadn't said to her.

"Good-by, Mrs. Hohenschuh. We certainly have enjoyed this."

"You come again. All of you. You just drop in any time you feel like it."

"Good-by, Mrs. Statzer! . . . And Maynard!"

But they had to remember to say that.

Mr. Drayton took the wheel, the big engine started humming, the car rolled ahead. They waved—they were going. . . .

"Well!" Mrs. Hohenschuh said gratified, climbing back onto the walk. "They was real nice folks! I don't see why you made such a fuss over having them."

"Look at your hands, mother!" Bert said bitterly.

"Ja, I know. I dug up them plants. Well, it don't matter now, they're gone anyway."

She waddled serenely to the house.

Bert stood looking after the car. She didn't know just what she had expected this dinner to mean to her. Anyway, she hadn't thought that everything would be just as it was before, that mother would be the one they got on with (mother, who hadn't really lifted her hand!), that she would just go back into the house with a lot of dirty dishes to wash. She didn't yet see what their idea was.

Spinster and Cat

THE birds were making a great chatter in the vines outside. As Toldine dressed she kept an anxious eye on the window. She went downstairs and opened the back door to the fresh green summer morning. Sammie was not on the wash bench, his place. Toldine looked anxiously over the dewy grass with its long early shadows under the apple trees. She thought of all the other cats that on some tragic morning hadn't appeared, and wondered how long they were going to let her keep this one. Then she heard "Miaow!" from inside the house. He had slipped past her skirts into the kitchen.

"Ach, you was here then?" she cried. "Was that why the birds made all that fuss—over you?"

"M'yow!" he answered her and jumped up against her skirt to beg her to hurry.

But before she fed him both must stop for their invariable morning rite of greeting. Toldine crouched and put her hand on his head, and Sammie lifted his head a little to meet the curving touch. The sleek gray floss of the fur was warm under the dry roughness of the palm; and beneath the pressure of the knotted fingers the fur was flattened down in streaks and then, rising softly back, crackled with fine electric life. A look of deep affection came from the mysterious, unchanging beryl-brightness of the eyes. The head ducked, the body arched and curved, Sammie began to purr, purr loudly.

"Was you glad to get in?" Then she accused him, "Where

you been? You been somewhere!" She tried to pull off the dry
cobweb thread that had entwined two of his whiskers. "You
don't like that! Ach, then you shouldn't get into such places,
come in with your whiskers mussed up like a stray cat. You
won't say where you been!" Then she crouched lower, stroked
his head again and her voice softened to the mysterious murmur of affection between them. The beryl eyes looked brightly
back at her. The purr deepened into a sound lower, richer,
more continuous, at the very heart of contentment. "Here he
is again! Got his paws wet. Ain't you ashamed to come in with
wet paws? No, you ain't ashamed of nothing, are you? Ja, he's a
nice fellow, ja, he's a fine fellow."

And then, all at once, Sammie was through. He wanted just
that much and no more. He began to claw at Toldine's skirt,
with piteous little reminders, as she rose staggering to her feet.

"You'll get something. You needn't be afraid. You don't get
left out. Not in this house. I guess you didn't catch nothing.
Had poor mousing."

When he saw her begin her neat little morning preparations
he was ready to be satisfied. She went out to the back step for
the bundle of twigs that she had gathered from all over the two
lawns the night before and broken into even lengths. She took
off the lid of the cook stove, with the incurved ribs of iron
showing clean and ashy-gray, put in the two-days-old newspaper, laid a criss-cross pile of twigs over that, and then, at the
right moment, just when the twigs began to crackle, she bent
to the hod and grabbed out three sticks of rough kindling from
the radio crate Carl had chopped up and let her have. If she
did this exactly as it should be done she needed no coal for her
morning coffee. When the fire was going, she put on the clean
but battered blue-granite coffeepot with the coffee left over

from yesterday noon. She got a fresh pail of slopping, shining water. Then she took down the miniature pie tin which she called "the cat's dish," filled it two-thirds full of milk, and set it on the stove after the coffee had boiled and when there was just enough heat left to warm it. "Ja, he has to have his milk warm. He won't take it cold," she said commending him.

Now came her little arrangements in the dining room. She laid a clean newspaper over her place on the Japanese tablecloth, put on her plate, one of the old German silver knives and one of the spoons (it wasn't necessary to dirty a fork in the morning), set on two slices of bread and a little saucer of butter. When there were berries in the garden she had berries. She laid the other half of the newspaper down on the rug beside her chair. Sammie marched over to that, yawning. Then she broke a little bread into Sammie's dish and brought it down to the newspaper, holding it away from him carefully when he jumped up too eagerly. He had been fairly patient before, but now that his milk was within reach he set up a terrible commotion of miaowing.

"Ach, you can't be that hungry! Well, now you got it."

She set down the pie tin, and then she heard with complacent pleasure the dainty, rapid, skillful sound of his lapping. The sound was "company."

She poured out her coffee, spread her bread, cut an oblong piece of cheese into four exact slices with her knife. She spread out her last night's Dubuque paper which Carl's little girl had brought over to her after Carl had finished with it, flattened it out with her hand, and began to read the society items which she had saved until this morning. She took a thick reading glass and moved it slowly from item to item. "Mr. and Mrs. G. Armstrong Davis announce the engagement of their daughter,

Ethelyn . . ." No matter how people kept after her, she could keep from spending her money for glasses. From time to time she laid a strip of cheese on a strip of bread, took a bite, a drink of coffee. Petunias were crowded into a jelly glass on the table, and a faint fragrance came from them. Woman and cat ate in almost noiseless contentment.

But when she was half way through, her sister Henrietta came over from next door with a plate of cookies and a hunk of suet.

"Ach, you're eating a'ready! You're earlier than them over there. Ja, I don't know, Dorothy she ain't one to get up, and Carl now he's getting to be just like her. I brought you these cookies you should eat with your coffee. This suet I brought along for the cat. I see it on the table. I thought he might as well make 'way with it. You let him eat in here?"

"He won't hurt nothing."

Henrietta threw down the suet. It landed with a thump on the paper. Sammie drew back startled and outraged, but under encouragement consented to sniff at it with his pink nose. Then, giving his white-mittened paw one delicate, utterly decisive shake, he turned his back and walked away. It described the suet perfectly.

Henrietta was astonished. "Look at that! I thought he'd gobble that up. I thought all cats liked meat." But her face was red.

Toldine said dryly, "No, suet he won't touch."

"You got him spoiled!"

Toldine made no comment.

When Henrietta left, Sammie came back to his dish and finished his milk with calm gusto. Toldine regarded him with deep sympathy. "Ja, you know how you wanted your breakfast!" They liked it better to be left together. Contentment flowed around them.

After breakfast Toldine carried out her small array of dishes to the kitchen, dipped warm water out of the reservoir, poured the coffee grounds about the roots of some plants. The cookies she had not touched. They were not needed for breakfast. Sammie followed her. He sat down on the linoleum in a square of sunshine and began his morning laundry work. He gave a few casual licks at his snowy chest, brief attention to his white mittens, and then set to work with concentrated ardor on a patch of seemingly spotless gray fur just behind his left shoulder.

Toldine regarded him with humorous and admiring appreciation. "Ja," she said, "you got to wash up, too?"

When she had finished, every dish used was in its precise place. Sammie was shining. His white chest swelled into a magnificent spotless shirt front. His white mittens were perfect. Spots of scrubbed gray fur were moist and flat. His whiskers rayed out from his fluffy chops majestically. He was satisfied with himself.

Every morning there were these preliminaries through which Toldine and Sammie both must go. Now they were ready for the real business of the day.

Henrietta, looking from the kitchen window of the other house, thought, half contemptuous, half baffled:

"What all does she think she's doing out there?"

Toldine was in the garden. She went about looking at plants with minute attention. She picked the withered pinks and threw them upon the little heap of plant débris she was piling up at the edge of the garden. She tied twine around the spread-

ing phlox. She found out just where the dry earth needed digging with her gritty little trowel about the flower roots. She
filled two wooden buckets (candy buckets, the store man had
given them to her, they had cost nothing), and then to and
from these she made excursions with an old tea pot and put just
the amount of water needed upon just the plants that must
have it. She began making bouquets for the house. Her array
of receptacles stood out on the wash bench: two jelly glasses, a
bottle, a saucer, an inkwell. "Such bouquets!" Dorothy said.
But, "Toldine, she's got her own way of doing things," Henrietta warned her. The saucer Toldine massed full of rose-
colored petunias picked from their stems. She stuck three
pansies—blue, white, yellow—into the inkwell. Into one tiny
cylindrical bottle that had once contained twenty-five cents'
worth of perfume she set a single tuft of sweet alyssum. She
had found the bottle "thrown away." This bouquet was her
triumph.

Once she made an excursion into the wood shed. She mounted
a dry goods box and stood for five minutes motionless, impassive, gazing with concentrated attention through a knothole
into the back yard of old John Carpenter's, next door, until she
had observed enough for her satisfaction. Then, with a small
dry smile, she stepped down from the box, left the shed, and
went back to her flowers.

"You coming out, too?" she said.

Yes, Sammie had now made up his mind to join her. Toldine
never urged him against his inclinations—even if there had
been any use in that!—but she was gratified when he chose to
be with her. He followed her about for a while through the
garden in the fresh morning sunshine. Certain matters called
for his attention, and others for hers. There was a patch of

warm earth where he must roll. It was necessary for him to keep
an eye on a gopher entrance. He was on the lookout for birds,
too, although this Toldine would never admit to Henrietta.
They praised him for bringing mice and then scolded him for
catching birds! "How are you to know?" Toldine demanded
in consoling indignation. But she guarded the birds from
Sammie as she guarded him from his larger enemies.

The street was waking up about them. The folks in the other
house were up now. Toldine didn't need to watch for that.
She had a contemptuous knowledge of it from their shouting
and banging about. The milkman came. As always, he grabbed
for Sammie and, as always, Sammie ran. "Whatcha wanta run
for? I wouldn't hurtcha!" the milkman shouted vociferously.
"Hey, fellow! I was just gonna have a little fun with you. Why,
our old cat, I rub up her fur the wrong way and swing her
around by her tail, and she likes it!" And as he set down the
pint bottle of milk on the wash bench, he demanded with loud
facetiousness, "Well, Miss Schönwetter, I hear you and Old
John next door have struck up quite a friendship! Now, don't
ask me where I heard it. I hear everything. You can't fool your
milkman. Say, don't you think it's pretty mean of you to deprive some nice fellow of your good cooking all these years?
Better let me find you some nice old bach when I'm out on the
route and bring him around. I see all these old baches."

"I guess not," was all that Toldine answered. He went away
whistling joyfully. But when he had left and Sammie came back
to the garden Toldine patted the cat's head. "Ja, you don't like
him. No, I don't neither," she said with great contentment.

Now the annoyances began. Enemies menaced them every
day; and even in this secluded garden every day was a struggle.
There was a steely alertness under Sammie's silken placidity.

He blinked his eyes in the sunshine, but always a bright slit was showing. Toldine was on the watch for that boy across the street—that tormentor. Then there was that big nondescript brown dog that usually came rampaging through the garden at some time during the morning. Toldine took the part of all animals against all people. But she couldn't really care for that dog, and she saw what Sammie had against him. Anything she fed him went down in a gulp. Just speak to him and he'd be all over you. Before you were through, you had to be cross with him; and Toldine didn't like that. He should have seen!—she thought.

And there were always people. Toldine did no calling except to visit the family graves in the cemetery. But people came to the Schönwetter place. There was a tradition that no plants did so well as those from the Schönwetter garden. Toldine had a knack. She couldn't tell what it was and made no attempt to do so. That, she thought again, they ought to have seen!

Some of these people Sammie accepted and some he didn't. When Addie Epperson came Sammie sat blank and motionless. She gave a little shriek. "I didn't know that cat was here!" She fussed and fidgeted around and asked nervously how Toldine could stand him. "I think cats are so creepy!" There was ineffable contempt in Sammie's immobility. He wouldn't even bother to walk away from Addie Epperson. All her effusions over the "wonderful flowers" did not thaw Toldine's silent, grim disdain. Fat, heavy, perspiring Mrs. Kaster was worse than that. "Shoo! Scat! S-sss! Get out o' here! I can't stand no cats around." She had no perception of Toldine's cold fury. She went around stepping on budding plants and asking for seeds just the same; and when she left she urged Toldine heartily, "Why don't you ever get out o' here and come over?

You want to be sociable. It'll do you good." There were a few
people of whom Sammie approved. There was Mrs. Williams,
just out of college, shy and lonely, the wife of the high school
Principal. He flung himself instantly before her on the warm
ground strewn with dry shreds of grass and sticks and withered
petals. "Look at your coat!" Toldine told him in mild accusation. But she sympathized. "Ja, he knows." The lonely young
couple, out of place in the little town and aware of criticism,
were pleased by this acceptance. Mr. Williams lingered a long
time talking with Toldine and trying to ask businesslike questions about gardening, of which he knew nothing. Toldine
didn't care what people said. She kept things to herself—to
the uneasiness, relief and the total miscomprehension of her
family; but all her life she had cherished a deep, calm, satis-
factory detestation of the heartily unconscious Mrs. Kaster.

Now she was getting deeper into her work and deeper into
the summer day. So was Sammie. Their paths were gradually
diverging. Sammie—like Toldine herself—followed a neat, pre-
arranged routine, changing somewhat from week to week, and
varying slightly to suit the weather. But on a day so fine as this
he could allow himself some leeway from his set rule of pro-
cedure. Toldine noted every so often with satisfaction that he
was still about. He was affectionate this morning. As she
crouched among the potato plants he came and rubbed his
head and then his whole soft length against her sun-warmed
arm. "Ach, so you like me, do you?" He blinked his shining
eyes in agreement. Toldine answered, in a mutter, an old accusation. "Lazy! I guess you ain't lazy! You don't have to tell
folks about everything you do." He kept regular office hours,
just like a man, in his mousing places. Only he was more sensible

than a man. When there was nothing to do he didn't pretend
to do it. He was leaving the garden, however, by stages. He
had got as far as the shade of the snowball bush now. He took
his time.

Little Varselles came running over from the other house.
Toldine welcomed all the little children—saved pieces of hard
candy for them from her Christmas presents and secreted funny
toys in out-of-the-way nooks about the house. Dorothy had
dressed Varselles in her Sunday dress which had got dirty. She
was barefooted and sucking sugar.

"Hello, Aunt Toldine."

"You up a'ready?"

"Yes, I *been* up." Then she asked just what Toldine was
dreading.

"Where's Sammie?"

Toldine said she didn't know. She went on working while
Varselles hung plaintively about her. Toldine saw the cat all
the time, but she made no sign, and neither did he. Then Varselles discovered him. He was sitting very upright in the mottled
shade of the snowball bush, and—oh, how fine he looked!
His gray coat glistened with sunlight. A tiny iridescence shone
at the tip of each hair. His eyes glittered green, with woven
satiny color under the glassy surface, a round of color dented
in to the intense slit of black opening and closing at the centre.
His white chest swelled out in fluffy majesty from under his
whiskered face, his white-mittened paws were set neatly on
the ground, and his tail was curled compactly around his
person.

Varselles was in ecstasy. "Look, Aunt Toldine! See! I've
found him."

It gratified Toldine that Varselles was always after the cat, but it worried her too, for she knew what might happen. "He looks so pretty. Oh, I want him!" Gurgling wildly with joy, she dived for him. Instantly Sammie retreated. His eyes had a baleful glare. He suddenly spat—knew he shouldn't have done it—was angry and didn't care; stretched out as long as an eel, ran, slid, and was lost in the berry bushes. Varselles plunged after him and then turned back loudly weeping.

"Aunt Toldine! He spit at me!"

"Ja, he was bad," Toldine admitted. "But it was the way you went after him."

"But I love him. I want him. Why won't Sammie let me get him, Aunt Toldine?"

"Ja," Toldine told her, "you love him too hard. That he won't stand for." Varselles was staring at her with tragic eyes. "You want to treat him—ja, as if you liked him, but just the same as he does you, not so much more."

"The dog likes me to like him!"

"Ja, but the dog ain't the cat. You got to know."

But she never would know, Toldine thought. Fond as she was of Varselles, she had already judged the child by her small inner tribunal. Too much fuss. Fussing, stewing, noisiness, rampaging, a to-do—all these things she condemned. That you only did when you couldn't get things done without it. Ja, and that Becker fellow from south of town—he was a bachelor, and he liked cats and wasn't so blustering around as most men. Toldine smiled a discreet little smile; ja, but him, too, Sammie walked away from. If the fellow followed he turned with one brief snarl. He admired cats too much and was too humble. No, you couldn't stand that kind of a fellow all the time. He would be in the way. Toldine and Sammie had their own little hard criterion.

She was glad Henrietta wasn't around, however, or Dorothy. "That cat spit at Varselles. You ought to get rid of it." She could hear them saying that. It would be one more black mark in the long list of their grievances against Sammie. Ja, because he was hers, Toldine supposed—belonged to her and paid no attention to them—they could never rest until they had made her get rid of him. She had given Henrietta what she demanded of the family belongings: the big skillet, the leather chair, an immense platter for which neither of them had any use. She even let "those two" gather the best apples. But she fought to keep Sammie. All morning she kept warily out of sight of that kitchen window.

And it wasn't only the folks in the other house. In spite of the praises Sammie received—"Fine cat!" from men and "Will he let me pick him up?" from women—in spite of that radiant, innocent delight of little children—Toldine knew that there was always something working against him. "Well, Toldine's alone there, she gets lots of company out of her cat," the family said to other people in tolerant shame. But she knew how they resented her having him. Boys in the neighborhood were on the alert to torment him. Mrs. Judge Lawson went around telling people that cats must be destroyed if the birds, "so much more valuable," "man's little helpers," were to be saved—ja, when she wasn't stewing about the minister, or the school Principal, or the town garbage! There were all the women in town—old maids, too, some of them—who talked about "some child" and grudged Sammie his food on principle. It wasn't enough for her and Sammie to live off here by themselves minding their own business. Other people wouldn't allow it.

The worst was that old John Carpenter. Ja, and if she were to tell what she knew about him! The folks in the other house would try to make her get rid of Sammie; but they would never dare do it themselves. There were things of hers that they wanted. And after all, she lived next door and belonged to the family. John Carpenter said he had had enough of that noise. It was disgraceful. If the owner wouldn't get rid of that cat, some night he'd do it himself. Rousing the neighborhood when Christian folks were all in bed! Why did folks want to own animals, anyway?

And now Sammie was gone. "Ja, he got disgusted!" Toldine looked in his haunts—the nest of grass under the apple trees, a certain spot beneath the berry bushes. He was in none of them. She missed him, but she was relieved. There were other dangers —traps, dogs, poisoned rats—in the barns and pastures where he hunted. But until Varselles had forgotten he was better out of sight. Toldine went back and settled to the business of spraying the potatoes and worked hard until noon.

The afternoon was very hot. Toldine had got all her heavy work done in the morning. She took some sewing out to the shade of the big tree that grew between the two houses. From there she watched the "doings" in the other house. Fussing around ironing in that hot kitchen!

"Ja, you know better, don't you?" she said to Sammie.

She watched the goings-on with a scorn of which her thin, dark, impassive face gave no sign. Why couldn't that girl— she still called her nephew's wife "that girl" in her own mind— have got up a little earlier if she had all this to do? And if the ironing kept her so busy, why must she try and put through all that extra baking at the same time? Over there it was always a turmoil—ja, if not one thing, then another. And if two of them were so many for her to 'tend to, so that she flew at them and scolded them and couldn't keep them with clean faces, why did she want to go and have another right away? Henrietta living there with them made things all the worse. They must do her way all the time, and she must do their way. Henrietta ought to remember Katrinka, the little tiger the Schönwetters had had years ago. Toldine thought of that with a subtle reminiscent smile. When Katrinka had a batch old enough, then she cuffed them off and went back to her own business. Toldine was condemning the whole workings of the other house, its entire philosophy. Still, if Henrietta hadn't been living there, she would have tried to stay with Toldine. Some folks didn't know how to get on alone. So let her stay there!

She could see Henrietta in the dining room, working like mad, cutting out dresses. If folks would use what they'd got they'd be better off. Who needed so much anyway?

"No, you don't, do you?" she said to Sammie. "And you know how to have a better time than any of them!"

Always more, more, more, and then never satisfied!

She rocked. She and the cat had their own little arrangements for hot weather comfort. Sammie lay over near the pump where water had been spilled earlier in the day and where the ground still kept the faintest suggestion of damp coolness. The shade under the big tree was a vantage ground for observation of the neighborhood. Toldine's face was inscrutable. Dorothy always said, with easy patronage, "Aunt Toldine goes her own way, she never pays any attention to other folks." Henrietta said, "You don't know what all she sees."

Henrietta came over now. Toldine saw that she had her eye on Sammie. But she halted and said resentfully:

"You look cool!"

"I don't stew around in this heat."

Henrietta accused her, "You got only yourself to look after."
Then she remembered her purpose in coming. Her face
swelled and grew red. She made gestures with her fists.

"That cat went and spit at Varselles. She come in crying
and said that cat spit at her!"

Toldine made no answer. She bit off a thread, but she was
wary. The old, half-smothered quarrel between them was
flaming up in the heat. That silence of hers always infuriated
Henrietta, who couldn't keep still herself. Henrietta never
quite knew what was behind it, any more than she knew what
that witchy cat was thinking. His refusal of the suet still rankled. She burst out:

"You ought to get rid of that cat. If you don't somebody else
is going to do it for you." Her eyes were glaring. Dark hints
of old family passions were in her tone. There were two sides,
as there were two houses. "That cat'll do a mischief to somebody some day."

Toldine spoke with disdain. "He won't do anybody any
mischief." But she trembled inwardly.

"He won't?" Henrietta demanded.

"Not to anybody that lets him alone."

They were glaring now at each other, Henrietta's eyes in a
blazing fury, Toldine's just as furious but cold. In that one
statement the whole family quarrel was concentrated. Toldine
wanted to be let alone and Henrietta to manage. It all went
back to that—and farther, as the two old women only dimly
realized—away back to the father and mother, to the Schönwetter and the Kleinfelder, to the stormy demands of the father
and the wary independence of the mother, to the very birth and
conception of Henrietta and Toldine. Other things were en-
tangled in its now: which orchard trees belonged to which

family; misunderstandings that were always threatening to flare up into a "regular quarrel"; the constant threat of Henri-etta's coming over to live with Toldine, look after her, and get that cat out of the house. . . .

"Mother! Why don't you come back here and help me?"

The sharp irritation of the voice cut into the tense atmosphere between the two women and left them helplessly glaring across the chasm. Dorothy had come to the door with one of the little dresses in her hand.

"You've left all that work piled up on the table."

Henrietta was helpless before the demands of her son's fam-ily, whom she adored. Her new dress for Varselles must be fin-ished before evening. With an angry gesture she turned and went back into the hot dining room where Toldine could see her working furiously, grumbling, doing worse than grum-bling, all the rest of the afternoon. The "regular quarrel" was barely averted again.

Through the whole altercation Sammie had never blinked an eye. Now he got up with cold decision and went to the door.

"Yes," Toldine muttered approvingly, "it's better in there now."

The shades were down. It was dimly pleasant in the old-fashioned interior, never changed since the death of Mrs. Schönwetter years ago. Sammie slept on a cool strip of floor. Toldine went over her curious store of mending: rolled-up balls of lace from Carl's baby dresses, bits of silk pinned together, several colors of thread rescued and wound on spools. In here they were both safe.

But by four o'clock it had grown stuffy in the house. It seemed empty and lonely. Toldine called to Sammie, but he wanted to sleep and only flicked his ears. She could hear the

racket in the other house and she almost wished they would ask
her in to supper. Two meals alone were enough. She was glad
to see old Mrs. Graf coming up the walk—some one to whom
she could talk, one of her few accepted cronies. At the moment
that Mrs. Graf reached the door Sammie got up, stretched and
prepared to leave. But he could go now. They were busy in the
other house.

"Wo geht denn die Katze?"

"Ja, I don't know where all he goes." Toldine added, "Come
in, have a cup coffee."

"Ja, well . . ."

Mrs. Graf sighed, but it was for this that she had come. Every
so often these two must see each other. The intimacy between
them had been kept up for over forty years. Now they were
sure that they could rely upon each other. Mrs. Graf went to see
only Toldine now. On both the impassive faces there was a
taciturn glint of pleasure. Mrs. Graf took off her little black hat
with the black pansies, and exposed her round, smooth head
with the round ear-rings. Toldine lighted more kindling, put
on fresh coffee, got out the cookies, and they sat down to the
table. It was for Mrs. Graf that Toldine had saved all her obser-
vations.

"She, over there, is going to have another."

"Ja, so?"

"Ja. They haven't told it. But I noticed."

"But vot is den de last one? He is only—"

"Ja, fifteen months in October. Ach, I don't know! That I
wouldn't tell to any one but you. . . . It was true, Mutter Graf,
what I thought about John Carpenter. He goes to see that Jen-
sen woman. He goes out after dark and he comes back when
it is just light. She does his washing. I looked over and saw his

washing this morning. She'd put bluing in them sheets. That he would never do for himself."

"Ach, so?"

"Ja, that I wouldn't tell to anybody else, either. . . . I see by the paper a man flew in a flying machine over the jungle. Snakes in there thirty-five feet long! Ach, such things everywhere! Why does he want to fly over such places? What good does it do to him when he gets through? Why don't he tend to his own business? Those snakes they'll get along without his flying over to look at them. I stay to home."

"Ja, ja, dot is so," Mrs. Graf said. She sighed. She asked, "How is denn die Katze?" And when Toldine told her about the neighbors, about the other house, she advised:

"He's company. You stick to him."

Henrietta always resented having Mrs. Graf come to see Toldine. She hinted darkly, "When those two get together . . ." But she didn't have time to talk about it to-night. The new dress was finished, and so she and Dorothy and Varselles and the baby must all go to town—Toldine thought—to show themselves off. Henrietta had forgotten now about the quarrel; and Toldine and Sammie had his little time to enjoy the lawn all by themselves.

The evening was placid but hot and breathless still. Sammie sat on the edge of the cement along with the flower pots, viewing the evening landscape with the tranquility of a contented householder. Birds swooped low over the garden; but he was not after birds just now.

Toldine sat out in her little rocker and sewed as long as there was light, savoring the evening fragrance that came from the petunias. Once she muttered, "Ja . . ." She was thinking of something that had happened a long time ago. She almost forgot how the years had passed. At dark she went all over the two lawns through the fresh dew gathering her little bundle of sticks. Carl, before he left also for town, brought her the paper. She turned on the light and sat reading it, moving and moving her glass but saving the society items for the morning.

"Girl Bandit Robs Bank." All such things! Ten was her hour for going to bed. Before she locked the door she looked for Sammie. "Ja, he's gone. It's past his time now." He might be in his box in the woodshed, but who could tell? She ought to hunt for him, rescue him, shut him up in the house where he couldn't disturb folks. The night was warm and dark and breathing. Why interfere with him? He went his own way.

Toldine lay all night in one identical little spot in the bed. Those folks in the other house—she had made their beds, rumpled and tumbled and everything in a heap. That wasn't necessary! Toldine was a good sleeper. Henrietta said resentfully that she had nothing to worry her. Still she heard queer faint sounds—creaks, rattlings, breathings through the dark. The doors were safely locked. But everything was different in the night.

A growl, and then a long rising baleful yowl cut through the soft darkness, tearing into one jagged shriek at the end. Toldine sat up instantly, stiff with fear.

"They're at it!"

For long steady moments there was no sound again. She lay down cautiously, her eyes wide open, ready to get out of bed. But that couldn't have been Sammie, no matter how those folks in the other house might complain in the morning. Sammie, who was so nice in the house, so dainty and particular she could let him go anywhere, who on winter evenings sat furry and

soft beside the hardcoal burner and sounded all the warm contentment of the room in his steady, blissful purring. Ja, but in
the night, who knew what became of him? She thought uneasily, remotely, of dark haymows, dark, wide pastures through
which stealthy creatures glided, seeking the lives of the other
creatures. Sammie was different, outside, at night. In the winter
she tried to catch him, to bring him in and keep him warm, but
he kept flitting just ahead of her, just beyond the reach of her
hand, wary and elusive as a rabbit or a fox with the starlight
glittering wild and cold in his eyes, across the snow.

Again came that ominous yowl, and then the shriek split
through the air like a blinding zig-zag streak of vocal lightning.

Toldine got out of bed. She stood trembling on the cold floor.
A window in the other house banged up. "That cat!" she heard,
and, "Ought to be shot!" They wouldn't dare do anything to
him. But some one might—that old John Carpenter. . . . She
crept downstairs in her bare feet and opened the door to the
black night air. If it was Sammie she would catch him and save
him, keep him with her where no one could get him. Trembling and defensive she stood.

The sound was only a low growling now. She couldn't tell
where to locate it. She said, "Sammie!" The growling was still.
She felt about with her hands—touched something crouched
and furry. A snarl!—and then two forms flashed past her.
"Sammie!" Was one of them Sammie? She couldn't tell. He
had fled as if she were some one he had never seen before. She
didn't know Sammie from any other cat in the night. She stood
helpless, wringing her hands, hearing the sounds of conflict
that all at once dropped into stillness.

It had grown quiet, too, in the other house. Well, maybe they
would go to sleep now. If they could go banging and shouting

about all day, why should they make a fuss if there was a little
noise at night? Not a sound from John Carpenter's. Anyway, it
was no use to go after Sammie. He wouldn't let himself be
caught. Ja, and that was all right, too! She didn't want to catch
him. The things she liked were the things that wouldn't let
themselves be caught.

As Toldine stood there barefooted in the dew, she felt a sudden strange pleasure in the flying sight of those two wild creatures. Even in the remembrance of the caterwauling that tore
through her very ears she took a grim delight. "Pretty kitty,"
that nice little Mrs. Williams said—yes, but only "pretty kitty"
when he wanted to be! Let folks complain! If she didn't interfere with their way, why should she interfere with his? After
all, Sammie was a cat. He would have to take his chances and
live his own way. She didn't blame him. It was good to be alone
here in the dew and the darkness with the little breaths of
wind that came from nowhere, and the fragrance, and the
stirring odors. . . . The locked houses stood about her silent
and discreet. Let them all complain, if they must, in the morning. She was going to let the cat run where he pleased.

She crept upstairs to bed again. She heard a sound from next
door and halted with her hand upon the bed, motionless,
minutely intent. In the other house the baby was crying. But
that wasn't it. Old John Carpenter was just sneaking into his
back porch, too late to hear the caterwauling, or to make any
trouble to-night. Ja, this old John Carpenter—she had watched
him! Now in the daytime folks could see he was "looking
around" again—nice widows, nice spinsters not too old—but
he thought no one knew where he spent the night. Well, let
him think! Folks were all so careful, and they all thought no
one knew. In the morning they complained about the cats. It

wasn't decent. It was a shame. "You ought to get rid of that cat. That cat ought to be shot." Well, she wouldn't get rid of him. She would keep him as long as she could. Toldine got into bed. She muttered with grim amusement, thinking of old John Carpenter and his complaints—of all of them and their complaints:

"Ja, you needn't say so much, either!"

She turned then in her cool bed and went to sleep.

A NOTE ON THE TYPE
IN WHICH THIS BOOK
~~~ IS SET ~~~

*This book is set on
the Linotype in Granjon, a type which is neither a copy
of a classic face nor an original creation. George W.
Jones drew the basic design for this type from classic
sources, but deviated from his model wherever four
centuries of type-cutting experience indicated an
improvement or where modern methods of
punch-cutting made possible a refinement that
was beyond the skill of the sixteenth-century
originator. This new creation is based prima-
rily upon the type used by Claude Garamont
(1510–1561) in his beautiful French books
and more closely resembles the work of the
founder of the Old Style letter than do
any of the various modern-day types
~~~~~ that bear his name. ~~~~~*

SET UP, ELECTROTYPED AND PRINTED
BY VAIL-BALLOU PRESS, INC., BING-
HAMTON, N. Y. BOUND BY H. WOLFF
ESTATE, NEW YORK. PAPER MADE
BY S. D. WARREN CO., BOSTON